S...
e...
l...
South Africa and ...
lives with her partner and t...
on her second novel.

Praise for *Look at Me*:

'An assured and sensitively written debut' *Observer*

'Unnerving, absorbing and wincingly well-observed, this is an accomplished debut' *Sunday Times*

'The simmering tension and painful misunderstanding of Duguid's debut lingers on my mind . . . seductive and chilling' *Stylist*

'With characters that are sharply observed with a beady eye for detail, this is a haunting study of family, grief, and loss' *Daily Mail*

'Exquisitely written, with a beautiful balance between darkness and humour' Joanna Cannon, author of *The Trouble With Goats and Sheep*

'Full of wonderfully acerbic humour, a fantastic debut' *Sunday Mirror*

'Sarah Duguid's debut is light on its toes, a delicate, elegant examination of a complicated family situation where emotions are unpredictable and connections are tenuous' *Daily Express*, *S* Magazine

'This slender novel puts a fragile family under the spotlight with great effect' Cathy Rentzenbrink, *Bookseller*, Editor's Choice

'A book to fall in love with . . . captivating, creepy and beguiling all at once' Colette McBeth, author of *The Life I Left Behind*

'A hugely enjoyable novel – astutely observed, witty and original' Sarah Rayner, author of *One Moment, One Morning*

'Its astute observations about family means it packs a punch' *Good Housekeeping*

'A witty and touching take on grief and how families pull together to cope in its wake' *OK* Magazine

'A clever exploration of family and grief, which will appeal to fans of Harriet Lane' *Red* Magazine

'A tense, gripping and beautifully descriptive tale of grief, revenge and family secrets' *Heat*

'Duguid brings to life the nuances of family life with ease' *Grazia*

'This debut is about to go massive and it has us hooked from the get-go' *Look* Magazine

'Suspenseful, tautly written and unnervingly psychologically astute' Alison Mercer

'It reminded me of *Hausfrau* in tone, somehow. Startling and sad' Sarah Franklin

'Enchanting and creepy, *Look At Me* filled me with a delightful sense of unease' Sarah Chapman, Bibliomouse

LOOK AT ME

SARAH DUGUID

TINDER
PRESS

First published in Great Britain in 2016 by Tinder Press
An imprint of HEADLINE PUBLISHING GROUP

First published in paperback in 2016 by Tinder Press
An imprint of HEADLINE PUBLISHING GROUP

1

Cataloguing in Publication Data is available from the British Library

ISBN 978 1 4722 2987 8

Typeset in Sabon by Avon DataSet Ltd, Bidford-on-Avon, Warwickshire

Printed and bound in Great Britain by Clays Ltd, St Ives plc

HEADLINE PUBLISHING GROUP
An Hachette UK Company
Carmelite House
50 Victoria Embankment
London EC4Y 0DZ

www.tinderpress.co.uk
www.headline.co.uk
www.hachette.co.uk

For my mum and dad

I love to think of those naked epochs
Whose statues Phoebus liked to tinge with gold.
At that time men and women, lithe and strong,
Tasted the thrill of love free from care and prudery,
And with the amorous sun caressing their loins
They gloried in the health of their noble bodies.
Then Cybele, generous with her fruits,
Did not find her children too heavy a burden;
A she-wolf from whose heart flowed boundless love for all,
She fed the universe from her tawny nipples.

Charles Baudelaire, *Fleurs du Mal*, 1857
Translated: William Aggeler, 1954

prologue

Just the tips of four fingers were visible from the bottom of the stairs. The hand dangled from the top step, the slender fingers tapering towards the perfect arc of a woman's nail. No polish. Across the hand fell strands of hair; the head turned face down. The white nightdress she wore rode up her thighs so artfully it might have been staged. A piece of theatre; a fallen ballet dancer. In the background, the blue light of an ambulance thumped the white sitting room wall as the paramedics fought to save her.

ACT ONE

He told me that the ways of love and the ways of his loins weren't things that could be constrained by convention, that only the fearful lived like that.

ACT ONE

the letter

ON THE SIDE TABLE, FRAMED IN SILVER, MY FATHER DANCED. NOT A becoming kind of dance: his arms flailing, knees bent, one foot twisted in the air. He wore a multi-coloured top with wizard's sleeves and looked as if he could have done with a wash.

The photograph was taken back then – in his heyday – during the years he spent swanning about in silly clothes, smoking weed. I could imagine him, the man he used to be, slithering up to girls with talk on his lips of the new experimental ways with love. All wiry beard and long, greasy hair. Temptation itself.

I turned to look at him now, luminous with suntan, fresh back from the South of France, wearing his white trousers rolled up at the ankle. His teeth looked whiter when he had a tan. His dark hair had a decent cut and he wore a pressed linen shirt with an extra button undone into a deep 'V'. He sat on the grey sofa; behind him hung a picture of a nude, the lines of the body in electric blue etched into thick white paint. If I'd taken a photograph of him now, with his unsocked feet and smooth, dark hair, you'd take him for an Italian art dealer.

He pressed his bare ankle against the glass corner of the coffee table. It looked painful, the meeting of cold glass and

5

bone. His foot dangled over the edge, his brown toes scrunching and unscrunching as he talked. He hadn't so much as flinched when I showed him the letter.

'Elizabeth, it could happen to anyone,' he said.

Dear Julian,
   This letter may come as a surprise to you. I am writing to tell you that I believe you are my father. My name is Eunice. I was born in Charing Cross Hospital in the unmarried mothers' ward and adopted by a couple from St Albans.

'She's younger than me.'

'Oh, calm down, Elizabeth,' he replied. 'You're being way too hysterical and middle class about this.'

'You were married to Mum at the time.'

'Yes,' my father replied. 'But it was different back then.'

I remained still. He turned his head skywards, ran a hand through his hair and refused to be excited. The way he looked at me was nonchalant and carefree, all white linen and suntan. He told me that the ways of love and the ways of his loins weren't things that could be constrained by convention, that only the fearful lived like that. He was that hippy again, poking at 'people's narrow assumptions'. I wanted to ask him what was so wrong with basic decency, but I knew he'd have just snorted. I pointed at a paragraph further down the letter. 'She said you shouldn't feel guilty.' I raised my eyebrows at him. 'She's an optimist.'

'There's a bottle in my suitcase. Fetch it out for me, would you? I've had a long day. The flight back from Nice was hellish.'

* * *

6

I found the letter the previous day when my father called from his holiday asking me to find a phone number for him. 'It's a beautiful day out here,' he said. 'I'm sitting on a sun lounger. I'm like a lizard on a hot stone watching some wonderful girls. They're leaping in and out of the water in tiny bikinis. If they start going topless I don't think I'll ever recover.'

I laughed.

'This phone number. It's scribbled on a receipt. It'll be in my office somewhere. Just go and search.'

My father had built his office in a shed pushed up against the old brick wall in the garden. From the outside it looked nice enough, painted green to blend in with the ferns and bamboos, but inside the place had something of the caravan about it. A laminate floor, a bare strip light, nasty lilac curtains hanging from a single plastic-covered wire. Little of my father expressed itself in there. His chair, perhaps. Designed by Eames, it was dark green leather and stood on chrome spokes. The lamp, another giveaway. In the evenings, he sometimes read in his office. The soft light of an Anglepoise lamp in stainless steel made the place feel cosier but, still, it smelled of pinewood and paint.

My father left the office key in the lock so he couldn't lose it. He only had a cheap computer, not worth stealing, a few notebooks, a telephone, nothing he couldn't live without. I turned the key, pushed open the shed door and went straight to his desk. I searched through the piles of paper on top but found nothing. Usually, he hid the tiny key for the desk drawer in his pocket or pushed under a corner of carpet but that day it, too, remained in the lock. He'd left in a hurry. The position of his chair said it all. It showed the trajectory of the journey he'd taken the previous Friday. Not tucked under the desk but

7

rather flung back, almost at the back wall at an angle, pointing towards the exit. Five o'clock came; he pushed back while seated, stood up, strode out of the office without a backward thought. In his haste to leave for his holiday – a long weekend in the South of France, which he optimistically described as a working holiday because he'd be trying new grape varieties – he'd forgotten to lock the drawer. Next to a batch of receipts, an old cinema ticket and a blue stapler, sat Eunice's letter folded into a pink envelope. I opened it, curious at the pink, at the feminine handwriting, at a whiff of scent that still hung around the envelope's flap.

The words didn't connect. I had to read the letter two or three times. Did another man called Julian Knight exist, a chap who might have been the kind to receive something similar? After the third reading, I fell into the chair, like I'd been pushed; a spinning column of wind had come from nowhere and taken me off my feet.

Was it worse that she was female? Isn't being a sibling always an act of supremacy that's tempered if just two of you exist? What would my brother Ig and I do with a third; what would I do with another woman?

Back in the sitting room, I put it to my father: 'The postmark shows you've had it for over a year.' But the conversation went no further. I was small-minded. He was a heroic exploder of social mores. He cocked his leg. His tanned, bony foot buried itself in the sofa cushion. He plinked ice cubes into a glass of wine. 'Smell it,' he said. 'The vines are grown so close to the sea that salt dries on the grape skins. The scent of it takes you right back to the coast.' He held aloft the thin crystal glass, frosted with condensation, examining the colour in the light. He dunked his nose into it. He breathed in loudly, flaring his nostrils, a rush of air entering them.

'Strange you couldn't wait for such a nice wine to chill,' I said.

He dropped in another ice cube. 'Thoroughly wonderful,' he replied, taking a sip.

That evening, Ig made dinner. He didn't usually cook. He opened all the cupboards, slid around the floorboards in socked feet, irritated that he couldn't find anything. It's a ruse, I thought, so he doesn't have to face Dad. The day before, when I showed Ig the letter, he told me I had to keep it quiet. He became furious, threatened to tear up the letter, to burn it. I'd stuffed the thing down my top, running from him while he tried to throw me on to the sofa to grab it back.

Sitting opposite my father, I pinged one of the four metal lamps that hung equidistant over the long oak table. The shape of rice hats, in bright orange, they made a deep gong sound with each flick of my middle finger. The letter sat in the middle of us. It gaped at the fold, bobbing open and shut as the air stirred, like a clam shell gently nodding in the underwater swell. I carried on pinging the light, to make my father look over, but he ignored me, too busy explaining to Ig about his marvellous, salty wine.

Dinner ready, Ig slid the plates in front of us. At the head of the table, my father's chair had a high back, an arch of chrome curving around his shoulders. He looked as if he sat on a throne. The king of his own little North London kingdom. Ig had overcooked the asparagus. It drooped from my father's hand, a limp, sluggish green. He dangled it into his mouth to chomp the head off it. Still chewing the asparagus, he folded a pink slice of Parma ham on to his tongue.

'I might get in touch with her,' I said.

'Just leave it, Elizabeth,' my father replied.

'Why?'

'It's in the past.'

'Have you met her?'

'Twice.'

'Did Mum know about her?'

'Of course she did,' he replied.

'Did she mind?'

'It was different back then,' he said.

My chair clattered to the ground. 'I'm going to write to her,' I said. Ig had a look of both fear and impatience about him. I heard him call me petulant as I rushed out of the kitchen to find the writing pad. I punched my words on to a sheet of it. I'd show him.

From the doorway, my father watched. 'Not on the Basildon Bond, Elizabeth,' he said. 'Your grandmother would be turning in her grave.'

'What would Mum be doing in hers?' I replied.

Dear Eunice,

I'm sorry to read in your letter to Julian that you haven't so far managed to find your mother, and glad to hear that we at least form half the puzzle. I hope that's some consolation. I noticed that you and he had exchanged a few letters and he told you about Ig and me. Perhaps you'd like to learn more? I would be interested in getting to know you. We're related, after all. We must have things in common. I've often thought I'd like a sister. Did you meet up with Julian? I hope he hasn't disappointed you. He can be so vague. He's like that with everyone. So if you feel he has let you down, please don't take it personally.

Anyway, please do write back to me.

With very warmest wishes,
Your sister, Elizabeth

I scribbled the address then stalked off to the postbox before I could change my mind. Outside, the quiet of the street surprised me. I don't know what I'd been expecting, applause perhaps. The leaves on the trees shook in the breeze. The wide four-storey brick houses, withstanders of two world wars, just stood there. I rushed down the street like a madwoman but no one seemed to notice me. A woman walked beside a man who pushed a bicycle. The trees continued their rustling. The houses remained stoic. I almost felt relieved when I turned into the main street to find the thunder and rattle of the traffic outdoing me. I posted the letter.

Back at home, I sat at the table to finish my wine. I knew I looked defiant. Bolt upright, my elbows resting on the table, I turned my head away from Ig and my father. All they'd see was my profile as I stared out of the window, willing them to dare to speak. Neither of them did. I rippled with energy but the two of them remained still.

the audition

THE SUN SHIFTED AROUND THE HOUSE. EVEN IN THE DEPTH OF WINTER one room always had the light no matter what the time of day. In the mornings, the sun chose my studio bedroom, flooding it with light as if someone had peeled back the roof and opened me up to the heavens. In the height of summer, I organised blinds to go over the skylight or taped up thick bits of card but still the light came in. It trickled under the cracks in the door, slipped around the fabric of the blinds, poured in through the small frosted glass of the bathroom.

A spring morning, just before seven, the light nudged me awake. Up with the sun for yet another audition, yet another morning of standing around with a hundred other failing actresses, all of us hoping the doors of showbusiness would throw themselves open and eat us up. I pulled on a pair of black leggings, my eyes only half open. I stood in front of the mirror trying to correct the angle of the light. I'd thrown a rubble of make-up into the sink beneath me. I wondered if I had the energy for all this any more. I toyed with the idea of finding an office job. A simple monthly credit into my bank account, no uncertainty.

I pulled my face with my fingers so my skin stretched. What to do with myself?

You learn how you look when you're an actor. Casting directors talk as if you're not standing right in front of them, as if all actors could leave both their capacity for hearing and their capacity to feel at the reception desk. I wished I could. They talked about me as if I were a new sofa or a jacket they might buy. But would it fit? Would it be money well spent? Is she worth it? After eight years of doing this, I was under no illusions about myself as an object, of how I might look sitting on a shelf with passers-by admiring or criticising me.

I knew what I was in terms of the construction of my flesh, of how one part fitted into another, of how my nose appeared, of the lift of my eyebrow, the length of my leg, the line of my torso. Whether, with the right make-up, I could pass off as a schoolgirl, a siren, or a bored, knackered housewife about to give up on it all with a bottle of pills. I knew what my bones and skin had made because they told me constantly.

They told me I was handsome. Female casting directors described me that way. That annoyed me in itself. Men don't call women handsome, only other women do that. She's not one of us – she's handsome – as if they wanted to tell me I was practically a man.

Men would call me sexy. 'She's the sort of girl that blokes would want to fuck,' they said, to my face, more than once, first by a man who wore faded jeans and a grey sweater pushed up at the sleeves. He had blond hair and raddled skin. He tapped his foot against the stage floor and said 'yeah, definitely fuckable'. I looked back at him, steely and furious. I never got these jobs. Sometimes I wondered if the way I glared at them put them off, made them decide I might be more trouble than they could be bothered with. Perhaps they could read my thoughts?

I listened to this stuff week after week, feeling like a piece of steak on a butcher's chopping board. Meat being slapped down, turned over, prodded, examined. Will she be tender? Will she be tasty? 'Her eyes are too small,' a casting director once announced. My eyes are just eyes, I wanted to yell back at him. How could they be 'too' anything. I didn't wear glasses. Eyes were only there to see. Mine did that.

I was handsome and sexy with small eyes. I was slim but not muscular. I didn't have the frame of a woman who exercised, rather that of one who ate very little. I was pale and better off that way. Most casting directors agreed I wouldn't look right with a tan. They thought I'd look less intelligent. Being pale gave me a glassy quality, they said; something icy, English, elegant. But I'd got something around my face, signs of life, one of them called it, which sounded a little medical to me. What else could I have had?

They could see character in me too, something that would make people laugh.

So there it is, I am handsome and sexy, with too small eyes and a sense of humour. That's what I am.

I drew a black line around my small eyes then leaned in closer to the mirror, until my nose almost touched the glass, to examine my skin.

At drama school, I had held a future within my gaze. We all had. Prancing our way through our degrees in black leggings and long, cosy cardigans. We talked endlessly about the kind of work we imagined ourselves doing: what we'd say yes to, the things we'd refuse. The teachers reminded us every day that we were attending one of the best drama schools in the country. When the moment came, I assumed I'd have the things I wanted. I thought I'd have enough money for a nice home of my own somewhere with ivy and wisteria dripping around the windows. Three happy children would dip in and out of the pond at the bottom of the garden. The man in the picture I'd drawn for myself padded around our acres, spending his mornings in the garage making sculptures out of driftwood and discarded metal. By the time I'd reached thirty (the kind of age I assumed I might want that tranquil kind of life) I'd fund it with all the acting work I'd won.

The reality was that I started the day with a swim at the local pool, then spent the rest of it in my father's house wondering what I would do with the hours yawning out in front of me. A day feeling like a week. Everyone else so busy, so fulfilled, the world beyond full of people going from one thing to another while I stayed inside, trapped by these walls, the calendar stretching ahead, whispering failure, as I approached that age – my thirties – when an out-of-work actress can really begin to gather dust.

No one told us we'd have been better equipped for the world by studying something else, something useful. The teachers filled us with ideas. We went searching for our emotions the way other people search for matching socks, or their house keys. But once I found them, I didn't know what to do with them. We all shouted about how we'd reached a crisp, perfect authenticity, and yet underneath it all, I wondered if we weren't just making it up. 'Wonderful!' the teacher sang across the stage at Penelope as she groaned, bellowed, then mewled to depict the depths of emotion she felt at the love she found and immediately lost. The rest of us twisted across the stage with outstretched arms turning like windmills, dressed in all-white muslin, imagining we were germs. It all felt so serious, so necessary. No mention of decades to come living in bedsits, lifetimes in flatshares with damp soaking the carpet, summers spent with ten people sleeping in a rusty caravan eating nothing but sliced bread and margarine. As students we went on tour:

nightly performances to three tired-looking people who hadn't removed their raincoats and never laughed in the right places.

By eight o'clock, I stood in a line of actresses waiting one behind another in the chill spring morning, all of us hoping today might be different. We kicked at the pavement, chatted, smiled, tried not to betray our ambition. Outside we were on the same team. Friends, we talked about how awful it was, laughed at the misery of it all. Only once we got in front of the director things changed. Lined up like specimens, they pitted us against one another. We scored each other, eyeing up each other's bodies, legs, breasts, as if we were retail stock in a supermarket.

A weary-looking woman, large as a sideboard, bored at the very sight of yet another line of pert young actresses, opened the door to the theatre. 'Come in,' she sighed at us. We filed through underground corridors, past rows of dancing shoes and old props. There was a papier mâché dragon's head wedged in between three dustbins and the wall. Covered in dust, it bared its teeth at us.

'Don't touch them,' the woman said as we passed a pile of the theatre company's flyers. She had her back to me. I don't know how she knew my hand had reached out to take one. She deposited us at the side of the stage without a word. We stood together, forming a line, each one of us wearing black leggings as instructed, hands behind our backs.

The director went up and down, eyeing us by turn. He was small with short hair – too short hair, I'd have said if I were casting him – barely a centimetre long. I could see smooth, white scalp through it. He wore a slim-fitting T-shirt. His arms were thick at the tops and bell-shaped. A miniature bull. Some theatre men look like they're made of milk – all liquid, willowy arms – but the director was definitely made of meat. You could have butchered him into discernible cuts.

He paused at me, working the length of my body. I gazed back at him, taking in his frame, the appealing way his chin seemed dented, the perfect form of his lips, the way they parted as he thought. He appraised me more than the other women. I counted in my head. He stayed a full thirty seconds longer, letting his eyes rise and fall along the length of me. What was going on in his head, I wondered, in the way his eyes squinted, in the way he kept cocking his head from side to side, the way he squished his lips outwards as he carried on looking at me. He caught my eye and held it for just a moment longer than he ought to. Silently, I begged him to pick me.

'Why are you an actress?' he asked.

'I love the work,' I replied.

He said nothing, seemed about to walk on, as if my answer had bored him. 'I like to be noticed,' I called out after him. 'I want to be seen.' He turned, appraised me one last time, nodded, then moved on.

I kicked myself at my answer. I should have said something else. To be seen, I thought. Why the hell had I said that?

The audition ended with the fat woman coming back to herd us out of the way. 'You'll hear,' she said, closing the theatre door behind us.

the reply

BY HALF PAST TEN I WAS HOME AGAIN, SITTING IN THE KITCHEN FOR a morning of nothing. I whizzed the Kenyan coffee beans my father buys in the small spice grinder we've had ever since I can remember. Same house, same chair, same cups. Why had I chosen this for myself? Why had I believed the lie my parents told me: that the creative life was the only one worth living. I stared out of the window at an overcast sky. I spooned the coffee grounds into the pot, waited for the kettle to boil, opened one magazine after another, searching for auditions.

Then I saw it, just as I settled on a chair, pen in one hand, coffee in the other, upcoming productions page open. An envelope, waiting for me. Pink, the handwriting rounded, the stamp carefully placed to be exactly aligned with the envelope's edges. My name written in real ink, the faded oak of the table and a shaft of sunlight falling in a beam just above the letter. I kept reading the envelope. Elizabeth Knight, 82 The Old Row, London, NW3. I felt a tightness in my throat. I realised it hadn't occurred to me that I'd written to an actual person, someone who had a postman, a doormat, a home she lived and slept in. I hadn't thought that she might actually write back. Might want to start a relationship, and naturally assume from the words of my letter that I did too. I'd thought of my anger at my father, of his cavalier ways, of his refusal to face anything and his guilty insistence at his own embellished view of the past. I'd thought of the mother we no longer had, of the way she looked at the end. I didn't know how I connected wanting to find justice for her with the writing of a letter to her husband's secret child. Why had I thought she'd have wanted me to do that on her behalf? I barely dared open the letter, written on pink stationery. The writing littered with exclamation marks and kisses. The fool I'd made this girl, responding with all her heart, pouring herself on to the page because she believed I'd been thinking of her and not the father I wanted to goad and the mother I wanted to be returned to us.

'You were brave to contact me!' she wrote. 'Julian had told me about you and Ig when he responded to my first letter to him. I wish I'd been the one brave enough to have made the first move!' She confessed to having written letters to me she'd thrown away. Each time, she'd torn them up and despaired, feared she might never know us. She never knew how to begin or what she ought to reveal. 'But please don't misunderstand,' she wrote. 'I'd been desperate to contact you! I wanted to know you and Ig and know where I came from!! I wanted to find my real family. I always had a part of myself missing and I'm happier beyond words that you've been the one to make the first move!'

'PS,' she said, 'I'd love to meet up!!!'

I wrote back immediately. The quicker I did it, the less painful it might be; like yanking out a stubborn hair. I'd agree to meet her. Get it over with. No more than three lines: a thank-you for returning my letter so quickly, suggesting a week next Thursday for lunch, asking her if she knew a restaurant. I sent the letter off before anyone found it.

When my father came in from his office, I said nothing. I told him about my audition, about saying something stupid to the director, about how packed the bus home was, but I said nothing about the fact I'd arranged to meet this daughter who he surely hoped would remain a piece of his past.

the meeting

AN ESTUARY OF TARMAC IN THE TOWN CENTRE, LINED ON EACH SIDE with red-brick buildings. A high street solicitor's office, a sandwich shop, municipal offices, then a single gap where a building had been knocked out, a tooth missing in an otherwise perfectly preserved Victorian smile. Eunice had written back, saying she'd be driving a Mini Metro, teal in colour.

Ig hadn't wanted to come. All the way to St Albans he complained. 'You shouldn't have gone poking about in his things,' he said. 'Not everything's a conspiracy against you. There may have been a good reason he wanted to keep things quiet.'

'I was thinking of Mum,' I said.

Ig snorted. 'Let's just listen to the radio and forget about it.'

I turned it up to drown him out. We listened to a competition: 'guess which year' from the songs they played. We were still listening as Eunice's teal Mini Metro beetled around the corner. She slotted into a parking space in one go.

I watched her in the distance fighting to get out of the car. The wind wanted to carry everything away with it. I hadn't realised the strength of it. The trench coat she held whipped the air. Dust danced around her feet. She abandoned the idea of an umbrella altogether. She threw it back inside, slamming the door behind her. The whole car shook. A string of pink plastic roses with neon-green leaves, tangled around the rear-view mirror, swung gently. She walked in my direction, across the tarmac towards the white estate car I'd told her Ig and I would be in. I felt the wind. It whirled around the buildings with a low drone. I shuffled my feet against the beads of gravel. I felt a knot tighten in my stomach.

Eunice saw me. She waved, beginning to walk more purposefully, smiling all the time, bright and perky. I stayed where I was, just watching her. Cheerful, friendly, flammable. She came towards me, all synthetic cerise sweater and bubblegum-pink lipstick. Wispy hair, a mouse-coloured frizz, pinned with two grips decorated with fabric roses. The clips pulled her hair flat against her head, then let it bush out at the back. Clicking across the tarmac in mid-heels that didn't seem right, as if they should have belonged to someone older. A crystal heart stitched into her sweater glittered as the light hit it. When she reached me, she just stood there, stopping my attempt at a smile with the intensity of her bright blue gaze.

'Eunice,' I said, feeling my voice falter. My mouth refused to make the shape of a smile, no matter how hard I tried. I just stared, words sticking in my throat. I must defuse the moment with a smile. A new sister! Shouldn't I be happy? Wasn't that the normal reaction? Couldn't I at least appear pleased? But I felt stunned, caught in that brief moment of stillness between being hit and realising you've been hit.

Eunice gulped away a breath. Eyes fixed on to mine. Her hands shook at her side. She obviously wasn't lying about where she'd come from. That nose, those diamond-shaped nostrils made her so obviously my father's child. I could see the biology of it.

'I'm overwhelmed,' she said finally, opening her arms.

'Wow.' She looked me over again, up and down the length of me, gathering herself. 'Should we hug?' She pulled me into an embrace. Wisps of her hair tickled my cheek. I wanted to push her away. 'I've imagined this moment my whole life and now I don't know what to say,' she said.

'Me neither,' I replied.

'Siblings! *Real* siblings!' She threw her hands out beside her, laughed, a shot of incredulous, happy laughter. A tear rolled down her cheek. She dabbed at herself, then grabbed my arm in her hand and held it. 'My life's always been a jigsaw, with a piece missing.' Her lip wobbled, she seemed to be trying to compose herself, but couldn't. The tears overcame her.

Ig stepped out of the car, moving towards us in a determined kind of way as if he'd made a conscious decision to seem confident and welcoming. Eunice seemed unsure as Ig zoomed towards her with his arms thrown open, like a child being an aeroplane in the school playground. Her face tried to register him, as if she hadn't known he'd be with me, trying to work out who he was.

They looked an odd pair as they hugged. She, all decked out in pink, shivering with nerves, sniffing away tears, and he, thin like a stalk of bamboo. He was so tall and skinny, he could have swayed in the wind, bent almost double with each gust, rooted only by his great lumps of feet. His hands were enormous and seemed incongruous, out of proportion. They splayed all across Eunice's back, his arms like thick tentacles sucking her in towards him. I heard him tell her there was no need to cry. His hair stuck up like old hay.

We stood together, the three of us, making a triangle. I stared at the mascara streaked down Eunice's face and loathed myself. Ig looked as if he'd been slapped. The wind battered us for a few moments longer until Eunice told us she'd booked a table for lunch somewhere nearby.

Inside the restaurant we shuffled along the brown suedette banquette. The waitress handed me a menu, still damp from being wiped clean.

'Lovely fabric,' Eunice said, smoothing her hand over the seat. 'Nice like suede but it doesn't stain. Mike and I have suedette on the sofa at home, but in deep purple.' She paused, holding our gaze, as if she needed to gather our attention for her to say something terribly important. 'Purple, along with pink, is one of my favourite colours.'

Would that be it? I wondered. Exchanging the colours we liked, the foods we ate, lie-ins or up early, pubs or bars: the whole of our lives condensed into preferences.

'And we chose scatter cushions in chocolate,' Eunice said. 'I've loved doing the house up. We've only been married six months and the place is totally done. I got obsessed. Completely obsessed.' She pored over the menu. 'I'd bought all the magazines, watched all the programmes. Mike got sick of paint charts and fabric swatches. I told him we could have a weekend away when the house was done. I just wanted to get it right.'

Mike had owned the flat before he met Eunice, apparently. She stripped it out when she moved in and started again. Ditched the plastic leather sofa, the enormous television, the black metal shelves. 'The flat's contemporary and I like something more homely. I don't like sterile. I filled it with colour. Accent walls, a huge purple sofa, the cushions.' She kept talking, describing all the things she'd done, the colours she'd chosen and why, the fight she'd had with the downstairs neighbour over the wooden floors she wanted to install, how the new floors were her way of stamping her identity on the home Mike had bought as a single man.

A girl who'd stepped from childhood to adulthood in one go. All the sensible choices. Job, flat, husband. No drama school for her. No imagining she was a carrot working its way through the digestive tract of an anxious rabbit. She'd never spent an hour and a half *being* a chair. Hadn't pretended to give birth to triplets on a metal trolley borrowed from the catering department. She hadn't spent days staring at the bottom of a wine glass trying to make an internal map of the feelings she could draw on for her work.

'Sorry,' she said. 'I'm talking too much. It's because I'm nervous.'

I wanted to run away from this sticky restaurant, past the tables laminated with the previous day's food, push past the staff in their short-sleeved black shirts with aprons tied around their middles. Pocket for pad, pen, cloth, bottle of cleaning spray – if only they'd use it. I could pelt outwards into the fresh air, drink it in, gulp it down. Anything to get out of this stale, dim restaurant with its vinegar-scented air. Next to us, a table was littered with ketchup, crumbs, screwed up napkins. That particular aftermath of a lunch with children. Half-eaten mouthfuls, soggy morsels of bread, remnants of chewed chips. I kept looking at the exit, while Eunice kept looking at me, all happiness and incredulity. Beaming. We were really here!!!

She could smile but I couldn't. Something wrong with me. Did I have a blockage on the pathway that ruled human connection? A faulty synapse so that I knew, in an abstract way, how I *ought* to feel but my neurons were impeded. While I was here, and Eunice was there, nothing formed a bridge between us. Surely if I could pretend to be a carrot, I could pretend to be a sister. But she wasn't a sister. No way close to it. Rather a stranger, who I didn't want to touch, or hear, or see, pondering whether she ought to have chicken or fish. If I were normal, wouldn't the neurons be galloping, wouldn't they make me leap over the table towards her, thrust us together, fuse us into one glorious, happy, healthy family? Wouldn't we be gaily enjoying a third hug, the way they do on the television?

It seemed so one-sided. Was she even telling the truth? Could she honestly know in an instant that we were her siblings, then christen the moment with tears?

I studied her some more, taking the chance while her eyes ran over the menu. A flesh, blood and bone betrayal of Ig, my mother and me sitting in front of me, deciding that she might skip the main course and go straight to dessert because she could only eat sweet things when she felt overwhelmed.

Nothing on the menu tempted me. Not the chicken goujons, the deep-fried brie, or the burgers. I wondered why I'd thought lunch was a good idea.

'Can you recommend something?' I said to Eunice.

'The breaded chicken's good,' she said. 'Mike always has that. It comes with wedges.'

'What are the salads like?' I asked.

'Diet?' said Eunice. 'I was like that before my wedding. Watching my figure like a hawk.' Then she paused as if looking at me anew. 'No. You're an actress, aren't you? Julian told me in his letter. He and I met once, a couple of years ago, but he asked me not to contact you both. He didn't elaborate. He just said it was a bad time for the family. He said he'd tell you about me one day, when he felt the time was right. Look at your lovely thick hair. You *are* gorgeous,' she said. 'You look like an actress. I was thrilled when your dad told me that. I couldn't believe my luck. An actress! Boring old me, with an actress for a half-sister.'

'That's kind of you,' I said.

I picked at a plate of iceberg lettuce gone brown at the edges – it came with raspberry dressing. Eunice had a cheesecake. 'I shouldn't,' she said. 'But I need it for my nerves.'

'You're young to be married,' I said.

'Married by twenty-two. I suppose it is young,' she said. 'The thing is, when you don't have a family, a proper one, you crave it. It's all I wanted in life. A home, a family. To have two children who knew where they belonged. Then I met Mike and I just thought, this is it. He's my family.' She moved backwards for the waitress to place an enormous slab of cake in front of her. 'I knew instantly with Mike,' she said.

'You work in a shop?'

'I'm the manager. I order the goods in, arrange where they go. I'm quite creative. I can see where I get it from now. I love doing the window displays. We're the most popular gift shop in St Albans.' Eunice sprayed aerosol snow at Christmas, scattered small chicks across fake grass at Easter and tied huge pink bows for Valentine's Day. Mike's mother owned the shop. 'It's an ideal job for me,' said Eunice. 'Apart from the Saturday girl, I'm there all on my own, able to run things almost as I want.'

Eunice paused, a naughty twinkle about her. 'I bet I was a shock.'

'Yes.'

'It's not your fault, Eunice,' Ig said.

'I must have come out of the blue.'

We nodded.

Eunice dug the prongs of her fork into the cheesecake and licked. She didn't take full mouthfuls, just sucked at the fork in between gulps of wine. I looked at the crystal heart, at the hair grips, at her wide eyes. I abandoned the idea of eating the salad when I found a thick blond hair coiled around a piece of the goat's cheese. I pushed the plate away.

'She's not with us any more.'

'Oh,' replied Eunice. 'Can I ask—'

'She died. Almost three years ago.'

Eunice drew breath to ask another question, but I spoke before she could.

'She had an accident.'

'Oh,' replied Eunice, before going back to talking about her own life. She told us about Judy and John, her adoptive parents, about St Albans. She loved John, but not Judy. 'We don't get on. We fell out after some very unkind things she said to me before my wedding. Things about my past. And since my father died last year, I can't see the point of her.'

We both nodded. She took after my father, I thought. Her inability to self-edit, the endless talking. A female version of him without the smoothed edges.

When we'd finished eating, Ig refused her attempt to pay, 'It's the least we can do,' he said, thrusting her hand out of the way.

As we got to the door, Eunice turned to us. 'How do you feel? Now you've met me. Do you think we're going to get on?'

'Of course,' said Ig, putting a hand on her back to guide her through the doorway and out into the fresh air.

'I hope so,' said Eunice, bunching her shoulders up towards her ears. 'I really do. You both seem really nice,' she said.

a proper part in a decent play

IG LAY ON THE SOFA WEARING THIN COTTON TROUSERS THAT LOOKED like pyjamas. His work uniform. Exhausted, he sighed loudly, making sure we all knew it. He spent the day practising Reiki in a healing centre. For two years, Ig had been a Reiki master. He was sought after. A man who had healing hands, someone who could fix people with his energy. He'd work from eight in the morning until eight in the evening, seeing one client after another. He'd come home so exhausted he barely wanted to move.

'I'm knackered,' he said, drinking Mexican beer from the bottle.

I threw down my bag and sat next to him on the sofa. He handed me his beer, to offer me a sip. 'Me too,' I replied.

That day, I'd worked for my father. Every Thursday, my guaranteed weekly work, flexible enough that if an audition came up I could skip off. We did a loop, going first to Primrose Hill, through Islington, then up to Hampstead and down to the City, in his black delivery van.

It seemed to suit my father, driving around in a van. I sat up front, next to him. He talked the whole way round. Telling tales of himself as a young man, full of ideas, fresh out of Oxford with a history degree, touring the world in a camper van. He went to festivals, spent half a year living in a commune in San Francisco, drank ayahuasca in South America.

He and my mother set the business up when they first married. She had the idea that wine would be the thing to sell. They toured vineyards in France and Italy, trying to learn everything they could. Thursdays provided him with one day a week to hand on his knowledge, to train me, to make me share his enthusiasm. As we went from pub to pub, he explained this grape and that vineyard to me, why we sold at a particular price, what the wine would drink well with.

The pubs my father targeted were similar, each one run by a man in jeans and a navy blue sweater over a striped shirt who wrote the day's menu in chalk on a blackboard, listing venison, shanks of lamb, black pudding, steak and kidney pudding, sauces containing blackberry, and salads using beetroot and kohlrabi. A traditional pub, stripped out. Bare floorboards, scrubbed oak tables, mismatched chairs and wine glasses slotted between metal rails, hanging upside down from the ceiling. Another place might be painted differently, slate grey instead of midnight blue, but there'd be the same stripped oak floorboards. One pub had single words written in gold italics: *eat, dance, joy, friendship*. My father, a dapper-looking tradesman in his blue corduroy jacket, wheeled in cases of red wine and champagne. I hung back while the paperwork was done. At our last stop, a small place in the City, we always pulled a stool up to the bar, drank a glass of my father's red wine and shared a plate of charcuterie. He paid, and called it 'your wages'.

Today, we had an extra stop for a new client, east of the City. The landlord had contacted my father because his customers were changing, people had begun to ask him for different wine varieties. Inside the pub, the carpet was a confection of brown, mustard and orange, lights on fruit machines flashed, the ceiling was low and made the place feel cramped and stifling. Silent male drinkers stood with pints. My father and I waited at the bar for Steve. He had a smoker's face and wore grey trousers, grey shoes, had grey hair and grey skin. He nodded at my father and told him to sit. My father tried to crack jokes with him but the man didn't laugh, obviously suspicious of men like my father, men with hairstyles, men who wore sky blue. 'I'm not into wine,' he said, looking my father up and down. He wanted to taste a couple of cheap whites and a couple of cheap reds and see how they sold. But my father pulled more bottles out. He got the landlord tasting glass after glass. 'Let me explain these wines, Steve,' he said. 'I think I can convince you.'

On the sofa, I refused Ig's beer and instead spooned vanilla yoghurt from a pot into my mouth. 'Dad was true to form today,' I said to Ig. 'A shameless old hippy. He ripped off a new customer.'

I laughed but Ig didn't. He disapproved of my father's antics, of his willingness to deceive people.

'I didn't rip him off,' my father said. 'I was just better at haggling than him. It's business. Anyway, I'm teaching Lizzy.'

Ig sighed and rolled off the sofa. He padded over to the side table on bare feet and handed me a sheet of paper with a name and number on it. 'Someone phoned for you while you were out,' he said.

It was the theatre I'd auditioned at. The note said they'd be in the office until nine that evening.

'Who is it?' my father asked. I ignored him and went into the kitchen to dial.

'We have some good news for you,' the voice said. 'You've got the part of Katy. The director loved you. He'll see you for the first rehearsal next Monday morning. Eight sharp.'

I stood in the doorway and gripped the frame. I let my head fall back. 'I've done it,' I said. 'At long last, I've fucking done it. A proper part in a decent play.'

My father rushed off to fetch champagne. He called me 'my Lizzy', and whooped when the cork shot out, hitting the wall. He poured three glasses. We drank until the bottle was finished then opened another.

Across from us, opposite the table, a black-and-white photograph of our mother stood propped up against the wall. A huge picture. Her face must have been enlarged to four times its real size. She was diagonal to the frame, her mouth, full lips, flawless teeth, near the bottom left corner. She looked young, probably my age. My father liked it there on the floor, propped up against the wall. My Margaret, he called her. My wonderful Margaret. Ig and I thought the picture should be hung but my father disagreed. He was adamant about the way our mother should be preserved in people's memories so we hardly dared touch the picture.

That evening, in the shadow of our mother's image, it felt like the four of us together again. 'I've just had a wonderful memory. The warm evening, with the doors open, has reminded me,' my father said.

He gave us this scene: my mother's feet against the bare floorboards in the kitchen. Summer. The doors open, the room all light and air. My mother at the stove, wearing a long patterned dress in navy blue and rust. My father sat at the table taking her in. He loved her feet – 'little, pink, soft feet against the rough-hewn floor. She wouldn't put shoes on. It was sexy.'

A wonderful cook. Instinctive, creative. 'An artist!' my father said. When she'd finished cooking, they ate outside. He sat on a blanket under the mulberry tree. She brought the food to him then afterwards they lay on their backs to smoke a joint. They gazed at the tree against the sky, stoned, fascinated at the sound the leaves made in the breeze, watching them flicker and rustle, the smell of marijuana mixing with the freshly mown grass. 'It was a perfect day,' he said. 'We were in love. We'd decided to begin children. She wanted nothing more than to be a mother. It was all she wanted from life. To live in a lovely, busy home, full of little people running around. She had plans. She'd cook, make bread, sew clothes for them, design a wonderful secret garden by the wall, hide little goblins and pixies in it. We laughed at the thought she might have ten babies. Or eleven! Just keep having them. We thought of her spending her days padding about the house like Mother Goose, her little goslings tripping along behind her. We were so stoned by then, the thought of her with all these children made us laugh and laugh. We couldn't stop. It wasn't that funny but we were off our heads. We laughed until our insides hurt, until we couldn't take any more, until we both thought we might split in two.' My father sipped his champagne, his eyes distant. 'We were the envy of people,' he said. 'Margaret and I. The way we were. So free. So true with one another.'

theatre

I WAITED OUTSIDE THE THEATRE UNTIL THE DIRECTOR CAME. I WORE little make-up, my hair tied back, flat shoes and loose clothes. I wanted to look like a blank canvas, like someone he could do something with, but when he arrived rushing up to the door, he barely glanced in my direction. He jostled the key in the lock, complaining it was stiff, then let us both in. I touched my hair to check everything was still in place. As we walked into the theatre, he didn't say 'good morning' or ask how my journey was. He didn't say any of the things I imagined he might have said, the things I'd practised my answers to, so I said nothing either. We went through a side door and I raced to keep up with him, my legs no match for the great strides he took along the corridor.

Backstage smelled of damp. We sat on wooden chairs, our knees almost touching, the script on our laps. First he told me about the play. The story of an unhappily married woman. A poignant comedy, sad but redemptive, he said. My part would be small: a difficult person in a café. 'You represent loneliness,' he said. 'The atomisation of society, a world where no one touches anyone else, an urban world where everyone lives in the dark.'

I nodded as he spoke, looked at him eagerly, wanting him

to know I'd do whatever he asked.

'Your part is small, as I said, but I like you. You have a certain quality. I have something else in mind.' He stood up to cross the theatre. 'Been on a trapeze before?' he asked.

'No.'

'We have to do this early before the theatre's in use,' he said. 'We need the trapeze. And we need to be quick.'

He raked through a cardboard box, finding a harness, a black figure of eight shape, with a circle for each leg. 'Here,' he said. 'Step in.'

I hesitated.

'Don't worry. It'll be fun. The very best kind of fairground ride.' He seemed suddenly eager, as if I had been just the thing he'd been waiting for. 'You're adventurous,' he said. 'I can tell. You and me are going to have fun together. I knew it, as soon as I saw you.'

I didn't know how to reply so I just smiled at him. I took hold of the harness with one hand, held his shoulder with the other and stepped in. His shoulder felt firm and solid. Broad, safe shoulders. He bent to tighten the belt. His head rested close against my stomach, his ear almost touching my belly button. I wondered whether he needed to be so close.

'I haven't used this before,' he said, looking up at me, laughing so I could see a row of perfectly white little rectangles for teeth. His eyes twinkled as he pressed his hand into mine, promising me I'd be fine. His hand felt warm and dry. When he took it away so he could pull the tabs and the harness, it surprised me to realise I'd wanted him to stay like that with his hand in mine.

'Are you sure you know what you're doing?' I asked.

'No,' he said, 'but look.' He yanked hard on a thick, bright yellow canvas strap. 'That's the safety harness. Nothing will get through that.' Click. Everything in place.

He went to the side of the stage where he sorted through ropes hanging from the ceiling. The harness jabbed my thigh. I jerked upwards, just off my feet, then thudded down. I squealed. The director laughed. 'You're safe as houses, Miss Knight,' he shouted from the wings. 'Don't worry your pretty little head with thoughts of falling.'

I wanted to be swept up by his confidence but instead I felt a trickle of sweat slide down my back. The director pulled the rope again. This time, I rose more gently, trying to control myself. I stayed there, about three feet up, my legs swinging beneath me.

'Very undignified,' he said. 'I am sorry.'

I was meat, tipping in thin air, while the director wandered the stage, suddenly serious, explaining. 'The trapeze scene represents the leading lady's fantasy,' he said. 'Imagine that. Feel that as you are up there. A woman viewing another version of herself, running away through the air. Sexually alive, vivid, energetic. Temptress instead of drudge. Wearing a diaphanous white dress rather than her usual marigold-yellow rubber gloves.'

In front of me, red velvet chairs swept back towards the far wall, curving right and left. A full crisp packet that some-one must have lost during a performance lay at the edge of a chair by the aisle. I rolled my feet, turned my ankles, rotating them in thin air. The harness dug into my groin. I wanted to come back down. The director searched for his glasses. I felt the blood supply to my legs cut off. I pulled my legs together and leaned back so I made an arc. I urged myself forwards and back holding on to the ropes either side of me. My head fell back. The arc grew until I moved at speed. I took the clip out of my hair and shook it.

'Good girl,' the director said. 'I knew you'd be good. I knew you'd get it.'

Higher and higher, swinging forwards until I flew over the chairs, then going so far back I felt the backdrop curtain ripple against my feet.

When I fell still again he yanked at the pulley sending me six feet higher. 'Try doing a somersault,' he said. I tilted my legs upwards. My head rushed towards the ground. I pushed through until I jerked to a halt with my body upright.

'Wonderful,' he said.

He pulled me higher. 'I want another somersault.'

He cranked and turned so that I was high up, maybe thirty feet. I tried to remain calm but I could feel my chest tighten. The director below held the script in one hand, the pulley in the other. Almost level with the scaffolding that held the lights, I stiffened. The coloured gels, the gaffer tape, white sticky labels with handwritten notes on the back of lights. A labyrinth of tiny walkways going between the lights. Dust covered it all.

'Don't think about it,' the director shouted.

Sweat flooded down my back, a river of it, a torrent of fear. I dabbed moisture from my forehead with my sleeve. I peeked my head forward to check the drop. The height of a house, higher maybe. The director, hand on pulley, waited.

I took a deep breath in then flung myself forward. My stomach fizzed and jumped, I kept my eyes open. The stage floor rushed past me. Then I jolted upright again, my breath quick, my hands shaking.

'You're a little stiff up there,' the director said. 'Do another and loosen up.'

I went again.

'And another.'

Again, I turned.

After ten somersaults, he let me down. My stomach churned. My throat felt hard. He undid the harness and I stepped out, unsteady on my feet. I stumbled, he held out his arm and I grabbed it. Then he pulled his arm right across my stomach and held me tightly in a kind of strange, sideways embrace.

'I need a glass of water,' I said.

In the cloakroom, I scooped handfuls of water over my face. Still panting slightly, I looked at myself in the mirror. I'd turned a shade of split-pea green.

When I came out of the bathroom, the director was at the door. 'I'm sorry,' he said. 'For making you feel sick.' He put an arm around my waist, pulling me towards him so my head rested on his shoulder. 'That wasn't very nice of me, was it?' he said. 'I'll have to make it up to you.'

visitors

MY PARENTS HAD DIVIDED THE HOUSE IN TWO. MY FATHER DECORATED downstairs, my mother upstairs. Along the corridor, she hung lithographs of flowers, positioned vases on windowsills so that upstairs felt like a cottage. The pale blue carpet along the corridor left a slice of dark wood exposed on either side of the uneven floor. The antique door handles were spheres of brass covered in small dents. She had constructed something of her own, using the discarded pieces of other people's homes. Her legacy, the mark she'd left behind.

She disappeared off for days at a time to shop. She found everything in reclamation yards: the battered old floorboards, the iron handles on the windows, the oak beams. She took the train out of London to spend the day buying and I'd wait behind, sitting on the stairs, aching for her to come home. The day seemed so long without the sound of her swishing through the kitchen. Only my father to get lunch. All he'd manage was an old bit of cheese or an apple. We'd be starving by the time Mum came home.

When I did finally hear the gate click, I rushed to help her in with her boxes of stuff. While she drank her tea, I sat in close to her, my legs touching hers so I could feel the warmth of her, holding her arm so she couldn't go again. She went through the box of old prints she'd bought, or sifted a box of brass, showing me handles, levers, switches, small squares of metal grille, everything covered in dirt. Things bought at car boot sales, at antique shops or funny little bric-a-bracs her friends ran on the coast. It baffled me why she bought this dirty old stuff when the shops were so full of new things. But then she'd polish a handle, bring it back to life, make us all see the beauty in it.

'I made this place too,' I remember her saying one night, when I heard them arguing bitterly.

The house had felt alight when she was in it. She whisked through the rooms, smoothing and tidying, making the whole place better, aiming at perfection as if my father's love depended on it. In the evenings, she smoked a joint, her legs flopped across my father's lap.

Upstairs, we couldn't throw her away. We kept her in my old bedroom, the place I used to sleep before my father built us separate studio flats in the courtyard. We kept her folded up with tissue paper so she didn't crease. We covered her in plastic sheeting to keep the dust off. So crammed full of her, we could hardly open the door any more. I had to push it halfway and squeeze through if I wanted to sit with her. Hanging in my old wardrobe, the sheepskin coat she always wore, the long dresses, the blouses with pearl buttons. It smelled of her in that room, her own warm scent, a mixture of lily of the valley and biscuits. I could bury my face in an old sweater, smell her as if she was still wearing it. I spotted a cardigan with a curl of hair still clinging to the fibres. I looked at the hair but didn't remove it from its place. A memento as precise and direct as that seemed too precious to pull off and hold. We packed her away so we could have her when we needed.

She used to lie in bed sewing. 'When I sew,' she told me,

'I'm calm. I don't have to think about anything.' She could spend a whole day like that. Her own enormous bed felt like a room in itself, its own place, a vast ocean of white with coloured silks and needles thrown around the counterpane. I wanted to jump in with her but she told me to be careful, not to upskittle her threads or spike myself with a needle. I wriggled under the warm covers. Our bare feet touched, mine icy cold from running around without shoes on, hers hot and dry. I lay close in to her; a milky, sleep smell about her. All wrapped up in the duvet, I felt like we were little sardines packed in a tin. I wanted someone to close the lid, seal it down, so I could stay there for ever.

I still kept the wooden box, inlaid with mother of pearl, full of her lipsticks. She had none of the ugliness that my friends' mothers had: the toenail clippers, the horrible stinking creams to remove hair, the pumice stones with a skim of slime across the bottom, strange pink sponges to protect sore toes. My mother had jars of creams that smelled lovely, little jewellery boxes full of rings, big chunky ones decorated with crystals or bright green or blue stones, thick wooden bangles, everything beautifully stored. Even my friends agreed: her things were special.

We kept so many of her clothes, they wouldn't all fit in that one room. The overflow hung in Ig's old wardrobe in the spare room. Her wedding dress, a fur jacket, the black dress with the halter neck. She wore it for my father's fiftieth birthday party with a gold headband and bare feet. Her hair had come right the way down the smooth skin of her back.

Because my mother took up all of my old room, we only had Ig's old bedroom for guests. A quiet and empty space with a swept wooden floor and a bed covered in a white cotton counterpane, something church-like about it. Cool inside, smelling of dust. I loved the view from up there, out over the mulberry tree and the shed. All I could see was garden, wall and more trees beyond. I could pretend London didn't even exist. Just our green and pleasant land, an oasis, the only people around for miles. Not street after street full of rot and empty cans.

I picked off a dead moth from underneath the counterpane. Its legs contracted and bunched together like a single false eyelash. I shook it out of the window then made the bed up with fresh sheets. I'd bought a bunch of tulips from the shop across the road – five quid, I don't know why I did it. Purple tulips, a tight bunch of them held together with an elastic band. They had thick green stalks that leaked white sap where they'd been cut. Shouldn't it have been my father buying flowers, making an effort?

The tulips rested in a vase on the windowsill. I wiped around the pine table that served as a dressing table and sat on the edge of the bed. Everything in the room was light, except for the dark wooden wardrobe next to the door. The tulips looked somehow correct where I'd placed them.

I had one foot in the shower, about to bring the other one in when the doorbell went. Irritated, I wrapped my towel around me and looked outside. She stood on the doorstep, suitcase in hand, hair hanging in neat curls as if she'd been at them with a pair of heated tongs. She wore a red cotton shirt and a pair of jeans. An hour early, with a man standing next to her. I hung out of the window of my studio. 'Eunice,' I said. 'I need to get dressed.'

One weekend, I thought. It'll be over before I know it. I resolved to handle the weekend like an amusement. Embarrassing relatives arriving from nowhere, demanding to be tolerated. I could do that. Only two nights.

'We'll wait,' she replied.

I pulled on a pair of trousers, a white sweater, and went outside to greet them.

'This is Mike,' Eunice said. 'He's not staying. He's just dropping me off.'

Mike seemed solid and still, smoothing a hand down his cotton sweater. Eunice reminded me of a nervous, scatty greyhound. Everything they wore had been pressed. I wondered if Mike had done it, had stayed up late the previous night, making sure the jeans, the shirt, the light sweater hanging over Eunice's arm were all as good as new so they'd make a good impression. His own petrol-blue sweater had all the hallmarks of careful laundering. Maybe that's what they both did. They spent their evenings ironing and washing, giving everything the once-over with a lint roll before bed. The leather bag she carried was a perfect, unscuffed shiny brown leather with a gold buckle. They looked to me like two children buttoned into adult costumes.

When Eunice called to say she'd be curious to see where we'd grown up, I was caught off guard and couldn't think of an excuse. She felt our home might be a piece in her jigsaw. She asked me why none of us had called her after our lunch. 'We didn't want to intrude,' I said. I kept everything I told her contained beneath a patina of small untruths. I gave her the kind of picture she might like to have had. An image of people who cared about her but who appreciated she might need a little distance. I didn't say the obvious: we had nothing in common and could carry on quite happily without her.

'I'm going to have to get properly dressed,' I said.

'I did say to Eunice we shouldn't come early,' Mike said.

I rushed back to my studio, dried my hair, put a different sweater on. It took me no longer than five minutes. When I went to find them in the sitting room, Eunice was perching on the long leather sofa with a cup of tea in front of her. Mike stood beside her, not touching anything. 'I helped myself,' Eunice said, pointing to the tea. 'I didn't think you'd mind.' She took a half-eaten chocolate bar out of her bag then peeled back the wrapper to reveal a thick stub of chocolate with nibble marks around it. She finished it with her tea.

'I like this place,' she said, folding the wrapper into a square and putting it under her cup. 'It's very cool.'

She turned the pages of one of the photograph albums my father kept on the coffee table. 'Have you seen this?' she asked, pointing at the book. 'Those flares he wore should have been banned.'

'I should go,' said Mike.

'Why don't you have some tea too, Mike?' I asked, not understanding why I didn't want to be alone with Eunice.

Eunice stood up and clapped her hands together. 'No tea, Mike,' she said. 'Come on. Let's have a look at this place.'

I paused.

'You've got things to do,' said Mike. 'I can tell.'

'I have to close up the office. Shut down the computer. Make a couple of phone calls before people go home.'

'I'll wait with Eunice until you're ready,' he said.

I rushed out of the room to the office, then sat at my desk and held my head in my hands. I breathed long, slow breaths in and out. The air in the office was cool. There was something safe about the place, something ordered and predictable. Everything could be put away in filing cabinets or trays. I sat. I had nothing to do. I just needed to be away from them. A trespasser picking over my life. I'm not a private person and I don't mind guests so why did she bother me so much? How much time could I take before I had to go back in there?

When I finally went back into the house, nearly an hour later, the afternoon had begun to fade. From the kitchen, I could hear Eunice and Mike arguing in whispers about whether or not they should turn on a light. Eunice for, Mike against. I paused to listen. *You can't behave like that in someone's else's home. It's just a light. You're taking liberties. It's not as if they can't afford it. That's not the point. Well, I'll leave ten pence then, on the sideboard, to pay for it. Don't be an idiot, Eunice.*

I coughed sharply before entering the room, finding them both on the sofa, staring ahead of themselves into the gloom. I switched on the light, making them both blink and squint.

'We shouldn't have come so early,' Mike said.

'It's fine,' I replied.

'I was impatient,' Eunice said. She looked up at me from the sofa, her blue eyes open wide, her head cocked to the side. 'No, I was excited,' she said in a small, irritating voice. Then she tapped herself across the wrist. 'I always get it wrong,' she said.

'Make yourself at home. Come and go as you please,' I said. 'I just had these few things to do that were urgent.' I reached for Eunice's bag. 'Let's take this upstairs.'

'I'll carry that up,' said Mike.

In the guest room Eunice stood in front of the window and looked down the garden, admiring the mulberry tree. Its branches were covered in small buds just on the brink of un-furling into new, fresh green leaves. We were lucky, she declared, to have such a wonderful garden, such a large piece of land in London.

Mike said he'd drop her bag upstairs, then leave. Somehow he seemed too big for the room. Only a tiny space between the

45

wardrobe and the bed, barely room for one person to squeeze through to the small desk. We were crammed in there so closely, I got a noseful of his aftershave: heady, thick and musky. Mike's big white trainers kicked against the legs of the bed as he tried to manoeuvre himself further inside.

'Lovely room,' he said.

'Purple,' she said, noticing the tulips. 'My favourite colour. Did you buy them?' she asked, her eyes full of longing and gratitude. 'You're so kind. Really kind to do that for me.'

'It's just flowers,' I replied.

'No,' she said, 'that's really thoughtful and welcoming of you.'

She heaved her overnight bag up on to the bed, unzipped it and begun taking things out. First came her washbag, put on the side table next to the bed. Then a silk blouse, a long cardigan, a denim skirt. She turned to the wardrobe and opened the door. 'I'm a bit fussy about my clothes,' she said. She paused as she noticed the wardrobe already full of my mother's clothes. Then, without another thought, her hand reached up to grab the coat hanger closest to the end. She yanked it across, shoving my mother's carefully preserved things aside a foot or so. She hung her own four items in the space she'd created.

'Creases,' she told me. 'They ruin an outfit.'

Mike laid out her pyjamas, a tube of shower gel and a pair of slippers on the bed.

'Enjoy yourself,' he said, making for the door.

Eunice now looked at me, expectantly. 'I'd love to have a look around,' she said.

Eunice's head darted right and left, taking it all in. Her eyes flickered over pictures, rugs, collections of books. Outside, we walked through to the bottom of the garden. She spotted the door in the crumbled old red-brick wall.

'Can I look through it?' she asked.

But the door was locked and the key inside, in the same place high up and out of reach since we were children. It led out into the park beyond the house. I showed her the office, the door to the cellar, the patch of gravel where the cars were parked and finally my studio, the self-contained flat where I slept. Eunice's eyes flickered around it.

'Dad built them for us,' I said. 'One for me and one for Ig.' Eunice went over to the small sofa my aunt Valerie had given me, covered in green fabric, just big enough to fit two people. She peeked inside the cupboards, sat on the old kitchen chair on to which I threw my clothes. She climbed three or four rungs up the ladder to my mezzanine bed to investigate. 'Only a mattress,' she said. 'No frame.'

She came back down, poked her head into the tiny kitchen, separate from the main room.

'It seems very new, your kitchen,' Eunice said.

'Never used,' I replied.

'But these studios, they're across the courtyard,' she said. 'They're not even connected to the main house. Were you safe in there as children?'

'Safe enough,' I said. 'The big front gate locks. It used to be a car park before my father put these up. He thought it would be a good idea for us once we reached our teens, to be able to come and go as we pleased. He wanted to make us independent. And here Ig and I both are, almost into our thirties.'

'Why haven't you left home?' she asked. The words just seemed to leap out of her, unedited, making me wince at her directness.

The tight little walls of this studio had never let me go. It was supposed to be my halfway house, a step between home and independence. I could tell her I liked my studio. Where else in the city would I find a place whose entrance was a stable door of thick wood, painted deep burgundy? Where else could you leave the top section open to see the sky and feel the air, lie in bed and look out directly on to a garden full of green, even in winter? Where else could I pad outside barefoot into the courtyard, then through a metal gate to the garden at the back of the house where I could lie in a glade of silver birches and read a book while my father rattled down the garden bringing me a pot of tea on a tray?

'It's expensive, Eunice,' I said. 'Rent in London. And acting doesn't pay well.'

Eunice went back towards the mezzanine level, noticing the skylight above my bed.

'It's lovely at night,' I said. 'Looking at the stars.'

'It's what I would have had. One of these.' She turned a full circle, still looking upwards. 'It's wonderful.'

Lucky me.

As we turned to leave, her eyes fell on to the clothes piled over a chair. 'I'm messy,' I said.

I showed her Ig's studio. Different to mine, warmer, colour everywhere. Every shelf, windowsill and table covered by things he'd collected. Crystals stacked into a pyramid on a table. Four pictures of Ganesh, elephants studded in multi-coloured jewels, things from India, from Thailand, from Vietnam. Cellophane cylinders containing hundreds of cheap joss sticks. The smell of sandalwood hit me as soon as I opened the door. No bed on his mezzanine, just a cushion that faced a sculpture of the head of a male deity from Cambodia with its eyes closed. He used it to meditate. He slept below on a sleep mat he'd bought in Vietnam. An imprint of Ig remained on the mat, a ruffled bed sheet at one end, a joss stick still burning out in its holder.

Two large masculine hands landed on Eunice's shoulders. My father kissed her on the cheek from behind. 'Boo!'

Eunice jumped. 'Oh it's you,' she said, giggling. 'I love your house. Elizabeth's been showing me around. You didn't tell me you were so cool.'

'You know, Eunice,' my father said. 'When I bought this, nobody lived in these kind of places. It was before the fashion for lofts. It was unusual to live somewhere full of concrete and exposed pipes. Higgledy-piggledy, the way this is. Everyone still wanted nice, neat houses.'

'It's so creative,' she replied.

'People thought I was crackers. I remember Margaret, Elizabeth's mum, being terrified about telling her own mother she was coming to live with me in a converted garage in North London. Even the night before she moved in the old trout took her by the arm and said: "Are you really sure about this, dear?" And Margaret told her: "It's got a wonderful garden at the back, Mother. With a gorgeous mulberry tree. It'll be perfect for parties." Margaret was as crackers as me.'

Eunice, listening to my father, seemed a woman in love, in the most dangerous sense of the word. She seemed to have no edges. She threw back her head and laughed, an out-of-control, wild kind of laugh. She couldn't stop herself. She just looked so delighted. I wanted to tell her it was never a good idea to love like that.

She told my father she'd looked through his photographs. She made the same joke – that those trousers he was wearing should have been banned – and my father told her proudly that he'd been the height of appeal in them. He told her the girls couldn't get enough. Then he darted over to the cupboard by the front door and came back carrying his old leather jacket. 'You'll recognise this, then,' he said to Eunice. In the album there was a picture of my father at the train station, smoking a fag, louche and unattractive in a long, dirty hair, bad teeth kind of way. My father held the jacket up, displaying it, proud and delighted. 'Look at that. It's aged beautifully. I was quite the thing in this jacket.'

He put the jacket on and twirled, self-mocking and delighted. Eunice laughed and laughed again. I wanted to catch my father's eye, to tell him to slow down. What was he thinking? I wanted to take him aside, tell him to keep his distance, that a girl in Eunice's position would need a very clear line. We'd all need to make sure there was a very clear line.

'I like it,' Eunice said. 'I could see myself in it.'

My father held it for her to try on. It was orange brown – dun, you'd call it, perhaps – with two large pockets on each breast and a wide, rounded collar, large, leather-covered buttons and a dark brown lining. Eunice slipped her arm into it.

'How do I look?'

'Marvellous,' my father said.

Some people disappear in a bad jacket or an unflattering dress, it's they who look awful rather than the clothes, but with Eunice, the jacket seemed to sit upon her. She outshone it. She made the jacket seem more appealing. I looked at her afresh in that jacket. Her hair curled and feminine, her delicate nose, the two nostrils chiselled into perfect little diamonds, the clearness of her skin. The ugliness of the jacket brought all that into relief. She didn't look like the girl from a provincial town in Hertfordshire. She looked, well, she looked like she fitted in. She looked as if she could have been one of us.

'I'd take it off if I was you, Eunice,' I said.

My father had pulled Eunice towards him. His hand ferreted up the sleeve and emerged bringing with it her hand. He then rolled up both sleeves so that they weren't too long any more. 'I think it suits you,' he said. 'I always thought it was an ugly old thing but actually you look good in it.'

Eunice went to the mirror and stood for a while, turning right and left.

'I bought it in Kensington Market. I had to save up. There was a black one exactly the same cut and I agonised over which one I should get. But in the end, I got the brown because I thought it looked sharper with my beard.'

'It's nice,' said Eunice.

'I went to a party the very same night I bought it,' my father said, brushing the collar of the jacket even as Eunice still wore it.

The afternoon passed, the jacket was back on its peg and we were debating the evening. Ig was home from work. He lay on the sofa, looking exhausted. 'How can you be tired?' my father said. 'All you've done is ponce about in a beauty salon all day.' Ig's feet were on the coffee table, great bare chunks of flesh melting on top of my father's wine books and albums, explaining to Eunice what a Reiki healer was. She seemed confused as Ig explained it was all about the movement of energy, that we're all energy. You can't always see it but illness is caused by an underlying energy blockage that he can shift by tapping into the parasympathetic nervous system and unlocking the energetic pathways within the body. If you could find it, you could fix it. Ig hadn't been able to save our mother but every day, six days a week, he saved other people by holding his hands over their bodies to find the pulse within them that he was sure had set them off balance.

'It's about creating profound shifts in people's wellbeing and unlocking their true health within. We all have the potential to be healthy and happy, it's just that things get in the way – toxins, negative emotional energy, the pace of life today. They all have a depleting effect on the body's integrity and its natural ability to heal itself. Sometimes people are ill in a way you can't really see, or diagnose, or treat. They just have an imbalance, something that puts them off kilter, something that might even have happened in the delivery room at birth that just sets them out of rhythm. And if you can get to that, you can save them.'

My father appeared, showing Eunice a bottle of white wine. 'This is the stuff I sell. I'll get it cracked open and you can try.'

He sank a bottle opener into the cork and filled the four glasses he'd arranged on the table. 'Cheers,' my father said, pressing his glass against Eunice's. 'Welcome.'

We all smiled. Welcome.

'Hang on,' said Eunice, putting down her glass. 'I've got something.'

She ran upstairs and came back carrying a white plastic carrier bag.

'You didn't have to do that, Eunice,' my father said.

She put the carrier bag on the table and began pulling out wrapped presents.

'I couldn't turn up empty-handed. Not someone who works in a gift shop, of all people,' she added.

To my father, she handed a present wrapped in deep burgundy paper, tied with a pink ribbon that fell in ringlets. She watched my father as he unwrapped the package. Her eyes fixed on him, hopeful, wanting to catch his reaction at the start, at its most authentic before he could gather himself and pretend to like something he didn't.

'I couldn't have brought wine,' she said. 'Because you know so much about wine. I thought, I can't take him wine.'

My father pulled out of its wrapping a wooden plaque. He turned it over and looked. 'How lovely, Eunice. Thank you,' he said. He held it up to show to us all and then stooped to kiss Eunice on the cheek. One side of the plaque was wooden and the other brown laminate. On the laminate side were printed the words 'Good Friends and Good Wine Make for Good Times'. My father went to the windowsill and placed the plaque there, in between a black-and-white photograph of a woman curled around the body of a man and an old poster for the movie *Performance*.

'It's from Mike's mum's shop,' Eunice said.

I looked around the room at the long industrial window with a bare metal frame, the white-painted brick, the leather chairs with stainless steel legs, the painting of a nude, the black-and-white photographs in razor-thin frames; and Eunice's plaque with gold curlicue framing the letters.

Eunice had bought Ig a book of the walking routes of London. 'Your father said you liked travelling,' she said. She handed me something oddly shaped, wrapped in pink tissue paper. 'Careful,' she said. 'It's breakable.' I unwrapped it to find a blue ceramic duck with a bright yellow beak and large, sad eyes.

We thanked her by clinking our wine glasses against hers.

'It's lovely to be here,' Eunice said. 'Thank you so much for having me.' She shrugged her shoulders up to her chest, looked around at us all, with an elfin, sweet, naughty little smile. We all told her again she was very welcome.

I left my father and Eunice finishing their wine and went into the kitchen to make a tart for dinner. Next door, I could hear Eunice asking my father if he had a picture of her birth mother.

'She was very beautiful. With dark hair. She was a wonderful girl. She had a zest for life,' my father replied.

'But do you have a photo?'

'She had beautiful green eyes,' he said.

'But what was she like?'

'She was kind. And lovely. I remember we'd all been somewhere for the weekend, to the coast, Brighton, I think. There was a big group of us. And she had a guitar and she played it all the way home on the train.'

Didn't they all play the guitar back then? I put the tart in the oven and watched it through the glass door as it bubbled and began to turn golden.

'I don't blame you for anything,' I heard Eunice tell him. 'If you're worried about that.'

Sunday morning, the weather was sunny and crisp and so was my father. He loved Sunday mornings. There was something of the schoolmaster about him as he commanded the kitchen units and stovetop, frying eggs, juicing oranges, rubbing butter into a chicken ready for lunch. He sang 'good morning' to me, thrust a glass of homemade juice in my direction and slipped two eggs from a pan on to a white plate. I didn't want them, not fried in butter. I dipped a piece of dry toast into the yolk and nibbled. By mid-morning, still no sign of Eunice. My father wanted me to check on her.

'I can't go into her room. It would be inappropriate,' he said.

'But she's your daughter,' I said, raising my eyebrows at him, a ripple of anger washing through me at the thought Eunice was his fault. 'You can do whatever you want. You could sit on the edge of her bed and sing lullabies if you wanted.'

'Just check if she's all right,' he said. 'It won't take you long.'

Upstairs, the smell of Eunice's sleep wafted into the corridor, a musty, thick, acidic smell. Her door was open, just a crack, and I peeked through it. The little red shirt she'd worn the night before hung neatly around the chair, her shoes were arranged side by side beneath it. Two earrings and a gold ring formed a careful triangle on the dressing table. Deep asleep, her lips parted, she had the sheet wrapped up around her face, a small corner of it in her mouth, sucking it as she slept. In the other hand, she held the edging where my mother had embroidered tiny red and black ladybirds in silk thread.

I wanted to step inside the guest room and kick one of Eunice's shoes. How would she like it if I stuffed her shirt into my mouth? How would she feel if she woke to see me, standing over her, my face made of two staring eyes, a nose and a large gaping hole, where my mouth might have been, the remains of her red shirt poking from it?

'Eunice,' I whispered. 'It's getting very late.'

She turned over in bed, sighing, her face all crinkled up like a newborn baby, as she registered the light hitting her eyes.

'You're missing the best part of the day. We're almost ready for lunch.' She murmured something I didn't understand. 'Time to get up.'

She seemed to be going back to sleep, so I just gently put my hand to her shoulder and rocked. 'Time to get up,' I whispered again.

She stirred, her eyes opened, squinting at me.

'What time is it?' she asked.

'Late,' I replied. 'We were beginning to worry.'

'What a comfortable bed,' she said. 'What a lovely, quiet room. I love it here.'

55

* * *

The metal tray clattered as it hit the floor. The wire rack inside fell and the raw chicken thudded out against the wood. 'Shit,' my father said. Eunice laughed. On the ground, the pink, flabby chicken was upended, lying on its breast with its legs pointing upwards towards the ceiling. It clasped a half of lemon through its rear end. The second thing he'd dropped that morning. Earlier half a lemon had skidded across the floor, flying away as he brought the knife down on it.

Eunice wanted a bucket of potatoes to peel, or an apple to slice, or a few dishes to wash, because she didn't want to be staying in the house and not helping.

'You're a guest, Eunice,' my father kept saying as he tried to remove a peeler from her or take a cloth out of her hand. 'Elizabeth will peel the potatoes. You're a guest.' He kept saying it. That word guest. Eunice planted herself on the white metal stool by the window, her ankles looped round one another, chomping an apple. She reminded me of a candlestick, made of two coils twisted together, or ivy rooting into a trellis.

'I'd imagined all this,' she said. 'Where you guys must have lived. What you did on a Sunday. Or a Monday, or a Tuesday for that matter.'

She jumped down from the stool, walked around, letting her eyes flicker along a shelf of cookbooks, looking upwards to take in the huge steel cylinder that travelled the length of the ceiling to serve as an extractor fan. Her eyes travelled to a line of pegs with steel pans of all different sizes hanging. She ran a hand along the table. 'Beautiful wood,' she said. She drank us in, putting flesh on the bones of the life she said she'd imagined.

She was still wandering round the kitchen, when a face appeared at the glass of the kitchen doors. Then a hand, waving vigorously. The face was smiling, the way toothless, inane

56

people smile. The door opened to reveal our aunt, Valerie, still wearing the yellow sweatshirt and trainers from the keep-fit class she'd been to.

Valerie hadn't expanded with time, the way some women do. Instead, time had sucked the fat from her bones. She appeared keen and brittle. Her skin was papery and dry. She looked as if she might break. She came into the room, kissed us briefly then slumped back in the high-backed green chair by the door. She looked like a colourful old bird in a tree, her yellow sweatshirt vibrant against the green of the chair and her nose sharp like a beak.

'This is Eunice,' my father said to Valerie. Valerie seemed about to say something – she had an enquiring look on her face – but my father cut in before she could speak. 'She's here for the weekend,' he said curtly.

I wondered how it might go, my father introducing Valerie to Eunice. Valerie, the sister to his dead wife, the woman who still needed to come here, nearly three years on, to check up on him.

Next, my father's old friend Tom arrived, tripping through the door holding a bottle of champagne. A friend from back in the day. He knew who Eunice was. I could tell by the way he and my father exchanged glances. Valerie spotted them, immediately insecure, her eyes darting right and left. What weren't they telling her? She surveyed Eunice, then squinted at my father, then Tom, as if hoping someone would enlighten her.

'Lunch!' my father said, holding a cooked chicken on a plate. The potatoes were placed proudly on the table, a pile of spinach in a white bowl, a bottle of red opened. My father took the head of the table. We fanned out around him, Tom to his left, Valerie to his right. Eunice, Ig and I sat further along.

My father began demolishing the two roast chickens. He stripped the flesh away from the breastbones, ripped the leg bones from the main body. We passed our plates. He doled us out our meat. There was something about the way my father looked, his eyebrows raised and his lips pursed together, that gave him an air of self-conscious insouciance. He couldn't have been scared of Valerie, could he? Not my laid-back father, the man who can do whatever he wants, the man gnawing on his chicken leg and telling Tom how much he loves chewing on bones.

'It feels so animal. It reminds me that I'm an animal, that we're all just animals,' he said. He gnawed some more.

'There's still no greater pleasure for us humans than chomping on another animal,' said Tom.

Eunice glowed, drinking it in, her face blank and open with wonderment, watching my father as he sucked at his lips, drawing in the chicken fat that had settled there.

'As if you needed reminding, Tom, that you're an animal,' said my father.

Tom guffawed and swigged at his wine. 'What was it that Kingsley Amis said? That the thing he loved about sex was reminding someone who was an animal but liked to think she wasn't an animal that she was indeed an animal after all. Something like that.'

Valerie rolled her eyes.

'Sorry about this,' I said.

Eunice shrugged, looking thrilled. 'Don't be.' Valerie kept looking over at Eunice. She seemed to want to strike. She had a question. Any moment she'd slap it down on to the table.

We ate the chicken, finished an apple crumble, passed around a plate of cheeses. Empty wine bottles gathered. Eunice held

58

out her glass for more wine. Greedily swallowing down gulpfuls.

About to take her coffee to her mouth to sip, Valerie stopped, changed her mind. She held the cup aloft and turned to Eunice.

'And how do you fit into the picture?' she asked.

'Eunice has come to see us for the weekend and get to know us,' my father replied. 'She's my daughter.'

Valerie winced. The word flew through the air and landed on her cheek with a sharp sting.

'Right,' my father said, clapping his hands and jumping up from the chair. 'Who's for a smoke?'

He took out an old leather pouch cracked with age from the drawer next to the cooker. He removed a ball of dark resin from it, the size of a golf ball, wrapped in cellophane. He laid out a thin sheet of cigarette rolling paper on the table, a cigarette lighter and a cigarette. He cranked at the lighter, holding the block of hash in the flame until it singed. He flaked two layers of hash shards on to the rolling paper.

'Do you smoke, Eunice?' he asked. Valerie kept looking sideways at Eunice.

'Have you met any other of your relatives?' Valerie asked.

'I'm still searching,' Eunice replied.

'Who for?' my father said.

'Well, for my mother, of course,' Eunice said. 'The agency are having trouble locating her. They think she must have moved a lot.'

Valerie stared at him, her hands drumming at the table. My father singed the block again with his lighter. He licked down the seam of the cigarette to unwrap the tobacco then dropped it on top of the flakes of hash. He took the joint up to his mouth and ran his tongue along the adhesive edge.

'Oh, that's good,' he said, inhaling deeply. 'Who else wants?' He held the joint out. Smoke wandered away from its red end in a thin trail.

Valerie clipped the joint from my father's hand. The red end glowed as she closed her mouth around it, sucking the smoke down, a thick white curl of smoke rolling around her rocks of teeth. Her tongue lolled about on her bottom lip as she swallowed. She shaped her mouth into an O, expelling smoke in a single column.

My father carried on smoking, then passed the joint on to Tom, who took two or three good puffs interspersed with sips of his wine.

'And how old are you, Eunice?' Valerie said.

'I'm twenty-three,' Eunice said.

'You're twenty-three.' Valerie looked over at my father. 'She's twenty-three,' she said, enunciating the words slowly, moulding each one into a weapon she could hurl at him.

'Yes,' my father replied.

Valerie held out her hands. She took back the joint which was now heading down the table from Tom towards Ig. She puffed deeply, scowling as the smoke hit her eyes. Her nostrils flared as she stared down my father.

'You're a liar.' She said it softly.

My father put out his hand and touched Eunice's. Valerie raised her eyebrows. She turned her head away from him quickly, like someone flicking away dust.

'I'm not a liar, Valerie. There are no lies,' he said.

Eunice twirled a spoon. She spun it, then let it go, watching it land. She picked the spoon up to do it again. She'd transfixed herself on to the spoon. She didn't look up once to watch my father and Valerie.

It wasn't unusual for Valerie and my father to be rowing.

60

Tom, Ig and I had watched this kind of thing often enough. Bottles of wine, then weed, and soon after the two of them would start going at each other. She'd rake the past over, sieve it for spoils, search for a gem she could hold up into the air. A nice nugget of something solid and incontrovertible. Something he absolutely couldn't deny – a mystery daughter might turn out to be the winning diamond.

Silence. It seemed they'd stopped. Who to speak first? But then they started again. *The thing that's wrong with you is.* My father had stubbed the joint out into the remains of his crumble; it burrowed like a paper maggot into the cooked apple, all wrinkled and squashed.

The row was building the way a wave does, gathering and gathering. Ig looked ashamed. Valerie told my father he was promiscuous. His retort: 'I wish.'

He was selfish, a liar, a rat, no husband at all. Valerie was a sad old spinster, couldn't get a man, bitter, jealous, living vicariously. He'd endured all these years of her policing his life, her face pressed up against the glass, eyes squinting into their happiness. He'd never been able to get rid of her, and he still couldn't. *I have to. Who else is going to keep an eye out for Ig and Elizabeth? Someone's got to get cross with you because Margaret never did. You're always complaining. I don't have to let you come here.*

My father rolled another joint.

'Afghan black,' he told Eunice. 'Bloody difficult to get hold of these days.' He drew in another long puff. The grey-blue smoke rose off the end in an opaque, wandering line and dissolved into the air. 'Damn, it's good. Clear and clean as anything. Not like the stuff nowadays that's sending everyone psychotic. Just a good old-fashioned high, this is. Go on, Lizzy. Have a puff. It'll do you the world of good.'

61

Valerie finished her coffee, said she'd see herself out.

'Sorry,' my father said to Eunice.

'They warned me about this kind of thing,' said Eunice. 'That we can put a spanner in the works.'

My father smoothed his hand over Eunice's. 'It's just Valerie,' he told her. 'It's not you. You're not the spanner.'

'Valerie's a nut,' said Tom. 'She's always been like that.'

In the kitchen, we sat around, finishing the wine. My father opened some port. He was stoned and drunk by now. The light outside had faded to evening. The table riddled with rivulets of spilled wine. Rosy-cheeked, a little slower, at Eunice's insistence, my father said he'd tell her what had happened.

My father had met Eunice's mother on a trip to Brighton. He'd gone down there in a van, leaving my mother at home. 'Tom was there,' he said. This woman he met worked in a café. He was already married to my mother. The woman brought coffee to the table then settled into a chair to read a book while Tom, my father and the others drank the coffee. 'She was all limbs, that girl. Bare arms and bare legs, curled in a chair like a cat in the sun. She didn't look at me once. I was intrigued so I went over to her.'

They'd had three months together, he and this new woman, Louise. An affair. Margaret knew. He told her. Came straight home and told her he'd met someone and wanted to pursue a liaison.

'We were very young when we married and it seemed the way to do things. We thought we were being very modern, very daring and open. Relationships were too controlling. Families were little units in thrall to capitalism. We were humanists. We loved people and the body. We believed the body should be free. Margaret and I believed we were so in love, we could handle anything. Bigger than convention. Margaret loved this idea.' My father stopped, smiling. 'You've seen Valerie. That's the way Margaret's parents were. Margaret fled that. She wanted something different. We both did. We explored the way we could be, pushing the boundaries, being different. Love was one thing, the body another. Margaret and I never lied about who we were.'

Louise knew he was married, knew the arrangement and she didn't care. 'I don't think there was ever a question of me leaving Margaret,' my father said.

My father and Louise met here and there. He whistled down to Brighton on the train to see her for an evening. She came to London. They wandered down the King's Road together. They had a few overnight stays. It was an experiment, the first time he'd gone that far. 'She was lovely,' my father said. 'There was a freedom to her. She had a wildness I found beguiling. But one time, in the morning, I returned and I saw the way Margaret looked at me. She hadn't slept. Hair all over the place. I realised I had to stop seeing Louise.' He looked at Ig and me, spoke emphatically. 'Margaret was solid. The thing we had was something you could touch. Louise was just electricity, a flash of something exciting.'

My father told Louise he couldn't do it any more. The only time he heard from her again was a letter from her to say she was pregnant. My father wasn't sure he believed her, so he did nothing. Now he looked Eunice straight in the eye. 'I am sorry,' he said. 'I am sorry about the way I treated your mother.'

'She did want me,' replied Eunice. 'She didn't want to abandon me. She wanted to keep me. She loved me, it said so in the social worker's report. She kept me for five months before giving me up. She tried everything to keep me.' She paused, looking round the room at us, a little triumphant. 'I was breastfed,' she said.

'I'm not proud of myself,' my father said.

The afternoon wore away. Eunice finished another glass of red wine. 'Apparently, my mum – my real mum – found out where I'd been sent and came to the house.' She played with the stem of her glass. 'Judy let her hold me. After that, she asked if she could come every Saturday to spend the day with me. She said she'd only take me to the park around the corner. Just a little walk and the chance to hold me. But after the first time, after my real mum dropped me off, I cried and cried. I wouldn't stop. So Judy told her she couldn't come any more. Judy said that it was too unsettling for me. We'd be best off left alone to build our own rapport.' Eunice paused, searching our faces for a reaction. 'In fact,' she said, her voice filled with indignation, 'I found out recently that Judy then reported her for finding out where I was to ensure it didn't happen again. Judy called it a clean break.' She slammed the glass back on the table. 'I uninvited Judy to my wedding and haven't spoken to her since.'

'Perhaps Judy thought she was doing the kindest thing at the time,' said my father.

'But the good thing is,' said Eunice, ignoring my father, 'she really spurred me on to find my own family. That's why I'm here! She gave me hope. My mum risked all the upset of coming to Judy's house, of seeing me, having to give me back. She did all that for me. It shows how desperately she wanted me. Can you imagine how thrilled she's going to feel when I find her?'

Outside in the car park, Mike fiddled with the lock on the boot while Eunice jigged at his side telling him what a wonderful weekend she'd had. Alight, eyes bright, fizzing with energy, she told him how welcome we'd all made her feel. 'You don't realise what you've all done for me,' she said. 'Letting me come for the weekend. It's been amazing.'

My father put Eunice's case on the ground next to the car. Wine stained his lips now. A little unsteady on his feet, eyes hooded from the smoke, he looked a mess. Scruffy strands of dark hair fell into his eyes, blue linen shirt falling open at his chest, a joint still in his hand, the backs of his brown leather shoes broken, his feet slipped into them like slippers. Mike could barely contain his disapproval as his eyes flickered along the length of my father, this ridiculous man his new wife had just fallen in love with.

'I think this weekend's been good for Eunice,' he said. 'She's imagined all this, you lot, her birth family, where she comes from. She talked all the time about it, about what she might find here.' He threw the case in the back of the car. 'And now she knows. She's had the chance to see what you're all like.' He slammed down the door of the boot, wound up the car window and without looking back, drove off with Eunice by his side.

ACT TWO

I wish I had beautiful things like you've got.

the trapeze

THE DIRECTOR TOLD ME OVER THE PHONE HE HAD SOMETHING HE thought might loosen me up on the trapeze. 'An exercise,' he said. 'You'll enjoy it. But we'll have to do it together at my flat. I'll expect you at six thirty p.m.'

I chose a duck-egg blue sweater, black jeans, a simple loose jacket. I didn't tell my father or Ig where I was going. I just shouted through the door to them that I'd be home later. As I walked to the bus, I stopped my mind from leaping forward. I kept telling myself, it's a small part, five minutes on a trapeze. Nothing special, nothing noteworthy. I had no reason to be excited. Obviously, the director liked me or he wouldn't have invited me over but I wouldn't ruin everything by letting my fantasies run away with themselves.

At a concrete block of flats by the river, I pressed the buzzer for number thirty-two. The building, like the director himself, was stout and stocky, built to last. A solid, immoveable lump of gristle. The thin glass buildings either side made it look even sturdier. His voice came through the intercom, telling me to come straight up. Fourth floor. When he opened the door to me, he had wet hair and bare feet. He wore jeans with a pale blue shirt. He'd rolled the sleeves of the shirt up, revealing a glimpse of firm, thick forearm.

In here, he seemed smaller, his bare feet padding against deep, fluffy, mustard-yellow carpet. 'I inherited the flat from an aunt,' he said, spotting me looking at it. 'It came with the carpet.'

'I wasn't thinking anything about the carpet,' I said.

He tapped me across one shoulder. 'You're a bad liar.'

Windows stretched the length of the sitting room. The river beyond was busy with boats. The water slapped and rippled, churned by the movement to the colour of milk chocolate. I stood waiting for him to offer me a drink, or a chair, or any of the normal things to make me feel I was welcome. He fiddled with his sleeve. 'There's something I'd like to do. To help you on the trapeze. I believe in you. I want to make this work.'

'I want this to work too.'

'It wouldn't be good to do this on a light head.' He grinned. 'We'll have a drink afterwards.'

He opened the glass door on to the balcony, beckoning me through it. At one time, the door handle must have been white, but all that remained were specks of the paint and a surface of soft iron where years of being touched had rubbed it smooth.

'Don't worry. I've done this plenty of times before,' he said, offering me his hand. He dragged a chair towards me and pulled one along for himself. We looked out across the water. The wall of the balcony was formed by a sheet of concrete so thick you could sit there, with a metal pole running along it to stop people falling.

'OK?' The director patted my leg. 'Stand up and come over here.'

Below, a determined rower on a slim boat swept through the water. Tourists wandered the riverbanks, hordes of them, in belted coats and rucksacks. The director put his hands on the wall to lever himself up. He put his feet under the metal railing, resting his shins against it.

I wanted to tell him that he had a low centre of gravity. It was different for him because he was short and firm. But I knew he didn't take refusal. I'd done my research. Actors with their own ideas didn't do well with him. The drop below was thirty or forty feet. 'Come on, Elizabeth. You'll be fine,' he said. 'No fear.' He waggled his hand at me, beckoning me up.

I slapped my palms flat on the wall, splaying my fingers as wide as they'd go. I leaned my weight into my hands then scrambled a leg upwards. Standing, the director put his hand out and took mine. I felt the pole jabbing into my shins, the only thing protecting me from tumbling forwards. My feet began to fizz and sting. The stinging changed into a dull pain, travelling upwards, intensifying as it went.

'My feet hurt,' I said.

'Let's stand for a while,' he said. 'Breathe.'

The rower passed. The director's hand felt warm and dry. My own must have been cold with sweat as I gripped his.

'You're terrified,' he said. 'Relax. This is safe. There's a pole.'

'It barely comes up to my knees.' I felt my voice choke. I swallowed away tears.

'Feel it,' he said. 'Don't react. Just observe where the fear is in your body.'

An image of home travelled through my mind. The image of the kitchen table, of everyone around it, my father at the head, talking about nothing; or himself, or the past, always the past. Ig slumped around the place.

'Give the fear a colour,' the director was saying. 'Watch it. Don't react. Observe. Feel it wandering your body.' He turned

71

sideways on to me. He spoke in a slow, nasal voice. His breath smelled of coffee. I imagined my father and Ig again, seeing me up here. I saw them laugh at me.

'Everyone's scared. All actors are. It's just the way a performer responds to fear that marks them out. If you learn to respond well to fear, you can go anywhere, do anything, be anyone on stage. You have to see the fear as just a thing, the same as anything else, the same as happiness or laughter, a state that will pass.'

I didn't speak. My legs were set apart, wider than my hips. I had bent my knees and I focused on the sensation of the metal bar pressing into my shins. A drop of sweat worked its way downwards through the centre of my chest, drawing the heat out of me. The cold began to find its way through me.

'Imitate a person who isn't afraid. You want to be seen, and yet to do that, you hide. An actress's life is only ever performance and imitation, revelation and concealment. You imitate someone but that person you're imitating is nothing more than an imitation of someone else. It's like mirrors reflecting each other back and forth.'

We stayed quiet for a moment.

'Tell me something you're noticing,' he said.

'This is really very dangerous,' I replied.

'It's fine. Come on. What are you noticing?'

'A smell,' I replied. 'Slightly sweet. It just came to me, on the breeze, just then.' I hardly moved my mouth, in case the movement made me topple off. 'It's gone. I could just smell it for a second. I can't find it again. No. It's definitely gone.'

'So let's keep going,' he said. 'Keep observing your surroundings. Keep finding the fear. Hold it. Turn it over in your hands. Be curious about it. Treat it as you would an interesting object.'

In my head, the image of Ig and my father laughing appeared

once more. I wished I'd stayed at home. What was I doing here? With a stranger. For nothing, for two lines in a play.

'You're not afraid of falling,' he said. 'You're afraid of jumping. You're afraid your feet might jump you off, against your will. That you might do something reckless. You're not afraid of an accident. You're afraid of freedom. The freedom to do whatever you want. You can't go through life being afraid of it, clinging to the safety rail.'

'I think you're pushing—' I began to reply but he cut me off.

'Have faith in your two feet, planted firmly on that wall. Trust them to look after you.'

More boats passed. A couple wandered up the towpath. I heard laughter.

'I bet you live like this,' he said, 'always terrified at the thought of something new.'

I tried to answer him but the words stuck.

'You do,' he said. 'You need to open up. Let life flow. Think of a woman who lives boldly and channel her.'

The director landed with both feet on to the balcony again, turning to hold his hand out for me. I stepped carefully down from the wall. He put his hand on my neck, touched my bare skin. 'You feel cold,' he said. He put his fingers down inside my sweater. 'Shall I fetch you something? To warm you up?' He touched his finger to my lips. 'You've got something. Something I can develop. I like you, Elizabeth.'

Inside, he poured out two glasses of whisky. 'This'll do the trick,' he said as he handed me a glass. He sat back on the deep sofa and rested his feet on the coffee table. I stood, holding the glass, unsure where to put myself. He patted the space next to him on the sofa.

His arm reached out like a proboscis, drawing me in next to him. His hand travelled back towards my neck again. His

73

fingers pressed in against the top of my spine and moved in small circles. 'You OK?' he asked. 'I wasn't too awful to you, was I?'

'I'm fine,' I said.

'I didn't mean to be awful. I just believe in you. I can push you, make you better.'

With the other hand, he swirled his glass. The whisky inside made a small vortex. His fingers moved against my spine; with the other hand his palm rested against the side of my neck, my jawbone pressed against him. 'I hope it's worked,' he said. 'Our little exercise. I do hope you can do the trapeze next time.'

'I'll be fine,' I said. 'I want this part. I want to do well for you.'

'I know you do,' he said. He sipped at his whisky. His hand continued to work at me, moving further down along my spine. 'It would be awful if we had to replace you because you couldn't relax up there on the trapeze.'

I sipped the whisky and lowered my head so my cheek moved into the palm of his hand. The director put his glass down on the armrest. He undid the top button of his shirt. 'It would be awful if we had to lose you,' he said again.

The slatted blinds at the windows made the concrete pavements, orange streetlights and black river water beyond visible in slices.

'I'll work hard for you,' I said. 'I want this. And I know I can do it.'

'After all this hard work. I know how difficult it is for young actresses. How hard it is for them to find their break, how easy it is for them to find themselves stuck in a rut, wake up one day and be too old for it, the possibility of a career just passing them by.' He moved his arm further so that his hand travelled across the back of my neck. His fingers rubbed down my spine, travelling well beneath the top of my sweater. 'It's tough out there, without decent contacts.'

'I know and I'm so grateful to you for helping me.'

I surveyed his face as it came close in to mine, his hot breath touching me. 'Do you like me too?' he asked.

He leaned in closer towards me. I hesitated but he carried on pressing in against me. I tasted the whisky on his tongue, like warm, wet earth, and I closed my eyes.

another visit

SINCE MY MOTHER'S DEATH, VALERIE AND I MET IN COVENT GARDEN every Tuesday. At first we met because it forced us out of the inertia of grief. The meeting made me take a shower, find something to wear other than a dirty old T-shirt and socks and have a go at reality for an afternoon. Now three years on, it had become a habit.

In the early days I travelled up on the top deck towards Covent Garden and felt like a carcass; just bones rattling together. It took me all my effort to buy a ticket, find a seat, remember which stop to change at. I used to wander off the bus without thinking. I'd find myself halfway up a street, blank and listless with no idea how I'd got there or why I'd even left the bus. I lived under a cloud of confusion. Nothing made sense, not even the idea of a bus stop.

But I must have appeared normal to the outside world, even as I wandered these familiar streets, lost. I wasn't marked out by a black armband. No one knew how they ought to treat me. People barged me out of my place, raced to grab the seat ahead of me. My sadness wasn't written on my face any more. No red, streaming eyes and unwashed hair. To the other passengers, I was unremarkable. Just a quiet young woman, sitting on a bus, going from one place to another. I didn't wear my madness in unkempt hair and dirty clothes. I didn't talk to myself or pee on the floor. But all the same, I could have done. I felt as if the inward and the outward had divided. I peered out to the world beyond where things happened that I couldn't understand. I bore witness to a series of moving images happening right under my nose but nothing made sense. I just stayed, ducking behind my eyes. In public, my body became my place to hide in.

I used to sit on the bus trying to remember my mother as something solid, but I could never make an image stay. She dissolved away and the harder I tried, the quicker she'd disappear. Instead, I made the house stay the same. I kept her within the solid objects, things that couldn't disappear. I didn't want anyone to move the rooms around. I needed to know that in every room something of her remained. I needed to see it, touch it, feel its solidity and know her warm hand had brushed that very piece of kitchen counter, or corner of table, or it had been her delicate fingers that had twisted a lightbulb into its socket. I touched the ends of my hair: that bit would have been here when she was still alive, I thought. I still struggled with a haircut.

Valerie and I wandered the streets that threaded around the back of the Opera House until we found a place with untreated, rough wooden counters, coffee makers that looked like a science experiment, tiny cakes studded with whole blanched almonds, everything from somewhere else: Sicilian lemons, Valencian oranges, cakes soaked in syrup made with Provençal lavender. Valerie sighed. They didn't do filter coffee so reluctantly she ordered a cappuccino.

'I said too much the other Sunday,' she said.

'It doesn't matter,' I replied.

'It does,' she said.

She hadn't been for lunch with us since that Sunday with Eunice. She and my father were in one of their frequent cool-off periods. A month or so of not speaking before she'd come back, returning to our lunch table as if nothing had happened. Round two. They would slip back into their roles like putting on a comfortable old piece of clothing. The uniforms they wore to fight in.

Valerie dragged a stainless steel spoon over the surface of her cappuccino. She sucked up the froth then scowled and snorted at the mention of my father. 'Someone has to have the courage to tell Julian what a total berk he is,' she said. 'Because Margaret never did.'

Valerie was skilled at anger but hopelessly inept at sadness. She was the opposite to our mother, who'd been a genius at sadness, yet never revealed to anyone what we'd learned since must have been bubbling away underneath. Valerie could shout, but she couldn't cry. She could rail at the world until I thought her head might explode but she would never show her weakness. She was angry, she said, because our mother hadn't known how to be.

Valerie said that my mother had inherited all the beauty. There'd been none left for her when she came along. There was not the slightest trace of envy because, as she told everyone, she was glad she wasn't beautiful. She said beauty captivated a certain kind of man. They would want to possess it, trap it under a glass to gaze at when they wanted. 'A woman is more free without beauty,' she said.

My father didn't believe her, but I did. It wasn't my mother's beauty that stood in Valerie's way, in spite of my father's bitter assertions about her envy; it was my father himself. Valerie had put him in her way as an obstacle for her tears. While she remained furious with him, she didn't have to cry. Even at my mother's funeral, she didn't cry. Her face was fixed into a furious grimace, bound so tightly I feared she might shatter. 'We lost Margaret the day she got married,' I heard her say. 'We always knew he'd destroy her with his strange ideas about love.'

At the service, Valerie and her parents kept away from our father. Ig and I stood beside him. The three of us knotted together. A sodden day, in an awful cemetery, next to a busy road. Cars trundled past, spraying dirty rainwater on to the pavements. I threw a rose over my mother and the earth swallowed her up, took her from us no matter how much we'd wanted to keep her. I barely noticed the day go by. Suddenly it was over. My shoes wet from the grass. No idea how I got mud up my tights.

Valerie stirred the remnants of froth into the coffee then drained the cup in one go. 'I wish I'd kept my mouth shut,' she said.

'No, you don't, Valerie,' I said and she laughed. The laughter made her face break into lines and creases, the brittle expression she'd been wearing suddenly shattered.

'He infuriates me,' she said.

'We know,' I replied.

'He just blithely carries on.'

'Why didn't anyone tell us about Eunice?' I asked. 'Mum knew yet she didn't say.'

'It wasn't her secret to tell,' she replied, turning to the window, suddenly agitated. 'It's just so typical of your father.' She twisted her napkin around her finger. 'To have some idiotic young woman turn up at his house.'

Back at home, I lay on the sofa, about to read a book, when the phone rang. I opened my book, left it ringing. It wouldn't be important. The ringing stopped but then immediately began again. Then, just as I was about to touch it, I saw the sandwich Ig had made for lunch on the kitchen counter. I knew what the voice would say: could I bring it to the clinic in the next ten minutes. He'd drag me away to take red pepper and hummus to him. I looked back at my book, sipped my tea. The phone rang for the third time.

'Elizabeth.' A breathy, desperate voice. 'Elizabeth,' it said again.

'Yes,' I replied.

'Everything's fallen apart.' The voice broke. Pellets of sound, little jags of crying scratched at my ear. 'I don't know who to turn to.'

'What's happened?' I said.

'Something terrible.' Her voice broke again. I told her it was OK. I said, 'Oh dear.' I hushed and ahhed. I knew I sounded insincere but what else could I do? I barely knew her. In the end, I stopped. I waited until she gathered herself enough to talk. 'Mike's ended our marriage. He's asked me to move out.'

I said nothing.

'I need to get away from St Albans. Just for the afternoon.'

I paused, drew a breath in. 'Well then, why don't you come over here?' I said. 'Come and have a coffee or something.'

Eunice knocked her foot against the front step, a finger in her mouth, sawing at her nail with her teeth. At the sight of me, she dropped her head and began shaking. 'Oh Elizabeth,' she said. 'I can't tell you how nice it is to see a friendly face.' I led her inside, plumped a cushion for her on the sofa.

'I've got nothing,' she said. 'Nothing.'

The thought made her shake again. Her tears seeped into a

tissue. I handed her the roll of kitchen paper and put some water in front of her. Tepid tap water in a scratched, cloudy glass that she didn't touch.

'Without Mike, I've lost my job, my house, everything.'

'I'm sorry,' I said.

The log burned away and the fire crumbled. I threw on more wood. Outside, the afternoon faded. White cloud turned grey, an orange mist of streetlight came over the wall. I switched on the steel floor lamp.

Eunice still hadn't said much. She cried. I offered to fetch her things. She refused, cried some more. Crags of candyfloss-pink polish chipped from each nail. She wouldn't eat anything, didn't want a bath, couldn't face a walk. She wanted to sit by the fire, stare at the flames, try to think of nothing.

Like that, the afternoon wore away. We were reflected in the cold, black window. Shiny, like two characters captured on photographic glass. We looked hyper-real as if we'd been posed that way to tell a story. Eunice's head bent low. I leaned towards her. My face serious; hers desperate. Soft, soothing peripheral light surrounded us in the sitting room. The fire glowed and crackled, the smoked, resin smell of burning logs. 'It's nice here,' Eunice said, leaning back into the sofa. 'It's relaxing. I feel calmer.'

'This is a surprise, Eunice,' my father said. Behind him stood Ig. He kissed Eunice hello, then escaped through to the kitchen. My father poured himself a drink, offered one to both of us. 'I'll do you a strong one,' he said to Eunice, the only acknowledgement that he'd noticed her puffy face and red eyes.

'Who's doing dinner?' my father asked. 'I'm starving.'

'I'll go,' I told him.

I opened the fridge but found only a packet of ham and some old yoghurt.

'There'll be something in the garden,' Ig said, looking up from the newspaper.

My father kept up my mother's vegetable patch. At the height of summer, he would come into the kitchen with his hands cupped, holding tomatoes, or beans. The tomatoes wouldn't be rich red but rather green and tinged. The beans would be thin with black streaks. But he didn't care about the quality of his produce. He never tried to improve it. I'd seen him barefoot, his feet sinking into the mud, just standing there in his vegetable patch, stoned probably. He'd go down some days and smoke. He'd sit on the bench for hours. Ig and I would find an empty wine bottle, its label worn away, sunk into the ground, as if it had sprouted up. On warmer days, he'd take cushions from the sofas and arrange them along the bench. He'd stay there, one hand cocked behind his head, and stare at the sky. Every so often, a thin line of smoke weaved up from his prone body.

I headed across the lawn carrying a small trowel. When I looked behind me, Ig followed. He had his feet half-in my father's trainers. He paced swiftly across the lawn, lifting his legs high like someone walking barefoot across hot sand.

'Elizabeth, wait. I'll help,' he said.

At the bottom of the garden, next to the empty rows with sticks and labels, Ig sat on the bench with his back against the brick wall, picking at a lump of moss. He held the torch and I dug into the ground, pulling up potatoes. I held the green tops, so that the potatoes dangled from the roots.

Ig and I both faced the house. The glass doors into the kitchen acted as a frame for the activity inside. Within the frame, warm, orange-pink light. Outside, cool and dark.

My father appeared in the right side of the frame. He walked across it towards the table on the left. He crossed back again, returning with a glass of water. Eunice took it from him. They pulled chairs out from under the table.

Ig and I sat side by side, close in together. I could feel the warmth of him. I wanted to press in closer. I wanted him to put his arm around me.

Eunice held a shred of tissue. Her head bent and her shoulders shook.

'What the fuck,' Ig said.

I stayed silent.

'I just want to come home in the evenings and be quiet,' Ig said. 'I just want calm and quiet.'

'It's my fault,' I said.

When eventually we went back inside, my father took the potatoes from me, shaking them from the roots.

'Nothing touched these,' he said to Eunice, 'other than a bit of natural fertiliser. Not a chemical on it.' He stuck them under the running tap.

Eunice was tear-stained. A sorry kind of dinner: slices of flabby ham and my father's buttered new potatoes. He doled the food out, standing over the table pronging pieces of ham with a fork. 'Get some food down you, Eunice,' he said. 'You'll feel better.'

She just stared at her plate as if she'd never seen food before. Instead of eating, she told us about Mike. She'd decorated his house, she'd made the very thing she wanted, a home, and then he'd taken it from her. 'I liked owning a home,' she told us. Shortly after he'd asked her to move out, Mike's mother phoned to tell her it was best she didn't work in the shop any more.

A drip dangled from Eunice's left nostril. It shook but never fell. When she finally realised it was there, she blew her nose and left the tissue on top of her potatoes.

'Eunice, all men are shits,' my father said.

You should know, I thought.

'A lot of men find happiness dreary. It's not you, it's not personal, it's the thing called happiness he didn't like.'

Eunice just stared at him.

'It's not admirable, it's just the way it is. I'm not excusing him,' my father said.

'I wanted a baby,' she replied.

'Have another glass of wine and stay the night, Eunice. Get yourself back together.'

Eunice drank the wine. Then she wanted something sweet, but the only thing my father had were apples from his own tree that were thick-skinned and dried your teeth. She reached over to the fruit bowl and took two out. She handed one to my father. He devoured it in four quick bites, saying it tasted like apples should. Eunice pecked at hers.

My father stood up, launched the core across the room towards the bin, and told Eunice he was going to the corner shop to buy her a toothbrush. My father was excellent at exit strategies. 'Elizabeth will make you some tea,' he said.

'Go through, Eunice,' I said. 'I'll bring you the tea.'

I went to empty the teapot in the bin. Nestling among the damp tea leaves and potato peelings was her apple. I hadn't seen her discard it, she'd done it so deftly. Still whole with just two or three specks of white flesh visible where the skin had been nibbled away. From the kitchen, I could see Eunice on the sofa, the back of her, alone in the space, sitting up straight. There she waited, head, neck, shoulders, silhouetted against the light of the television.

I put the tea on the table. She changed colour with the screen. She went from green to orange to bright white and back to green again. I was glad of the television. It saved us from any more talk. Ig was long gone. Straight after dinner he'd gone to meditate in his studio.

When my father came home with the toothbrush, he too sat with us.

'I've got nowhere to go,' said Eunice.

'You've had a big shock,' I said.

'I think I need to go to bed,' she said.

She waited by the door to the stairs while I ran across to my studio to find a T-shirt for her to sleep in. When I came back, she remembered she needed face cream. 'You go up. I'll bring it,' I said. I ran back out into the cold again.

In the guest room, I handed her the tube. 'You've all been so kind to me,' she said, as I handed her the cream. She dabbed her face with it. On the radiator sat a pair of white pants, washed out and drying for the morning. 'Thank you for everything,' she said. 'You've saved me. You really have.'

We were all up before Eunice in the morning. My father seemed convinced she'd leave as soon as she'd finished her coffee.

'But where to?' I said.

'She'll have a mate who can put her up,' he replied. 'Of course she will.'

But when she came down, saying she'd been awake for hours trying to take in the enormity of what had happened to her, there was no talk of leaving. 'Mike was my future,' she said. Instead, she sat on a stool, staring out to the garden. Eyes dabbed with red, hair a mess, hugging a woolly cardigan around herself. A small tragedy in the corner of our kitchen.

Pale and mousy, clutching a sodden tissue. Hard to imagine we were related to one another.

'Do you think he'll ask me back?' she said. 'Do you think this will all be a bad dream and he'll phone me up and come to fetch me home?'

My father hovered in the background, edging his way towards the exit.

'Elizabeth, will you stay with me today?'

'Eunice—' She held my arm, gazed up at me with a deep, intense, desperate stare. 'Eunice, I can't. I'll be late for my rehearsal.'

I chucked the remains of my tea down the sink, slung the half-eaten yoghurt in the bin and tore out the door. My father will shuffle her into a taxi. She'll be gone by the time I get home, I thought. He might even drive her. Anything. He must have done it hundreds of times before, in his heyday. Coaxing them into taxis first thing, pressing the fare into their hand, closing the door behind them.

But when I returned home in the evening, exhausted, my plimsolls nearly worn through, blistered feet and a bruise on my arm from the trapeze, I stopped sharply at the sight of her in the sitting room.

Same brown cardigan, sitting in the gloom. A piece of uneaten toast in front of her. Two red, swollen eyes. A pile of snotty tissues on the coffee table.

'Eunice,' I said.

'Julian's gone to get takeaway for dinner,' she replied.

While we waited for him, I opened a bottle of wine. 'Just a small one for me,' she said.

When my father came back with the food, I followed him into the kitchen.

'Why the hell's she still here?' I hissed at him.

'You invited her,' he said.

'Not for three days, I didn't. Just tell her to go. It's your house. Tell her to leave.'

My father pushed past me. 'I'm not saying anything. This is your fault. You tell her. I'm not doing it.'

In the sitting room, my father smiled at Eunice as he deposited aluminium boxes of curries on the table. He handed Eunice a spoon, told her to help herself.

'Come on, Elizabeth,' he shouted through to me. 'What's keeping you?'

We sat on the sofa with the red and green curries arranged in front of us, eating side by side, with the television on, barely saying a word to each other. When we'd finished, Ig took a mango to have in his studio. My father went to read in his office. Eunice stood by the stair door while I fetched her another clean T-shirt and more face cream.

'I don't know what I would have done without you,' she said. 'I really didn't have anywhere to go.'

Next morning, Eunice thought she might manage a small slice of toast. She'd slept better. She held her mug out for Ig to pour her a second helping of tea.

'Do you think your Reiki could help me?' she asked. 'Would it make me feel calm?'

My father munched his way through a bowl of cornflakes. 'So, Eunice,' he said. 'What's the plan?'

'I don't know,' she said, suddenly melting into tears again, caving inwards like something being demolished. Again, she mopped herself up with a tissue.

'Why don't you help Elizabeth and me?' he said. 'There's a delivery coming this morning. An extra pair of hands will be useful.'

For as long as my father had his wine company, we'd had the same delivery driver. The terminally unexcitable Pete. My father liked to think he looked after Pete. He chatted, offered him coffee, gave him a bottle of wine to take home after each delivery. Pete's expression always remained motionless. No sense that anything went through his head other than maps and directions. He'd accept the coffee, slosh three teaspoons of sugar in it, smoke, then tell my father he didn't drink wine but his wife would like the bottle. He always made the same joke. He'd hold the bottle up and say: 'I'll get a quiet evening if she drinks all that.' Then he'd put the bottle in his van. I couldn't imagine Pete having anything other than a quiet evening.

Eunice clutched a tissue. My father and I waited beside her, lined up to watch the van make its way into the courtyard, inch by inch, Pete's head hanging out the window looking back and forth to check he wouldn't scratch his van. He always had a difficult journey but he never complained. He swore, he perspired, he always lit a cigarette the minute he jumped out of the cab but he never outwardly grumbled.

The van came to a stop with a tyre dunked into the soil of a flowerbed. Pete swung open the door and jumped out of the lorry's cab. He leaned against the wall, cigarette in one hand, the other wiping sweat from his forehead. His belly hung over his jeans, slack like bread dough. Smoke flowed out of his nose and mouth as if his guts were on fire. Pete never helped us unload the wine. Loading wasn't in his contract. Driving was in his contract.

'We're dropping you in at the deep end,' said my father to Eunice. 'It's always a scramble getting this lot inside the cellar.'

The cellar smelled of wet earth. The air felt damp and it clung to my skin. I hated going down there, imagining the creatures that surely scuttled around. It didn't feel like part of our home, rather as though it belonged to the city beyond, to the grimy, unlit corners of London. A single bare bulb covered in dust and cobwebs lit the space just enough to see.

I picked my way down the rickety stairs with Eunice following. She jumped back with a gasp as her hand brushed past one of the damp walls. She held herself inwards, her cardigan pulled tight around her body. Her head darted about, right and left, searching for cobwebs. 'It's so *dirty* down here,' she said.

I began dragging the old boxes out of the way to make a space for the delivery while Eunice watched. Upstairs, my father levered a plank of wood through the entrance. He pushed it down the stairs to make a slide for the boxes. 'I'll push. You two catch,' he instructed.

Eunice and I looked up the stairs to him, two faces in the dark gazing at the rectangle of light beyond, our feet avoiding the puddles. My father let the first box slide down the plank. We held out our arms, feet astride to give us strength. We caught one after the other, taking it in turns to stack them on the wall behind. My father slid a box down the shoot without waiting for me to return. Eunice stood alone as the box skated towards her. She looked a skinny, terrified thing, her thin little arms frozen in the air. She shrieked as the box didn't stop at her arms. It carried on plunging downwards, forcing her to the ground then landing with a thud and the sound of smashing glass, beside her. A pinkish red stain spilled across the cardboard. My father rushed down the stairs.

Brown, dirty water covered Eunice's back as she sat up. Water dripped from her hair. Wine had leaked over her trousers. Bottles rolled out of the box, nudging at her feet. She bent to pick one up that seemed intact but the base of it had broken away. Red wine flowed in a torrent, splashing her cardigan and covering her feet. She threw the bottle to the ground, then sat back in the dirt, cross-legged on the wet floor, her head in her hands. She began to sob.

'Oh Eunice,' my father said. 'Whatever's the matter?'

In my studio, Eunice stood wrapped in a towel, cowering with cold. Her soiled clothes lay in a heap by her feet.

'I'll wash them,' I said.

'I'll never wear them again,' she said, picking the bundle up to dump in the bin.

I searched through my drawers to find something for her to change into, something old that I wouldn't mind lending.

'You've got such lovely clothes,' she said, peering over my shoulder as I hunted through my things.

I looked around at Eunice, catching those wide, sad eyes glaring down at me. The way she watched me steadily, clinging on to me with that look as if I was the one she'd chosen to save her.

'I wish I had beautiful things like you've got,' she said.

I opened the doors of the wardrobe wide. 'What would you like to wear?' I asked.

'Oooh,' she said, stepping forward, eyes round and eager. 'Can I really?' She leafed through the wardrobe. 'Anything?'

'Yes,' I said.

Eunice's fingers travelled towards my long cashmere cardigan in pale cream, expensive, my favourite.

'Anything?' she said again.

I nodded and she slipped the cardigan from its hanger. Next she chose a T-shirt made from crumpled silk. With both in her hands, she looked at me eagerly like a child testing the limits, waiting for permission to be granted. I said 'yes', just quietly, and she ran through to my bathroom to change.

When she emerged seconds later, I could see the outfit didn't quite fit. The cardigan sat a little too long, the T-shirt bagged around her neck. She looked even younger now, like a little girl dressing up in her mum's clothes. There! I'd done my bit. No one could accuse me of not trying.

The next day, my father and I left Eunice at home while we looped around North London in his van. We stopped, unloaded, carried on again with my father haggling over each new order. At the final stop, we polished off half a bottle of wine and a plate of ham, then drove back.

We arrived home to the sound of the oven whirring. I went to switch it off, thinking I must have accidentally left it running but inside sat two small baguettes being heated through. Close by, on the counter top, white plastic packets lay torn and discarded.

'I've done dinner,' Eunice said, appearing from upstairs. 'I wanted to help.'

She brought the plate to the table: two pale baguettes, soaked through with butter and garlic. Our cheap, industrial dinner.

'I won't eat these, Eunice,' I said. 'I've got to be careful with my figure.'

She stared at me.

'For the play,' I said.

'Just have a small piece,' she said, handing me some of the bread. My father crammed a slice into his mouth then washed it down with red wine.

At the cooker, I boiled an egg.

'Elizabeth's mother used to make bread, Eunice. Didn't she,

Lizzy?' my father said. 'Twice a week. Wholemeal bread. She never used a recipe. She could make it off by heart.'

I watched my egg clang against the sides of the stainless steel pan. The boil in the water moved it in circles, as if the egg travelled on its own.

'It all started with bread, Eunice. Bread was at the heart of it, back in the day.'

Here we go.

'Bread was part of our revolution,' he said.

My father must have been nervous. He always resorted to lecturing when under threat, letting the words form a wall that he hid behind, wearing openness as a disguise. He could spout to a roomful of people on any subject. Life, women, politics, feminism, car mechanics. Any subject. He could perform for hours in order to avoid something. The man at the centre of the party, rolling from wall to wall with his stories and laughter. Talk of his body, his drugs, the search for fine sex that led him to travel the width of the United States from the communes of New York to the communes of San Francisco, picking out the best creatures California could offer up for his unyielding appetite. Everyone laughed as he cantered around the room, poking fun at himself, letting everyone know he'd chosen adventure over safety while, at the same time, managing to hide – even from himself – that chaos wasn't the same as freedom.

'Elizabeth mocks me,' he said. 'But she has no idea. There was nothing silly about us. We were dangerous. People were scared of us. You only know us in clichés but we were a threat, the police were on to us. And we started a lot of things.'

My father glottal-stopped when he said 'a lot', as if he was back there, the posh boy doing Cockney.

'We started the health-food revolution, we started wholemeal bread. We put the body at the centre of everything. That's what we did. The world was all buttoned up, full of tight little stoic people, all pale skinny legs, bad teeth and braces, going slowly mad. Desperate for love, desperate to free their bodies.' My father held up his hand and clenched. 'Look, Eunice,' he said, 'it's like holding a big lump of dough in your fist. The harder you clench, the more bits of it bubble up out of the gaps in your fingers. That's what it used to be like. But we hippies let the spirit soar because we freed the body.'

'Please don't drink any more wine,' I said.

'Before us, people didn't think they could enjoy their bodies but we put the body at the centre and everything changed. We were all about physical sensation, physical existence. Brown bread, yoga, macrobiotics, looking after ourselves. We got high, we laughed, we danced and we fucked. We made sex wonderful again.'

'I don't know if you can lay claim to sex,' I said.

'Oh, but we can,' said my father, swigging more wine. 'We brought it out of the margins. We were a Romantic movement. We said to the world, "You've got a body, now bloody well enjoy it." It was those women in the Seventies who ruined it, who got all authoritarian with their rules and their communes. The Seventies was just a decade-long, bloody committee meeting. But we were Romantics, we swung about, just loving our bodies. We didn't talk about it. We just got on with it. The girls in the Sixties were lovely, they were the last generation of lovelies, before they became all bad-tempered in the Seventies.'

Eunice looked bemused, like someone who'd turned up at the wrong party, as if she was trying to work out whether she ought to smile and laugh because my father was joking, or be serious and interested, because she thought my father must be making some very intelligent points about life.

My father slurred: 'Social movements are like marriage. First Romanticism, then authoritarianism, then off again looking for Romanticism, then fucked again. It's the way. It's always the way and always in that order.' He stared into his wine glass. 'It's all just one search for innocence after another.'

Eunice opened her mouth, tried to speak, took a sharp breath in but no words came out. Just a sound from her throat, solid phlegm cracking, a small whine. She went silent again, embarrassed.

'I'll never taste my wife's bread again. That's a taste forever gone.' My father looked into the distance, extravagantly wistful. 'When I took that last morsel of it, I bet I didn't know it was my last,' he said.

After we'd eaten, Eunice said she needed to phone Mike. My father suggested she go into the sitting room.

I can't bear that we're over. It's a big thing, Mike, to end a marriage. I mean, just remember, you married me. We weren't just going out. Something told you I was the woman you wanted to spend the rest of your life with. You can't have just imagined that. Whoever this other girl is, this secretary or whoever she is, can't have what we had. She's just a passing thing. Someone to turn your head. It won't last.

'There was someone else?' I whispered to my father. He nodded. We filled our wine glasses, he sliced a piece of cheese. We fell silent, waiting for the next instalment.

How could you? How could you do this to me? You know what I've been through, finding my family, Dad dying, falling out with Judy and now this. All in the same year. What sort of person does it make you, to abandon me now like this?

It didn't seem to be working, because finally, she became furious. Rage spilled out of her, a storm within her that seemed to be chucking words out of her mouth, one after another.

I hope you and your silly, ditzy, thick, ugly secretary both choke.

I jumped at a thumping sound.

'Eunice,' I said, running into the sitting room. 'Are you OK?'

She stood, knocking the phone against the wall, leaving small indents in the plaster. 'Eunice,' I said, running, removing the phone from her. 'What are you doing?'

'Mike wants me to fetch my stuff,' she sobbed.

I led her back through into the kitchen.

'Oh dear,' my father said, the solemnity and control of his voice a sharp contrast to the woman standing in front of him, her hair tangled in threads, her face red and blotchy. Eunice fell into a chair, splayed her arms across the table and cried hysterically. My father and I hovered. She couldn't stop. She kept crying while we both looked at each other, unsure what to do. My father attempted a pat on her shoulder. Eunice turned to look up at him with pleading, wet eyes. 'I can't go back to Judy. Please don't make me. I just feel so lost and so alone. I have no one. No one at all.'

'I'll come with you,' I said. 'To fetch your things from Mike's.'

The next day at Eunice's apartment block, she and I took the lift up to the third floor. Inside the flat, an entrance hall gave way to a windowless corridor lit with halogen. Five bleached oak doors with steel handles led to a sitting room, a kitchen, two bedrooms and a bathroom. 'I always hated this entrance hall,' she said. 'You can't do a thing with it. It looks like you're in an office block. I wanted to paint it, but he drew the line at strong colours in a windowless corridor.' She kicked the door open into her bedroom.

Eunice's room had a large, double-glazed window looking out on to the car park below. Hooks made from small metal flowers studded with bright stones as the stigma held the curtains in place. Made of a sheer fabric, they shimmered red and purple. 'The colour on the walls reminds me of baby deer,' she said. 'It's lovely, isn't it? Fawn.' The wall opposite the bed had been painted in lilac. A picture of Mike, taken on the day he graduated, sat on the bedside table. His parents – I assumed – were standing either side of him. His mother wore a hat and a bright red suit.

Eunice searched for the things she needed, all the time scattering objects on to the duvet: small china ornaments, wooden boxes full of trinkets, shoes, make-up, a laundry bag. The pile mounting, she scanned the room. 'I didn't go to university,' she said. 'Not like Mike. I started work at sixteen.' She yanked a box from underneath the bed. 'It's all right for the privileged. They can throw people away like they don't matter.'

'Here,' I said, reaching to help her. 'Let me.' I dragged a suitcase down from the top of the wardrobe and opened it out on to the bed.

'I can't take that, it's Mike's.'

'He can give you a suitcase,' I said, opening it.

'His friends shunned me when I went out with them,' Eunice said.

I took a handkerchief from Mike's bedside table and wiped the case with it, moving aside the straps to rub deep into the corners. I held the white cloth aloft, brown with dirt. 'Shall we leave it here?' I said, resting it on Mike's pillow.

Eunice halted, then laughed. 'Oh go on, then,' she said.

'You're so much more daring than me. And you've been kind, helping me like this. Thank you for coming.'

When she'd finished packing, Eunice told me she wanted to sit alone in the room for a moment. I waited for her next door, my eyes flickering around the place. Not a curve or a hidden corner in the whole flat. Every inch of space had a purpose. Sharp edges. Everything spotless, newly painted. Vases, photograph frames, silk flowers, little china ornaments, all vied for space on top of the shelves. In the kitchen, a bright white cloth hung over the tap. A spray bottle of citrus-scented bleach the only thing visible along the black faux-marble counter. The sitting room was a riot of colour. The enormous purple sofa almost blocked the door. A huge white vase on the floor was crammed full of silk flowers in yellow, orange and black. Small figurines covered rows of dustless shelves.

We loaded her stuff into the car. 'That's my whole life in there,' she said, glancing back at the two suitcases, three cardboard boxes and five carrier bags. 'Who'd have thought I'd be twenty-three years old and that's all I'd end up with?'

On the drive home to London, we didn't say a word. She gazed out of the window, lost in thought. When we arrived back, I helped her inside with the cases then my father dragged everything up the stairs to the guest room.

'There you go,' he said, heaving the last box inside. 'Until you get yourself sorted out.'

'I can't tell you what a relief it is,' Eunice said, 'to have somewhere to stay.' She glanced around the spare room. 'And somewhere so nice, at that.'

As we left to go downstairs, she closed the door behind us. In the sitting room, my father poured himself a gin and tonic. We didn't speak as we heard the sound of the shower. Footsteps across the floorboards moving from the bathroom to the bedroom and back again. Thud, thud, thud. Silence. Thud, thud, thud.

My father was on his second drink when Eunice poked her head around the door and stepped inside. Scrubbed clean, she'd combed her wet hair back from her face. She wore a loose grey T-shirt with a deep neckline falling open around her chest. Rather than sit, as my father suggested she did, she wandered round, eyeing up our things. She picked up a marble bowl lined with gold leaf and examined it.

'Is that real gold?' she said, her eyes scanning the base. She moved on to the opaque glass orb that concealed a lightbulb, tracing her finger around the shape. Next, she picked up the only photograph of my parents, together on their wedding day.

'How did you two meet?' she asked.

In the picture, my mother had tied her hair up with flowers of soft, primrose yellow, cream and pale pink. Lengths of golden brown curls fell around her bare shoulders.

'At a party,' my father replied.

Eunice continued examining the picture, her eyes flickering over it. 'She's wearing a nice dress.'

'She made it herself,' I said.

'She's very beautiful.'

Still holding the photograph, Eunice turned to look at us both, drawing in breath, as if about to say something, but then stopping herself. Finally she spoke. 'When exactly did she die?'

My father and I stayed silent.

'So was it love at first sight?'

'There was something serene about Margaret,' my father replied. 'I was very sure.'

'You look a striking couple.'

Eunice put the picture back on the shelf with a sharp snap.

'Careful, Eunice,' I said. 'It's the only one we have.'

'She looks really lovely,' replied Eunice.

When Eunice went through to the kitchen for dinner, I retraced her footsteps. I moved the things she'd touched back to where they had been, so they all still sat in their correct places.

first night

THE STAGE MANAGER NODDED TO LET ME KNOW, IT WAS TIME. I TUGGED at the harness one last time, took a deep breath and jumped from the scaffolding hidden away in the wings. My feet disappeared into thin air. I flew across the stage while the audience gasped. A beam of light chased me, but I didn't squint even though my eyes hurt. The bright, phosphorous white picked me out, scurried after me wherever I went. The audience was just a haze of brown and red. I could feel their presence rather than see them. I swung, my dress and my hair blowing out behind me as I became a human pendulum arching from one side of the theatre to the other. I forgot my nerves. I forgot everything, my anxiety, my fear of falling, pleasing the director. I heard only the gentle ripple of claps as I flew around the theatre feeling like nothing more than a blur of glossy hair and diaphanous white. My back arched, my hands gripped the cables either side of me, my head trailed through the air. I could feel everyone looking at me as I flew: sexual, untouchable, backlit.

The beam of light snapped off. Pitch black. The sound of the audience seemed amplified in the dark. A cough, then a sniff. I almost heard them breathing. I hung in the middle of the stage with twenty-five seconds of darkness to arrange myself. The spotlight aimed at me, the gaze of a large gun; it would pop at me, ready or not.

A sudden flood of light. Long, scarlet ribbons unfurled from my white dress, so long they touched the stage. I turned in mid-air, one somersault after another, slow and controlled at first, then spinning faster and faster, my legs opened out wide, the scarlet ribbons rippling and dancing beneath me. The lights snapped off suddenly. The audience cheered. A stage hand tugged on the ropes, pulling me back to the scaffolding. He grabbed my feet, planting them back on the platform. I caught my breath. His arm around my waist pulled the rest of my body to safety. Working quickly, he undid the harnesses. With only the light from a dim head torch, he led me to the ladder to take me back down to ground level.

'You did it!' the director whispered as I scampered back into the dark warren of rooms behind the stage.

At the curtain call, we kept bowing, holding hands, blowing kisses to the audience, bowing and bowing. We couldn't stop smiling, none of us. One last time, we held our hands up. The audience cheered and we skipped away to disappear backstage. Afterwards, the actors milled around the wings, all of us buzzing with energy, kissing each other, elated. The director was thrilled. He rushed around the wings congratulating us all. I scooped my hand into a tub of cold cream, rubbing the pancake into my face to melt away the thick stage make-up.

The guests clapped as we arrived at the after party. Not a wild, raucous thunder of applause but the genteel tap of one hand against the back of another hand while it still held on to its glass of champagne. Barely any noise at all on its own, but with fifty people doing it at the same time it formed into a mild, restrained kind of praise.

The party was held in a small room with a low ceiling, a mahogany bar in one corner and walls painted red. 'It's how I imagine hell to be, all this red,' I said into the director's ear as I passed him. I leaned my chin on his shoulder. 'I keep expecting the devil to come popping out at any moment.'

He grinned. 'Here I am!'

As I moved through the crowd, making my way towards the back of the room, people brushed my shoulder, told me 'well done'. They passed me like a valuable object from one person to the next. A waitress fetched me a glass of champagne. Men in bold pinstripe suits speared canapés with toothpicks while the slim, blonde girls by their sides pulled the ham from pieces of melon to discard in the ashtrays.

My father, Ig and Eunice made a tight little circle in a corner at the back of the room. This was the kind of party my father hated, full of people he called 'twits'. He couldn't hide his disdain as he watched them all air-kissing each other, plucking the canapés and drinks from passing waiters. Eunice stared around the room looking amazed at the sight. Her eyes wide, she clasped a small handbag decorated with coloured glass beads, clamping it to her side. She gasped as she spotted the leading lady, Willow, slipping among the crowds. 'What's she like?' Eunice whispered. She rearranged her necklace, a string of huge red beads, the size of small potatoes. 'You were brilliant,' she said. 'That trapeze scene. Flying through the air, it looked magical, with all those amazing lights. Wasn't she brilliant, everyone?'

On the way home, my father complained. He didn't like men in pinstripe, he didn't like our definitions of worldly success, he didn't like girls who wouldn't eat properly. 'How about we just enjoy ourselves?' I replied.

'What was with you and that director?'

'Nothing,' I replied.

'He was very flirtatious.'

'He's like that with everyone,' I said.

'He's an idiot.'

On the back seat of the car, Eunice hadn't stopped smiling since we'd left the theatre. 'I think that's the best thing that's ever happened to me in my life,' she said. 'And you, Lizzy, were just totally amazing. I can't believe we're related. My sister is a famous actress.'

I stayed silent as the car veered through the quiet streets of night-time London. I don't know how I'd managed it, but I'd begun my path to a new life. Nearly three years since my mother had died and somehow I'd found my way to the other side. I'd shed the past that had clung to me for so long, dragging me down like a heavy woollen coat. Finally, I'd been zipped back up again after being so suddenly torn apart.

ACT THREE

I think, actually, my father had become rather fond of Eunice.

moon

IN THE SITTING ROOM EVERYTHING SMELLED FRESH. STRIPES WERE carved into the fabric of the sofa, from the Hoover. Eunice's magazines formed precise squares on the coffee table. Everything dusted. Clean and order; a calm cosiness to the room. The lamps bathed everything in warm, gold light. The muted red and black kilim rug was spotless, pulled taut under the sparkling glass coffee table. The rug seemed to soften everything. The tinkle of jazz in the background. My father stood at the sideboard, in pressed navy blue trousers and a pale shirt, scooping ice cubes from a glass bowl with his cupped hand. I hadn't seen the place look so clean in ages.

'Someone's been busy,' I said.

'I'm a whizz with a feather duster,' said Eunice.

'So I can see.'

'We're having gin and tonics,' she announced.

My father gave me the drink.

'Cheers, Lizzy,' she said, holding up her glass, rattling it to make a pleasing jangle with the ice.

To celebrate the arrival of summer and the success of my run in the theatre, my father had decided to take Eunice and me to his favourite Greek restaurant, in a small park near Hampstead Heath. He'd been going there since the Sixties. With my mother, he used to eat there almost every week in summer. They took Ig and me as babies tucked into our prams. Once, my mother apparently spent all evening pushing me around the garden, trying to soothe me to sleep so she could eat.

The restaurant had a corrugated tin roof and thin walls, practically no more than a shed, painted dark blue. Because it was so flimsy, it could only open for a few months of the year, when the weather was warm enough. Inside were four bistro tables and an open kitchen, no bigger than a bathroom. Outside, a small terrace covered in trellis threaded with fairy lights had space for ten tables. If it rained, everyone crammed into the tiny room within. Sometimes there'd be thirty people in there, eating dinner with their arms tucked tight to their sides. The moment the evenings grew colder, the restaurant would shut without a word. We'd turn up to find the door bolted. They just disappeared. The cold weather whisked them away. But even when it was warm, the restaurant might close with no forewarning. The boss would say he hadn't felt like cooking. My father never complained, even if he'd wasted a journey. 'I like a man driven by instinct,' he said, 'rather than commerce.'

Ig wasn't able to come with us as he had to work late, but my father had instructed Eunice and me to change and to meet him downstairs at seven for a drink before we left for the restaurant.

Eunice sat in a cloud of floral scent. Perfumed and lipsticked. Every time she moved, a puff of her fragrance wisped through the air towards me. As I went to fetch a lemon slice, her smile followed me around the room. Needy, eager, she didn't take her eyes off me. Her dress was made of stiff white cotton that fell just above her knee. She resembled a single sheet of blank paper with two little legs attached.

In the two months that I'd been working at the theatre, Eunice seemed to have appointed herself housekeeper. While I slipped in and out, barely spending more than an hour or two at home, she cleaned, tidied, made sure we always had milk in the fridge and bread on the table and constantly warned us – with a hopeful smile – that one day she would give us what she called a 'deep clean'.

My father appeared to like this newfound order. He no longer found himself having to run to the corner shop in his pyjamas because we'd run out of coffee or toilet rolls. As a consequence of his domestic life feeling under control I think, actually, my father had become rather fond of Eunice.

We took a taxi to the restaurant. My father hugged the boss, who pointed to the last remaining free table – meant for two, but he would squeeze in an extra chair. So we sat, the three of us crammed in, our knees pressed together underneath the table, that peculiar feeling of bone against bone. A single, skinny waiter whipped between tables, breathing in when the space was particularly tight. An empty plate gone from one, a jug of water deposited on another. He danced a waltz, somehow serving everyone as they needed. He swept past us. Three glasses, a ceramic jug of white wine, a glass jug of water left in his wake. A moment later, an ashtray gone, a bowl of black olives in its place. Eunice dived for an olive.

At the table across from us, a man in crumpled linen ate with a woman whose hair was held in place with a cream feather, its tip dipped in red dye. On another table, six teenagers threw tiny pieces of screwed up napkin at each other. The girls had messy hair and wore thick black eyeliner. On to their table, the waiter wedged in plates of chopped octopus, bowls of mussels, slices of cheese blackened under the grill.

'I feel like I'm in a private club,' Eunice said. 'You'd never know this place was here unless someone took you.' She pressed her tongue into the space where the olive's stone had been, and ran it along her lip. 'I see what Judy means now when she says the posh are different.' She drew the olive back inside her mouth. A moment later, it appeared again, thrust out: wet, pink tongue still inside the space. She lolled it against her lower lip, drawing it in and out. Each time she thrust the olive outwards, she pulled a silly face.

'You've let me in on your secret,' she said.

In the corner at a single hob, the chef tried to force an octopus into a tall pan. He removed the lid with a pair of tongs, a cloud of steam billowing out, his hand clawed around the octopus's head. He twisted it right and left, trying to ease the creature into the pan. A purple, suckered leg flopped away, refusing the water. The chef kept jostling it, forcing the whole creature inside. He clamped on the lid, turned up the heat dial.

The boss was a vast, well-fed man who laughed easily but looked as if he could have done with a day or two in the sun to brighten him up. He had fingers like sausages and a damp, hot-looking palm he kept slapping across my father's shoulder.

'Lovely place,' Eunice said. 'Is it yours?'

'This is my daughter,' my father said.

'But he knows who I—' I said, stopping when I looked up to see my father pointing to Eunice, who held out her hand for the boss to shake.

My daughter. The first time I'd heard him say it. What was he thinking? 'My daughter.' What was wrong with just calling her Eunice? She didn't need a label.

'My father was telling me what a wonderful place this is,' she said, 'and I just had to try it.'

'Your dad's been coming here for years,' the boss told her.

Shouldn't she should have a different word? That word – father – suggests a history. How about a word that suggested lack of history? A word that explained they had a simple biological connection, not a relationship built, fought over. A bond of bathtimes, stand-offs over a plate of vegetables, afternoons spent on a windswept beach hoping for a break in the clouds, or a strong, hairy arm clamped around a child's tiny, squirming torso to stop her running off. Eunice couldn't have crawled into my father's bed in the middle of the night to sleep beside him – it wouldn't have been right – but I could. So why should we share the same word? Shouldn't language be more precise than that? Doesn't language have a duty to spare my feelings, to differentiate between the weight of things, to separate biology from emotion?

'Lovely daughters you have,' said the boss. 'You're lucky, Julian.'

'Aren't I?' replied my father.

'I had four sons but we always wanted a daughter,' said the boss.

'You can adopt me,' said Eunice, laughing.

The boss held his arms out wide and grinned. 'You can come and live with me any time you like.'

Don't tell her that, I thought. Then: 'There you go, Eunice. You've had another offer.'

The waiter swished past. A slab of feta, sitting on top of cucumbers, parsley and tomatoes, arrived on the table. My father cut through the cheese with the side of his fork, a soft karate chop that broke it into three chunks.

'Go on,' said Eunice, leaning in towards us, conspiracy written on her face. 'What do you think of me? I've wanted to ask for ages.' She shuffled in her seat, looking at us, pulling her best face as if looking in a mirror.

We stayed silent.

'Go on,' she said.

'We think you've had a bit too much to drink, Eunice,' said my father jokingly, moving her glass and trying to offer her some cheese.

'I haven't,' she replied, taking back her glass. 'I didn't think I was good enough for you. But now look at me. In the midst of it all. Living in a posh house in London. Being taken out. Here I am! A London girl!'

'I think I'm going to have the octopus,' my father said.

The food arrived. Mussels for me, moussaka for Eunice. My father's octopus had been hacked into chunks. Now it swam in a shallow pool of olive oil. My father asked for another carafe of wine. When it arrived, he poured Eunice a glass. She giggled as he told the story of how he crossed into France on the ferry during his university holidays, going through immigration with an old girlfriend who'd forgotten her passport. She hid under coats and sweaters on the back seat. 'She didn't get caught,' my father said. They travelled across four countries and home again, with her hiding.

'Why didn't I ever meet boyfriends as fun as that?' Eunice said. 'I thought Mike was exciting because he took me for a night out in Stevenage, all the way from St Albans.'

We finished eating and my father ordered ouzo. The boss came over again, slamming the whole bottle down on to the table with another slap to my father's shoulder. The waiter zipped past, leaving behind water and a bowl of ice cubes. The teenagers danced on the patch of dry mud by the terrace, their long limbs flopping into unusual shapes. A girl draped her slim, brown arms around the neck of a much taller boy. Everyone was drunk, including the boss, who leaned against the wall with an ouzo and a cigar, his work finished for the night. Eunice rushed up to take the boss's hand in hers. She led him to the dance floor where she began spinning around him while he stayed rooted. He moved like an old tanker, not without rhythm, but heavy on his feet, a wall of flesh, using his free hand to twirl her around the floor. A warm evening, lights twinkling around us. My father and I sat back in our chairs, just watching.

The boss began to jig, the faintest kick of each foot as Eunice jumped around him. My father knocked back ouzo. I drank water. The boss puffed and sweated. Finally, he came over to our table, told my father he couldn't cope any more, insisted we take his place. Eunice still bounced to the music. My father drained his glass. 'Come on, Lizzy,' he said, taking my hand.

I liked watching my father dance. He made jagged movements, whirring like a robot. He looked strange but it was the way he always danced and it felt right. He buzzed around the dance floor. One of the teenagers rushed in towards him. He picked her up then threw her out so her legs spun round in a circle. Another girl wanted a go, so my father spun her too.

The floor wasn't made of pockets of tightly grouped people; instead it was thrown wide open. Everyone danced with everyone. I craned my neck to look up at the small fairy lights, weaving through the trellis. Tiny dots of white against the dark sky. The warm evening slipped around my bare arms and we all jumped. Collective joy, energy shared, everyone moving, everyone happy. Eunice spun so fast, she might have spun right off the dance floor and carried on spinning all the way to the bottom of the hill. We all looped arms to make a line. The whole restaurant, twenty of us, maybe more, doing the cancan, kicking our legs up, squealing and laughing. The boss watched, pleasure across his face, as he sucked on his cigar and dabbed sweat from his upper lip with a napkin.

The music and the lights cut. We hung, suspended, abruptly stopped, the throb of music still in our ears but not knowing what to do. The energy to dance but no music any more. We had to dismantle ourselves. Time was up. People fetched jackets, drained glasses. We looked around at each other. The pretty lights replaced with the orange glare of a distant street-light. The sky dark sea-green. In an instant it was just a drab park in North London and we were just tired people who'd sweated too much. Eunice looked a little battered by the night, her make-up sweated off, the dress tinged with grey. My father panted, looked stunned as if he'd just come up for air.

We left the park, then took a right turn down the main road. Up ahead I saw the waiter with his jacket slung over his shoulder, drinking water from a plastic bottle. We cut through another park for the short way home. In there, it felt cooler, the grass and trees had sucked up the heat. My father lit up a joint and the three of us walked side by side until we reached a barrier. My father cleared it in one jump. We crunched down a gravel pathway past a small pond where swans slept curled into delicate buns of white feathers. A monochrome scene: pale leaves, black lake, white swan. Repeated above: white stars, black sky, white moon. We emerged into a grassy meadow to another, more secluded pond. My father wasn't ready to go home yet. He wanted to cool off.

On the small pontoon, my father dropped his trousers and stood with his arms outstretched, his head falling back. Above him, a perfect disc of white moon coated everything in silver. He kicked off his shoes, wriggled from his trousers, tugged at his shirt. Naked, he looked like a man about to conquer something. His buttocks, white orbs against the night. A smooth back, nobbled spine, dark hair curling at his neck. He spun around, urging us to swim. His arms stretched above his head, pulling the flesh around his belly so he looked a few inches slimmer. The rest of him dangled like a bunch of deflated balloons.

Two young women fully clothed. My father in front of them splayed out as if doing a naked star-jump. Why hadn't he just jumped straight into the water? I wondered if Eunice was looking. I couldn't see in the light. She did start talking a lot, though, gabbling about swimsuits, camping holidays, her parents. I turned back to look at him. I didn't need to be shy. He was my father. His body practically belonged to me. Eunice began wondering out loud about the variety of the trees in the park.

I ran towards my father as if to push him in the water. A laugh, a small jump, and his straight body sliced the water at an angle like a toy soldier, his arms clamped against the length of his body. He outwitted me. He disappeared, then bobbed back up, blowing snot into his fingers. He kicked his legs making a froth of white, swivelling on to his front to begin swimming breaststroke, puffing and snorting like an old walrus.

Eunice tugged at her dress. It came off, prised over her head, underwear and sandals remaining. She didn't rest her clothes neatly on her shoes, folded, as I would have expected. She left them lying there, crumpled in a heap. She shook her hair out. And there she was standing in translucent polka-dotted lace underwear. Her hands travelled behind her back, unhooked her bra so that it fell away. Her nipples were dark little circles as delicate as the rest of her. I glimpsed the slender shape of her. The slope of her breasts, her smooth stomach with its taut nub of a belly button. The line of her body was like the confident, clean stroke made by an artist's pencil. Just one smooth sweep, not a lump or bump along the way, so the pencil line could go from her armpit to her ankle in one. I wouldn't have known a body like that existed underneath all the pink fluff. Sculpted, beautiful, standing naked with her hair falling about her bare shoulders.

Finally, she peeled down her pants and stood naked in front of the water, facing my father. I wondered about her shyness before and her confidence now. Was it a trick of the light? Was she returning the gesture? Or was it the heady love of the adopted child towards the newfound parent? With no rules and history to contain it, the love distorted into something else. She dropped into the water, felled like a tree, plunging in lengthways, a tomb of water rising up and covering her, sinking her down into the cold.

What was I doing here? I didn't want to play like this with them. I didn't accept her, and if I had fun, it might look as if I did.

At the far end of the pond, near a small boat that slapped the water, my father flipped over on to his back. 'Come on, Lizzy!' he shouted. 'Top marks for Eunice. No dilly-dallying, Lizzy.'

'I don't fancy it,' I said.

I heard the thud and slap of bare feet against the wooden pontoon. Two arms around my waist. Cold, wet against me. A joking threat: if I didn't go in he'd make me. I looked down to see my father's naked legs dripping on to the wood. A sopping head pressed against mine, arms squeezed around me, making my clothes damp.

'OK, OK,' I said. 'I'll come in.'

I undressed quickly, leaving my underwear on.

'One, two, three!' my father shouted.

I hesitated.

He began chanting my name, refusing to allow me to bottle out. I pinched my nose and jumped. I chilled in an instant, slapped all over by the icy water. My skin stung. My feet disappeared into something sludgy, toes dipped into slime. I bounced up to the surface, struggling for breath.

'Catch us up, Lizzy,' my father shouted.

I ploughed towards them, moving quickly to beat away the cold. My father in front – pack leader – Eunice and I, the little ducklings following, bobbing through the black pond.

'What better pleasure can there be than naked swimming under a full moon?' he said. He turned on to his back, shot water into the air then let it rain down on his chest.

On my back, I let my head sink. A crisp line of iciness made a circle around my hairline. A halo. Everything cold one side of it, warm the other. The line of trees made black clouds against the sky. A piece of moon visible, the rest hidden. I loved the smell of summer. A mix of grass and warm wheat. And the silence. Only the sound of our gentle kicks as we disturbed the water.

Afterwards, we lay out to dry. I felt the mild spike of grass on my bare skin. The moonlight picked us out against the dark undergrowth. The dim light made our skin look pasty. We were the colour of putty on black grass. White oblongs, like three of Ig's crystals laid out in a field. I had bits of pond sticking to me. My father peeled a strand of weed from his leg.

'In my teens,' Eunice said, 'I'd look at Judy and I'd think, thank God she's not mine. Thank God I'm not biologically related to her.' She plucked a handful of grass from the ground with a sharp rip. She gazed up at the sky, then flipped herself over on to her stomach, propping herself up on both elbows so she could look at my father and me. 'Judy wasn't mine. My whole childhood wasn't mine. As a baby, I was taken out of my own story and dropped into someone else's. Nothing about it belonged to me, felt like me, truly me. I always had something missing. But you know, in the back of my mind, I always knew I'd find something out there that *was* mine. A real home, a place to belong, somewhere I fitted in.'

At home, lying in bed, trying to sleep, my leg searched for a cool spot. I couldn't get comfortable. The top sheet had knotted into a ball. A shuffling at the door, just the faint sound of a hand rubbing wood. I sat up. Was it a burglar? Had I locked the outer gate? Should I hide? More rustling. The handle turned. The thin line of light beneath the door grew into a triangle. In the space stood Eunice, wearing her little blue cotton nightdress with a hairband tied around her head. 'Lizzy,' she whispered.

'Yes,' I hissed.

She started up the ladder towards my bed, her bare feet padding against the varnished rungs. A slice of night where she'd left the door open. A trace of coolness entering the room. 'I can't sleep,' she said. 'I'm worrying.'

'What about?'

'Can I get into your bed?'

'What?'

She slipped under the sheets. More heat. I felt a hot, tacky leg bare against mine. She quickly moved it, slid her hand under a single thin pillow.

'Can I just lie?'

I turned my back.

'I can't stop thinking.'

The bed was too hot with both of us in it.

'Nothing lasts for ever,' she said. 'Today's made me scared, Lizzy.'

'You'll be fine. You've just drunk too much.'

I shuffled and turned, trying to get comfortable, but I could feel myself sweating. I threw the covers off to feel cool but then I was too cold and picked them up again. I let my leg hang over the edge of the mattress to see if that worked, but I couldn't settle; I took it back in, rolled on to my front.

'Eunice,' I whispered. 'You're going to have to go back to your own bed.' No reply. She was already asleep. Deep, even sighs. Hot, damp breath against my arm, a film of moisture on her skin from the heat. She turned, harrumphed, fell silent.

It seemed like hours had passed. I still couldn't get comfortable. Sleep mocked me. My leg ached. My whole body ached. I couldn't be still. A sweaty lump beside me, taking too much space in the bed. I felt furious. The bed was a small double. She made the whole mattress slope in her direction. I kept rolling into her. She was a sweating stone. The heat clung to me as if the outside and inside had fused. Nothing marked me out. I was just heat within heat. I rocked her with my hands. I wanted to scream, to slap her, to smash her. I had to hold myself in. My eyes pulled. My head hurt with no sleep. I craved sleep. The whole world was sleep. And yet electricity flowed through me, biting rest away. I needed to fall.

Why should she sleep and I not? I swung my legs around, landed both feet with force into Eunice's back, flinging her from the mattress. Thud. She landed on the floor, woke with a start and sat up, gasping. 'My head,' she wailed.

'You fell out of bed,' I said.

'My head,' she said again, clutching it along with a handful of her hair.

She crawled back into bed, a heavy, tired lump, face crinkled up. Moments later, the sound of sleep. She breathed, heavy and deep.

dust

I WOKE TO THE SOUND OF MUSIC. LOUD, EXPANSIVE, ROOM-FILLING sound. I recognised it as an old record of my father's. Playing full tilt, the noise washed through the courtyard and probably beyond. I could hear it in my studio, through two windows. The majestic, crystal trilling of a female voice, holding the note at its height. The singer hung on so long, I thought she might smash like glass.

I looked to my left and saw the empty space in my bed. She must have crept out first thing. I wanted to lie a little longer, doing nothing. Finally able to spend a day in my pyjamas now the show had ended.

On closing night, the director had given us each a bottle of wine – the 'girls', as he called us, received an extra bouquet of flowers – before sending us on our way. As I left the theatre, the evening felt cool and fresh after the heat of the stage. I held the flowers, clutched the wine, felt a sense of purpose and possibility. I sat on the bus smiling to myself, occasionally dipping in to smell the apricot-coloured roses. The director promised to call. He had things in mind for me, he said.

The flowers were still fresh and alive, arranged in a glass vase on the windowsill. The sunshine flooding the room overwhelmed them with light, making the soft petals seem almost translucent.

I loved days like this. There was no better place to be than at home, with all the doors open, listening to music. Ig, my father and I together. On hot days, my father would set up the inflatable pool. It had a small semi-circle of wooden decking at one end and was just big enough to swim across, just deep enough not to be able to touch the bottom. Ig would move the speakers outside, we'd open wine, invite a few friends around and as evening fell, we'd light the barbecue. The house was a world of its own on those days. The outside didn't exist. It was just us and our fun.

Ig's head bobbed past my bedroom window. I envied him for not having come on our night out. I couldn't get the image of the naked swimming out of my head. Why had I even agreed to go? My father always pushed things to their very limit. Why hadn't I just taken a cab home, left the pair of them to it? Hungover. Full of shame. I hadn't wanted to go swimming naked with Eunice, hadn't wanted to give her the impression she could creep into my bed at night. I dreaded the thought of having to go inside and face her, smile as if I hadn't pushed her out of the bed in the middle of the night as she trembled at the thought of losing something – someone – again.

By now the music had retreated into the foothills of emotion. The voice low and deep and melancholic, anticipating woes to come. Ig loved the old turntable. It sat on the metal table beneath shelves of ageing records. My father's music collection had everything: psychedelic rock, Sixties rock, opera, jazz. He'd built it up over decades but barely listened to it. A few months ago, Ig hooked up new speakers to improve the sound. He made whole days disappear listening to my father's collection, a pot of green tea beside an uneaten piece of dry toast, his fingers drumming the coffee table. He had a particular look when he listened to music, midway between having a dream and an orgasm. I'd go inside and find Ig, have a cup of tea with him. I could manage to avoid Eunice. Shouldn't she be the one hiding?

I climbed down my ladder, and went into the house. Inside, a warm breeze flowed through the sitting room from all the open windows and doors.

In the kitchen, Eunice stood on a chair, stretching herself to reach into the uppermost shelves of the cupboards. A pink scarf tied around her head, rubber gloves on her hands, sturdy trainers on her feet.

On the kitchen table sat plates, cutlery, glasses, whisks, wooden spoons: the entire contents of the cupbooards. I scanned the stuff Eunice had dragged out, things I hadn't seen for years: an old casserole of my mother's, crystal glasses with a swirling stem we only took out at Christmas. Teacups stacked, an articulated worm of bone china veering to the left, threatening to topple and smash. The doors open, the cupboards empty. The smell of drying bleach made me want to retch. The house had been fine. We hadn't needed cleaning.

'What a night!' she said, turning to see me. 'How are you feeling this morning, Lizzy? Sleep well?'

'Fine,' I said.

'Let me make you a pancake,' she said, stepping down from the chair. 'We've all been having them this morning.' She nodded towards the door. Outside on the patio Ig and my father sat at the table, eating and drinking coffee.

'Ig tells me pancakes can cure a hangover,' Eunice said, laughing. 'Didn't you, Ig?' She went outside to glance into their cups. 'More coffee?'

'Oh yes, please,' my father said, holding out his cup. Eunice took it from him, then came back inside to fetch the coffee.

I went to fill the kettle for tea. Even that had been polished. She must have been up for hours doing all this. The white crust of limescale vanished, the inside of it bright and clear. The cooker hood twinkled. Tiles had been scrubbed bright white, the washing machine wiped clean of congealed soap. The inside of the fridge sparkled. Every mark, every stain, every splash of food, layers we'd built over years, scraped away. Even the wheels of the butcher's block had been scrubbed back to silver. The top of it, an undulating chunk of wood, had been exfoliated. There'd been four tomato seeds welded to the surface. They'd been there for ever. No one had ever bothered to scratch them off, but they'd gone. Eunice must have scored them away with the palette knife. I wanted to stick tomato seeds to her. I'd dab them in strong glue and speckle her with them, making her spotty.

'So much stuff,' she said, scanning the table. 'A lifetime of things. I'm cleaning it all for you like I promised I would.'

She'd been touching everything, all our stuff. She'd moved things, sifted through these objects, our objects.

Eunice had her hands on her hips, eyeing the teacups. 'Do you need that many cups?'

'Yes.'

'You're wasting an awful lot of space. I've counted twenty teacups.'

'We need twenty teacups,' I replied.

'When was the last time you used them? If it's more than six months, it should get thrown out. That's the rule of clutter.'

'It's not clutter, Eunice,' I snapped.

All the things we treasured, the precious stuff we barely dared use. The things we kept safely tucked away, not because we needed them but because they filled a space, kept a pattern of familiarity; gave us our sense of home. The padding between love and emptiness. Our history. The story of who we were preserved in teacups.

A grimy wire trailed from the wall to the middle of the room where the fridge had been pushed. Thick, grey dust stuck to the zinc backing, fluff sprouted from the vents. A splash of something brown and sticky down the side previously hidden from view had been sprayed with a white cleaning mousse.

She must have been at the three powder-coated light fittings that hung low over the table. They were brighter, more vivid, polished orange from being cleaned. My father's beloved lights. He bought them with my mother when he first turned a profit with his wine business. He still bragged about his impeccable taste, about how expensive, quality design looked good decades on. I ran my finger down the shade and a piece of paint flaked off, leaving a streak of bare stainless steel where the colour had been. Had he noticed? Surely he'd be annoyed. Surely he'd realise it was too high a price to pay to have a pancake made for you in the morning. I inspected the other lamps. All three of them had strips of paint peeling from the metal.

'It's a good job you've got someone to get you lot tidied up,' said Eunice.

She flung her arms out wide in mock drama, then danced the length of the room, guileless, unselfconscious. Happy! A long, silk blouse, in apricot, rippled and ballooned out behind her.

'Dance with me,' she said, laughing. 'Oh, come on. Dance with me.'

'No,' I said. 'Not in the mood.'

She spun around. 'Look, Lizzy,' she said, pointing to a chair.

I turned to see a stack of my clothes: two cotton sweaters, a pair of jeans, T-shirts for sleeping ironed and folded into a pile. On top, seven pairs of white, lace pants, tucked into small rectangles. Crisp from too much soap.

She must have had a scoot around the floor because my white bra and cream camisole hadn't even made it into the laundry basket. I knew I'd left them tangled on the sofa, where I'd taken them off. A genteel assault on my privacy. In my room, her arms cradling a pile of my dirties. When had she gone in? Where had I been?

'Isn't there just nothing nicer than someone doing your washing?'

'When were you in my room?'

'This morning. I spotted it, as I left. I slept in your bed, remember? It dried in no time in this weather,' she said with pride.

I picked up the stack of clothes and ran out of the kitchen and back to my studio. I flung the stuff on the floor, destroying in an instant Eunice's careful folding.

I closed the door, and took in slow, steady breaths. What would my mother have done with Eunice? Would she have gathered her up and moved her out of the house or been more tolerant? She liked strays. In Greece one year, she gathered all the thin, scrappy dogs in the village and we spent the entire week with our villa overrun with scratching dogs, nibbling at their mange on our whitewashed steps. Perhaps Eunice would have been one of her stray dogs. She'd have been nice to her, seen that it wasn't her fault, that none of it was her fault. But Eunice wouldn't have had the same power if our mother had still been there. Eunice wouldn't have dared empty the cupboards if my mother had been sitting at the kitchen table, keeping an eye on her. Eunice would have been forced to know her place. She'd have been forced to respect our home. What did she want from us anyway?

Through the window, I saw my father in the courtyard.

'Dad,' I called out, beckoning him into my studio.

'What the hell is that woman doing?'

'Oh, she's harmless. A bit crackers. But harmless.'

I said nothing.

'It's only a bit of cleaning. Someone's got to do it.'

'Do you think we should let her do our washing?'

'Why not?'

'She's getting a little comfortable.'

'She's got nothing else to do.'

'Tell her you need the room.'

'I can't ask her to leave.'

'You can.'

'It wouldn't be kind.'

'I'm sick of her.'

My father blasted air through his nostrils, a single shot, the sound of a whale coming up to surface. He pressed his fingertips into his eyebrows and pulled downwards into his eye sockets, pushing against the bone as he dragged both hands down his face.

'She'd crumble,' he said.

'I'm crumbling.'

My father rolled his eyes.

'Just come and eat one of her bloody pancakes and make a decision to enjoy yourself.'

'No.'

'It's a beautiful day. Come and sit in the garden. Ignore her.'

My father left. I went back inside and crept up towards the guest room. At the top of the stairs, I peeked through the hall window. Eunice lounged on a garden chair, topping up her coffee so I carried on towards our guest room – her room – to search for evidence, for something I could show to my father and Ig that might change their minds.

Standing in her room – feeling like a trespasser in my own home – I could see she'd carefully made the bed, creaseless, its counterpane stretched tight. Pairs of her shoes formed neat rows: sensible heels in red, pink and black. On the dressing table, a collection of sparkling brooches and cheap earrings sat in more neat rows. Everything clean, she left behind no residue. The room could have been a shop window display. No dust, or empty packet or small, innocent, half-crescent of a nail clipping left behind. Only her things, the things she needed. The bottles all wiped clean. No cream clagged into a waxy ring around a tube of cleanser. No dirty cotton wool pad slung in the wicker bin. No lone hair curled into a stave on the surface of the table. Even her hairbrush was hairless. I picked through the boxes on the dressing table but found nothing. She was clean. She didn't leave traces of herself.

She had an ornament in the shape of a bare tree on which she'd hung necklaces, maybe twenty of them, not tangled but dangling straight, brass, silver and gold with beads and coloured stones. I picked up an aerosol can of body mist in cherry red and sprayed some on to my hand. A sweet, thick smell that went straight for my head. No clues. No evidence of a lie. No stray piece of identity to tell me her name wasn't Eunice, that she didn't come from Hertfordshire, that she wasn't adopted but rather a conwoman, who tricked people, then moved into their homes and stole it all from under their noses.

I opened the wardrobe door. My mother's clothes – so carefully preserved by us – had been pushed to one end to make way for Eunice's clothes. Hers hung at a precise distance from each other, space between each hanger, whereas she squashed my mother's together, all bunched up like an afterthought as if it didn't matter that they creased. My hands went towards my mother's things, just to tweak them apart a bit, give them some life, some space, let them breathe. *If she came back, she might need them.*

I searched Eunice's clothes. I picked at the heart-shaped crystals on the sweater she'd worn for our first meeting. The red blouse she wore the day she came for the weekend, the maroon silk scarf she draped over her shoulders at the theatre. I leafed through them all, dipping my fingers into her pockets. Nothing.

I kneeled in front of the wardrobe, pushing myself as far inwards as I could, to search the far corners. Deep inside, I swept my arm around, searching. I felt a plastic bag, strained to hold it. My lips pursed into a thin crescent moon as I concentrated on trying to grab it and pull it towards me. Inside it, there were more clothes, folded and piled inside. With one hand inside the wardrobe, my tongue pressed against my lip, I continued searching.

'Elizabeth.'

'Eunice,' I said.

She looked at me. I looked at her, my arm still inside the wardrobe. We stayed like that, just staring.

'You don't trust me?' she said, wounded.

'No, I—'

'You were checking up on me.'

'Oh, for God's sake,' I said, pushing past her and out into the corridor.

'What is it, Elizabeth? What have I done to you?'

Eunice called after me as I ran down the stairs and back out into my studio. I shut the door firmly.

Someone began knocking at the door. 'Elizabeth, Elizabeth, let's not—' The door opened a crack and Eunice's face appeared. 'Let's not fall out.'

I turned my back.

'I'm not here to take anything from you,' she said, stepping inside.

'I'm fetching my swimming things. I'm going swimming,' I said.

I grabbed my towel from the floor, whipped my costume from the hook on the bathroom door and pushed past Eunice. I'd do anything to get away from the claustrophobia of her – go anywhere – yet all I had as an escape was the leisure centre, five minutes' walk from home. I'd have preferred the sea, the sound of waves, the fierce crash against the shore. I'd like to have seen my feet disappearing into sand, but instead I'd tread clammy tiles and fear verrucae. Eunice stood outside my studio, watching me as I fled out into the street.

I liked being underwater because of the silence. I swam – breaststroke – rising and dipping. The only thing I heard was the sound of my breath amplified in my own head like the mechanical rise and fall of an old medical contraption. At the shallow end, I batted my arms like wings to keep position. Through tinted goggles, I watched the water turn from clear to opaque milk-blue at the deep end. I blew bubbles. One after the other. Plop, plop, plop, rising to the surface. It's starting, I thought. I wanted everything to stay the same but Eunice is the beginning. I'm going to be powerless; I'm going to be forced to watch everything I love disappear.

naked

'I LIVE AT EIGHTY-TWO, THE OLD ROW. DO YOU KNOW IT? WE'RE IN the middle of the street on the side with all the lime trees. You go through a small gate. It doesn't seem like much from the outside, but it is once you get in. Ring the doorbell and I'll buzz you through.'

When the chocolate cake arrived by bike courier, Eunice set the large pink box on the table in front of me. She held a knife – a thin curve of glinting stainless steel – and offered me a slice. 'I ordered it as a treat for everyone for lunch,' she said. 'I need cake. Like an addict needs crack.' She hesitated, glancing at the knife, before sinking it through the soft chocolate icing. 'I don't think anyone will mind if I have a quick slice now, with my coffee.'

'It's your cake,' I said.

She cut herself a huge piece, opening her jaws to their widest to bite through all three layers of sponge. With her little finger, she pushed an escaped dot of buttercream icing back into her mouth. 'Everyone says cake's good for a broken heart.'

'You don't look very broken-hearted, Eunice,' I said.

'Oh, but I am,' she replied, sucking the icing from her fingers. Chocolate gathered in the creases of her lips as she offered me a piece.

'My body's all I've got. I can't eat that,' I said.

'Should I be good? Or should I have another piece?' she asked.

I felt a mixture of disgust and envy as I watched her gorge herself, taking one bite after another, sucking the icing from her fingers. I could only imagine the taste: the soft, yielding crumb; the thick buttery icing dissolving in my mouth; the rush of the sugar as it hit my blood; the chocolate taste lingering on my tongue for the rest of the afternoon. I wanted that cake but I wouldn't have it.

'Perhaps you should be good, Eunice,' I said. 'Cake doesn't heal broken hearts.' I closed the lid on the box. 'It just makes you fat.'

She grinned at me. 'I wish I could be like you,' she said, pushing the closed box away from herself. 'You're so—', but then she tailed off before she managed to finish the thought.

Would my father still have been able to march through the house with his head in the clouds if he had heard the way Eunice had given our address to that cake courier? The proprietorial tone cut straight through me like that knife through the cake. This place, stitched into my skin, an extension of my own body, the place that held my past within it. I didn't want an unfeeling idiot like her to be in a position to take it from me, to damage us all.

She might use our lovely home to fill the empty space within herself, use these walls – our walls – as a foil for whatever it was she feared she lacked within. She might need things – expensive things – to make her feel safe and important. She'd leave us exiled from our own lives. She'd break us in order to fix herself.

The thought of what Eunice might be planning filled me with a kind of animal fear. I feared she might be the sort of insecure woman who could only tolerate primacy. To that end, she'd work on my father, persuade him that it was right, it was time, for me to be forced to give up my studio to her. She'd do it behind my back all the time smiling to my face. But she wouldn't see herself as cold or spiteful or envious, she'd see herself as a victim. She'd believe she had finally received what was rightfully hers.

The thing I feared most was her lack of empathy, her hysterical self-absorption. I feared her absolute, demonic, all-consuming belief in the supremacy of her own needs. If she caused me pain, it wouldn't bother her. In fact, it might even give her pleasure. If she took what was mine, it wouldn't occur to her that I might miss it. I wouldn't even have the slight consolation of knowing that she understood what she had done because the part of her brain that should be able to imagine how others felt, appeared to be malfunctioning. I'd just be collateral damage; and she'd just be pleased that she had what she wanted. I feared that she was nothing more than a proper little manipulator, disguised in pink kitten heels, putting everyone off the scent with her tears while she told people she loved me like a sister.

'Do you think I could be an actress?' Eunice said.

She wore a T-shirt made of stiff cotton decorated with tiny flowers in broderie anglaise. Beneath it, a pair of shorts in bright pink with ballet pumps in the same shade. I didn't know what it was about her that irritated me so much: that little pug nose or the annoying colourlessness of her hair. *Help me*, those two hard little eyes seemed to say.

Eunice was still fretting about where to store the cake on such a hot day when the phone rang. It was the director, offering me a way out of the house for the afternoon and evening. I went to the garden, relieved to be able to tell my father I wouldn't be staying for lunch. He'd already started cooking the pork ribs over the fire for Tom and Valerie. He tried to persuade me to stay, told me Valerie would want me there, and I nearly changed my mind until I looked over at Eunice. She had one foot suspended in the air as she dabbed neon-pink paint on to her toenails. When the right foot was finished, she held it up, twisted it right and left, examining the colour against the glossy green of our garden. I closed my eyes and turned to leave.

The director answered the door holding a wooden spoon. He asked me to follow him through his enormous window-lined sitting room into the kitchen, a Seventies concoction of brown floor tiles and fake mahogany cupboards with lattice windows.

'I like your flat,' I said. 'It's spacious.'

'I don't,' he replied. 'I hate old things.'

'But you've got nice views,' I said.

He clamped his arms around my legs as if picking up a caber to plant me on the countertop. A small window above the sink looked out over Edwardian rooftops. Squares of light and dark slotted together. I sat there and felt awkward. We weren't used to this, eating lunch together with nothing else to think about. Neither of us seemed to know what to say. For the last few months, we'd chased each other around the theatre, ducked into the maintenance cupboards to kiss or found an old mattress to lie on once everyone had gone home, but here in his home, like this, I felt suddenly exposed. We were together in broad daylight and I wondered what on earth we might have to talk about. He carried on washing salad leaves, not speaking, shaking a jar of homemade dressing, checking on the oven.

'What's for lunch?' I asked.

'A surprise.'

The director wore white sports socks and no shoes. I couldn't understand the socks. They didn't match the rest of him. On top, he wore an ironed blue shirt a little open so I could see the beginnings of his bare chest, the smooth rise of two hair-free pectorals. He hugged me with one arm.

'So glad you came,' he said.

When he released me, I began looking through the pile of reviews he'd left on the end of the kitchen counter. I'd already seen them – my father saved them – but browsing them gave me something to do. My trapeze scene was mentioned in two of the reviews, but my name wasn't. 'It doesn't mean anything,' the director said and I believed him. He wiped something from his top lip and kissed me. When he'd finished at the cooker, he handed me a plate of salad and sent me through to sit at the dining table.

I shouted through to him that I needed the bathroom. He told me I'd find it by going through his bedroom, so on my way back to the table, I stopped to have a look around. The room smelled vaguely of aftershave. By the window stood a mahogany desk, inlaid with a paler wood border and a section of dark green leather. Two pairs of silver cufflinks – one in the shape of a theatre mask, the other a set of dollar signs – sat on top, arranged next to a black leather wallet and a set of keys. There were two or three books – editions of Bertolt Brecht – covered in blue and green cotton canvas. A pile of theatre magazines were stacked on the floor but the rest of the room was empty. Just a bed, the table, a wardrobe and an old trouser press. Nothing personal: no photographs or invitations, no letters in the drawers, just old gas bills. No relics from childhood, nothing to tell me he hadn't been born a fully fledged adult in a pressed pale blue Oxford shirt and loose jeans.

'What is taking you so long?' he shouted.

I dashed back and sat at the table. 'Sorry,' I said, setting about the plate of salad.

For the main course, he returned from the kitchen with two plates and a tea towel tucked into his waistband.

'Baby chickens?' I said.

'Poussin,' he replied.

I stared at my plate. He'd slit them down the backbone and flattened them out. Next to the bird splayed out across my plate sat a small mound of sautéed spinach.

'They look horrifying.'

'They're delicious,' he replied. 'Soft and tender as anything.'

After lunch, the director put on some music. He led me across to his huge corner sofa, covered with creaky brown leather. He poured us out another glass of wine. I laid my head in his lap, staring up at the ceiling while he told me about his plans for his next project. 'A short film exploring chance,' he said. I listened while he talked, leaning my head up every now and again to take a sip of wine.

Afterwards, he took me to his room. In bed, I lay underneath him and I couldn't get the image of the chickens out of my head with their soft, plump bellies facing upwards and their legs falling open.

The next morning, I walked along the river towards the bus station. The sun was just beginning to burn through the morning. The air felt on the cusp of warmth. I bought a takeaway coffee then walked beyond the first bus station, to the next.

As I walked, the director called.

'What are you up to?' he said.

I told him I'd decided to walk.

'Well, walk back to my flat,' he said. 'I'm lying stark naked on my balcony. I've got my cock in one hand, a vodka martini in the other and I'm thinking of you.'

I laughed.

'I want to see those glorious tits of yours again.'

'No,' I replied. 'I'm halfway home.'

I carried on walking, watching market stallholders set up, past lorries making their morning deliveries to the restaurants. I enjoyed the flow of people crossing London Bridge on their way to work, knowing I wasn't one of them. I just kept walking and walking until finally, by mid-morning, I was only three streets away from home and had formed the idea that I must talk to Eunice. I should tell her my concerns. I realised that I was the one who started this, therefore I should be the one to end it. I resolved to take control, to begin laying the foundations for her to move on. She wouldn't exile me; I'd exile her.

In the sitting room, there was no sign of her so I began up the stairs. I knocked softly at the guest room door. No reply again. She wasn't in my father's room, or in the garden or . . .

'Eunice,' I gasped. 'What are you doing in here?'

'You looked in my room,' she said. 'So why can't I—'

Standing inside my mother's room, she held a small white box in one hand. The lid off, she sifted through its contents: faded childhood photographs, our old school reports, art works of glittering easter bunnies holding messages in spidery, uneven writing. 'All this stuff,' she said, replacing the box. 'What a treasure chest.'

On the ground, a black holdall containing our mother's old shoes had been unzipped: sandals, ballet pumps, bright turquoise evening shoes, all scuffed, faded with dust. They began spilling out of the bag as she pushed her way through them, pulling out the ones she wanted to look at in more detail. Next, she discovered my mother's old washbag in black with tiny blue flowers. Inside, half-used pots of face cream, a toothbrush, a crumpled, empty box of Temazepam.

'What were the pills for?' said Eunice.

I grabbed them and the bag from her and carefully replaced them in the drawer of the dressing table where we kept them. Undeterred, Eunice carried on her tour of the room, her eyes flickering hungrily over all my mother's stuff. 'These lovely pieces of furniture, pictures—' She lifted the corner of a white sheet covering a rail of clothes to peek underneath. 'You should wear this stuff,' she said. 'What a waste, leaving it up here.' Her hand flicked down the line of coat hangers, pulling things out. 'I mean, look at that.' She unhooked a coat covered in black sequins, holding it up for me to see. 'That's probably worth a fortune now.'

'We're not going to sell them,' I snapped.

She searched the room like someone shopping, hungry with longing for all this stuff, as if she'd landed on a secret bounty that she wanted to possess. I could see it in her face: she wanted it all. She burst with desire. She opened up a small wooden box of my mother's old rings, began taking them out, starting with the large green ring my father had bought her when she turned fifty. Silver band; huge, uneven stone like a hunk of peppermint rock. 'Wow,' said Eunice, pushing it on to her desperate, lusty fingers until she found the one it fitted. She held her hand in front of her, moving it around, watching it catch the light. My throat hardened, thudded with pain, but I couldn't speak. I daren't tell her to stop. I couldn't find the strength to stick up for myself, to defend our right to privacy, our right to live as we wanted. My stomach burned with hurt and grief while

Eunice carried on opening up box after box, peering in.

'You know, a fresh pair of eyes could get this lot sorted. When the mess gets overwhelming, you can't see through it.'

A cloud moved. Shafts of golden sun sliced through the spaces between the boxes, making hundreds of straight lines of bright light. Within them, millions of tiny particles of dust swam about in the unsettled air.

'I'd be happy to help—'

'Eunice, please don't tidy this stuff up.' My hands began to shake. 'Please.' My voice faltered. 'We very much need it to stay the same.'

'It's a beautiful room,' she said, her eyes flickering around the walls. 'So much bigger than the guest room. Wonderful, big windows. If only we could see through them. This room could be so bright.'

'Eunice, we should go downstairs.'

Decisively, I took the box of rings from her hand, returning them to their rightful place on the dressing table, alongside all my mother's other boxes that she liked to keep her things in. I kept them nicely preserved for her. I didn't want her thinking that I hadn't looked after her stuff, that I'd just forgotten her and let all the lovely things she'd collected so carefully over the years go to rot. My mum didn't buy just anything. She was careful how she spent her money, only choosing pieces of jewellery she knew she'd love for years to come. She wasn't profligate or gluttonous with shopping the way Eunice was. Stuffing her face with new things. Rubbish that she loved for five minutes then slung out. My mother loved her things. They made her history. Her rings and necklaces told a story. Places visited, children born, moments she preserved within the fibre of a stone. I resettled the dust sheet around them and carefully tucked it in to ensure a good seal.

'It's very sad,' Eunice said. Then she looked at me: a moment of recognition. 'We're the same. You and me. We're both motherless.' I felt my shoulders contract, a tightness drew across my chest, a void opened up within me.

'Oh, Elizabeth, I've upset you. I didn't mean to upset you. Please don't cry. I was just looking.'

'I'm not crying, Eunice,' I said, wiping my face. 'I'm fine.'

She came in closer towards me. 'Maybe this is my purpose, Elizabeth. Maybe this is why I came into your life. Everything has a reason. You're not going to fix me. I'm going to fix you. Maybe, I'm not here to find my past, maybe I'm here to help you by erasing the bad things from yours. I'm here to get you to move on.' I could feel her hot breath on my cheek as she ran her hand down my back. 'At some point in our lives, we've all got to let things go. I've had to. I always believed that one day things would miraculously change. That my real mum and dad would swoop in and bring me home and everything would be all right again. I had to let go of the idea I was meant to grow up in a normal family and it was so painful. And maybe now it's your turn. You've got to let go. She's gone and you've got to carry on living. I'm going to show you the way. I'm not here to take anything from you. Believe me. Trust me.'

I said nothing.

'Come on, Lizzy. You're shaken up. Let me make you some tea.' She directed me out of the room towards the stairs. 'Julian told me that this week was the anniversary for your mum. So, I know. Don't worry. He warned me. I know why you've been bad-tempered with me and I understand.' She stopped on the stairs and turned to face me, giving me a creepy little smile. 'I forgive you for being testy with me.'

anniversary

DAB! THE PAD OF EUNICE'S INDEX FINGER LANDED ON THE END OF MY father's nose. A tiny pat, a shrug, a giggle. She removed her finger, leaving behind a trace of wholemeal flour.

Flour dusted everything: the kitchen counter, the floor, the apron Eunice wore. Her sleeves rolled up, a balloon of bread in front of her, she bashed, rolled, folded, all the time checking the magazine recipe open next to her.

'I'm making you all something,' she said. 'To cheer you up.'

In front of her, a great puffy swell of bread dough that made me think of a huge, soft arse. She sprinkled more flour then ripped the dough into two pieces. Checking the pictures in the recipe again, she stretched and turned until each piece formed a pale, circular mound. Breasts now, covered in muslin, swelling in the warmth.

Outside, the day sweated. Ig lay on a blue towel on the lawn. His long, bony legs crossed at the ankle, the black wire of the headphones trailing down his pale, thin body. Shutting the world out with his own private music. The lawn had dried to a crisp. My father meant to water it but not today, he said. He'd take it easy today. He'd water it tomorrow. Inside, while the bread proved, Eunice swept through the house with the

Hoover. She knew we had guests coming, she said. And she wanted to make it nice for them.

August 27th. The worst day of the year.

From the garden, I heard the din of the Hoover, industrial strength suction that threatened to drown us out. She swept past the windows, sucking up the flour and any other dust that threatened her path, the small, powerful machine imposing order on a chaotic world.

My father drained the last of a bottle of sparkling water into his glass. He swung the empty, pleading for me to go inside for more. In the kitchen the oven went at full tilt, making the room feel heady with heat. Eunice swirled around it, taking loaves out of the oven, rapping her knuckles against the bases, fetching knives and cheese, worrying at a plate of lettuce leaves gone limp in the heat. I found more water. Eunice shooed me out of the kitchen. She'd do lunch. We were all to sit outside and relax. 'It's your day today. You don't want to worry about anything.'

Hands inside a pair of thick oven gloves, Eunice swished down the garden holding a plate with her two loaves. 'Lunch, everyone!' she called out. My father peeked out over the top of his sunglasses. He folded his newspaper in half, slapped it down on the end of his sun lounger and sat up.

'Look!' she said. She held the tray up close to him, looking at him hopefully as she presented the two swollen loaves. 'Not bad for a first attempt.' Eunice arranged a small table, pushing cups and plates around until eventually her lunch of bread, cheese, salad, managed to fit. 'There's nothing says lovin' like something from the oven,' she said. She hovered, seeming to wait for a reply, but none came so she hurriedly began moving plates, checking everything really did fit the table.

'Slice,' she said, handing my father a loaf and a knife. 'I know it's what your wife used to do so I wanted to do something to help you remember the good things and stop you feeling so sad.'

She stood over him as he sawed into it, looking intently at the flesh of the bread as he cut away a piece. My father ate slowly, reluctantly. Eunice examined his face for signs of pleasure.

'Yes?' she said. 'Good?'

He nodded.

I didn't touch Eunice's bread. Something about it, the two hard little loaves with their clagging insides, made me stay away. Ig devoured four pieces without a thought, then sawed off extra cheese. I nibbled at a lettuce leaf, debated drinking a second glass of the wine my father offered around.

After lunch, my mother's oldest friend Anna and her husband David arrived for the special dinner to commemorate our mother. Anna was long and lean with pale, weathered skin. The unruly hair she had in the photograph on my mother's dressing table had been tamed by middle age into a neat, pale brown bob. A light denim shirt tucked into blue trousers replaced the flowing dresses and garish patterns.

My father put up the sunshade and dragged chairs out from inside. Eunice fussed around with a teapot while Anna and David displayed perfect discretion, nodding their heads in thanks as Eunice trickled tea into their delicate bone china teacups, holding up a hand to refuse her offer of a choice between a small sandwich or a small cake.

We drank the tea, talked about the heat, about the garden, about the fact that tea makes you feel cooler on a hot day, and steadfastly ignored the obvious subject. Ig told us stories about the woman my father called Ig's 'infamous client'. In her fifties, going through a divorce, she used to insist on having Ig, and no one else, for her sessions. A trophy wife, Ig said, always swishing in and out of the centre wearing cashmere and silk, thick make-up, unable to leave her house without a pair of heels on. She said she needed an hour just to lie and be nothing other than herself. She wanted to take it all off, the make-up, the jewellery, everything. Ig didn't care. He handed her tissues and lotion to clean her face, let her leave her pearls in a small box he kept in the cupboard. Perhaps she chose Ig because she could tell it wouldn't bother him. He wouldn't stare at her, assess her, hover his eyes over her, along with his hands. She'd alighted on Reiki to calm her through endless quarrels with her ex-husband. She'd turned herself into something for her husband, now she wanted to turn herself back, even if just for an hour a week. She wanted to feel like a real person, she said, rather than a carefully constructed fake.

'You should have given her one,' my father said. 'While you had the chance.'

Ig sighed. 'She wants to take me out for dinner.'

'Will you go?' Anna asked.

'Dunno,' said Ig.

'I could see you with an older woman,' said Anna. 'There's an intelligence about you, a quietness, an ability to listen, to let other people just be. You're like your mother, Ig.'

'Don't get any ideas,' said David, and Anna laughed, blushing. No, no, no, that hadn't been her meaning at all.

'Do you like her?' Anna asked.

She took the pot of tea to pour herself another cup. I closed my eyes to listen to the sound of it, the jangle of the cup settling back in its saucer. Anna's breathy voice – as if my mother had come back for the day.

'Maybe she likes you,' she said.

'I still think he should have given her one,' said my father. David laughed heartily. 'It could have been quite something. On a Reiki table.'

Ig rolled his eyes.

My father wished the anniversary of my mother's death fell in the middle of winter so the damp and gloom would match his mood. The arrival of the longer evenings and warmer temperatures brought with them dread for him. I preferred that the anniversary came in summer. Light everywhere. The possibility of warmth.

The day felt like a mad, messed-up need to get it right. Panic, guilt, veiled words about what our mother might have wanted. If we hadn't done enough in life to save her, at least in death, we did. My father contained the anniversary of my mother's death with rituals. He needed the solidity of them, something constant that couldn't change, something he felt in control of. They gave him a sense of order.

The evening would begin with a glass of Sancerre, my mother's favourite wine, drunk in the garden. Next, he would plant something for her. Last year a plum tree, this year he'd bought five tubs of English lavender to grow a scented bush. After the planting, we ate. Rock oysters to start brought by Anna, chicken and tomato casserole made by my father, strawberry tart from Valerie. After eating, we spent the remainder of the evening outside, talking, smoking, playing Scrabble.

They were my father's rituals but they weren't mine. I couldn't quite fit myself into them. The chicken brought back all the wrong images. I didn't like the idea of my mother reincarnated as a chicken casserole. I didn't like the way the meat felt in my mouth, all slippery and wet. I'd have preferred champagne before dinner. I'd have liked to think about something else, the happier times, to celebrate her, tell joyful stories, for each of us to go round the table and say something about her that would make us all laugh, even if we'd heard it before. I went along with my father, though, because in the end, I just needed to pass the day.

In front of him, my father piled the marble slab high with carefully weighed parsley. Pieces of raw chicken lay stacked on a plate. Tins of tomatoes waited to be opened. He turned the process of making my mother's chicken casserole into an exact science, following to the letter the recipe she'd handwritten. I wanted to pick it up to see her handwriting again but he buffeted me away. I might ripple the air, he warned. A few leaves of parsley could flutter away. 'It might change everything,' he said. I stood back, taking her writing in from afar. Neat and clear. Curled, careful letters. Detailed instructions, every step of the cooking explained. Three lines on the way the onions should look before the tomatoes are added. What 'browned' chicken looks like: crunchy, granular skin, the colour of an over-tanned woman, my mother had written. My father believed in the precision of these instructions. They opened a channel of communication direct from the grave to the kitchen counter. She first made it for him when they were both twenty-two, having dinner together at her tiny bedsit. She cooked it on a single ring, hooked up to a gas bottle, using white wine in with the tomatoes. She perfumed it with rosemary from her windowsill, then sprinkled the finished dish with crushed raw garlic and grated lemon zest. My father described it as a revelation. 'The first time I tasted that,' he said, 'fresh, alive, colourful, I knew she was the girl for me. She didn't make brown food. She made stuff that tasted of sunshine.'

I don't know where she'd learned to cook the way she did. It hadn't been at home, with my grandparents. There was no theatre in her own mother's dishes as she tipped gravy over shop-bought pies and limp, exhausted peas. My mother told me how bored she'd been growing up. An Edwardian house with rust and beige tiles patterning the hallway, stained glass window in the door, the ticking of a grandfather clock measuring out the evenings. Her father in a chair, stuffing tobacco into a pipe; slippers slapping the bottoms of her mother's feet as she stalked the house, whacking her and Valerie's legs with a wooden spoon if they disobeyed.

No wonder my mother went slightly mad when she escaped into a home of her own. Hers was a jerky kind of domestic perfection. One evening, we might have eaten a roast chicken with crisp, salty skin and buttery juices; the next a bowl of soggy pasta she'd barely had the energy to grate an old bit of cheese over. One evening, I came home from school to a table laid for dinner with petals, leaves and rose buds scattered wildly all over a white linen cloth. The room madly lit with tea lights. Tiny candles, all flickering innocently, in small clear glasses. She'd put them everywhere: randomly cast across the table, lined up on the shelves, grouped together on the floor in the corner of the room. With the electric lights off, we ate salads made from things she'd grown in the garden. She sat tall, at the head of the table, defiantly stabbing yellow tomatoes with her fork. The room felt heady with the scent of different herbs and flowers. The elderflower cordial infusing on the stove bubbled up, steaming the windows. In the darkness, with the flickering candles, the infusion felt like a witches' cauldron, as if we'd landed in the middle of a séance.

Another time, she strung fairy lights through all the trees, hundreds of tiny bulbs that made the garden sparkle. Ig and I sucked on ice lollies she'd made for us from homemade raspberry purée. Before handing them to us, she dipped the ends in melted white chocolate. She played loud, strange music while we tore around the garden until late into the night, nothing but ice lollies for dinner. She and Dad sat on cushions under the mulberry tree getting stoned, rolling joint after joint. Mum let us lick the sweet strip on the rolling paper the way other people's mothers let them lick the cake bowl. I had to heave myself out of bed for school the next morning. I went into their room to say goodbye but she and my father were out cold. I'd been barely able to keep my eyes open as I waited for the bus. But as swiftly as the fun arrived, it disappeared. In the blink of an eye, a grey cloud could descend over my mother. After school, we scratched around in the cupboards for cornflakes while she sat in a wooden chair, staring at nothing. If I stood close to her, wanting to talk, she just sighed. 'Leave me alone, Elizabeth. I'm tired.'

Even though Anna and David only came from Kensington, they always brought their caravan to sleep in. A small, vintage bullet, made of aluminium, parked in our courtyard. They'd been bringing it since the early days when my mother was alive and they'd come for a week in the summer. Summers were always like that. My parents had people staying every night, crammed in everywhere, always a full house. Inflatable mattresses blocked the doorways, overnight bags wedged under the sideboard, toothbrushes on the coffee table. All summer, we could barely move for guests. One year, a school friend of my mother's she hadn't seen for years had pitched up from Argentina. My father made lean-tos in the garden for people to sleep under. He draped old sheets over wooden stakes and left piles of blankets for them to wrap themselves in.

'I'd love to show you the caravan,' said Anna, tactfully guiding me away from my father as he grew increasingly over-wrought in the kitchen. 'I've had it refitted with new fabrics, bespoke storage and a tiny kitchen built to my design. We love the caravan, don't we, David? We could spend all summer long in it.'

'It's wonderful,' he replied.

At the door, Anna twisted the circular handle so we could duck inside.

'It's lovely, Anna,' I lied.

Decked out to look like a Cornish cottage, the floor was durable plastic to give the illusion of weathered floorboards. Seats covered in cream linen. Four white porcelain mugs hung from hooks over the sink. Pretty pale blue curtains in the window tied back with thick braided rope. Handpainted fish and shells in different shades of blue dotted around the walls. 'I wanted the interior to look like a fisherman's cottage,' said Anna. She pulled open a door to show me her clever storage system. All her clothes, shoes and make-up tucked away. The shelves moved like a conveyor belt, up, down and across when she wanted to access something.

'I'll light the gas and make us tea. You'll be my first guest in the new décor.' She fetched down mugs, took out her matching teapot. She lit the single gas ring and we waited for the kettle to whistle.

'So that's the half-sister,' she said. 'You'd have thought she would have taken herself off for the day.'

'Not Eunice,' I said. 'She'll be here, in the thick of it, *helping* us all.'

Anna put her feet up on to the bench the other side and we drank the tea. She told me she missed female company. A true friend. She liked the ease of having another woman around the place, someone who could sit at a kitchen table for half a day, doing nothing but drinking tea and talking. 'I still miss that,' she said.

In the garden, Valerie arranged glasses on the table. Ig swept the paving stones while David stacked logs into the fire pit, ready to light later. Everyone assembled, my father came outside with two bottles of Sancerre.

Behind him, I saw the plate first. An enormous white platter with Eunice propelling it from behind into the midst of us. On it lettuce leaves formed the shape of petals, cheese cubes piled in its centre. 'It's a Cheddar flower,' Eunice said. 'I read about it in a magazine.'

She picked her way across the uneven stone slabs to present her plate to each of us in turn.

'Thank you, no,' said Valerie, holding out her hand to Eunice, all but batting her away.

My father held a glass of wine, looked up at the fading sky and told it he still felt racked with longing. The sky remained silent. 'I want her back,' he said. Still, the sky stayed firm. No crack of thunder, no sprinkling of rain, nothing to tell my father it had heard him. He kept looking upwards until Anna put her arm around his waist and coaxed him back to earth. Only the mad talk to clouds.

He put his glass down to dab an eye with his white handkerchief. He scanned the knot of concerned people looking at him then reached for his glass, but before he could pick it up, he collapsed forward, felled by a sob that refused to be suppressed. Anna clutched him around the waist. David pressed his hand into his shoulder. My father struggled to pull himself upright to carry on with the evening. He searched for Ig and me, flapping his hands, asking us to stand close beside him, to plait ourselves all together.

'We're here,' whispered Anna. 'Everyone's here.'

In the garden, composed again, my father filled our glasses with more wine. The taste of it always took me back there, to the first days without her when we just sat around and stared at each other. The house felt so empty, so quiet. The three of us silent for hours, then out of nowhere, a furious argument with none of us knowing how it had started. We fought about who it was worse for; the pecking order of grief in which each of us struggled to find our position; where we fitted seemed to matter at the time.

It's easier to grieve alone. With collective grief, the group can never coordinate. You don't feel the same things at the same time, so you can't understand each other. The worst kind of loneliness. I'd think of my father's good days as a betrayal, his bad ones as indulgent. He did the same. One day I was insensitive, the next he thought it time I 'pulled myself together'. But then if I tried to hold myself in to venture out into the world, I'd always regret it. I'd come across some berk or other who'd say their mother had died when they were seven or a baby or just before their wedding day, so it had been much worse for them. At least I'd had twenty-six happy years, they'd say.

Valerie stubbed her fag with a grind of her foot against the paving stone. She didn't want any more Sancerre. She fancied a gin and tonic, which was what she'd always drunk with my mother. 'I think she preferred gin to white wine,' said Valerie.

She lit another fag. I went inside to fetch her gin. Eunice followed me inside, telling me she had something else for us. Outside again, I handed Valerie her drink. She drew up close to me. 'Crisps,' she whispered, looking at Eunice through the window, emptying packet after packet into a ceramic bowl. 'Since when did we have crisps?'

My father moved towards the spot near the office he'd chosen to plant the lavender. We gathered around. Eunice hovered, looking uncertain of herself, as she held up her offering of cheese and onion crisps that no one had taken. Everyone became serious while my father dug. He tapped the plant pots to release the lavender, dropped each one into the mud, then pressed around them compacting the plants into the earth. Just as he finished, a breeze rippled around the garden so the stalks of the lavender shivered, making the flowers quiver like tiny purple insects. In our madder times, we might have made something of that, told ourselves it was her spirit among us, dancing through the plants to give her approval. But now, all this time later, no one said a thing. They were just flowers; it was just a breeze.

David teased his blond hair back into shape, pressing his palms around his head as if moulding clay. Sunspots dappled the backs of his hands. As the group reached the kitchen, he swept along Eunice's back with his palm to coax her inside. She turned to thank him. A broad smile flared across David's face. His teeth were slightly bulbous, a line of grey running along the gum. Had he had veneers? 'I wouldn't put it past him,' whispered Valerie.

My father took up position in front of his casserole. Lemon zest, garlic, parsley arranged in small saucers beside him, ready to give his dish its final flourish. He checked my mother's notes again then dipped a spoon into the sauce to taste. Eunice dashed around the counter, spraying with detergent, whipping away my father's dirty spoons, giving everything a wipe down. She gathered up two halves of lemon to throw in the bin. My father jumped to save them. 'I'm not finished with them yet,' he snapped.

'Here, Eunice,' said Anna. 'Lend me a hand with the oysters.'

Eunice glued her eyes to Anna as she inserted the small, fat blade into the muscle of the oyster. A single sharp twist prised the shell open. 'Yuck,' Eunice said. 'It looks like snot.' Anna rested the oyster on a plate of crushed ice, to start on the next one.

'Margaret's favourite. Oysters,' said Valerie from her spot at the kitchen table.

Anna bound Eunice's hand with a tea towel, putting an oyster in the protected hand, the shucker in the other. She guided the blade in towards the nub of muscle. 'Now tease it inside,' said Anna, all the time watching Eunice's blade. Eunice jabbed, the oyster shell lifted. She looked thrilled.

'You're out of wine,' said David to my father.

My father downed his spoon and went to the cellar for more. Eunice glanced in the direction of the casserole. Anna held out another oyster, beckoning her to try again, but Eunice drifted away, not listening, heading in the direction of the cooker. She hovered for a moment, looked around at us, as if waiting for someone to say something. In a split second, she had the lid off the casserole, breathing in the smell of the sauce. Valerie crunched walnuts, one after another, from a small white bowl.

Eunice crossed the room, took a bottle of Worcestershire sauce from the fridge, lid off the casserole again, she tilted the open bottle of sauce, preparing to shake.

'Noooooooooooo.' My father ran towards the cooker,

pushing Eunice aside so hard he almost took her off her feet. He ripped the pan lid from her hand, slammed it back down. 'No,' he said again. Eunice gathered herself from her near fall, stunned, silenced, her face blank with shock. My father prised the bottle from her fingers, threw it to the counter with such force that the neck of the bottle shattered, splattering sauce over the tiles. 'Stop fucking meddling,' he hissed at her. He stood between Eunice and his casserole, his arms outstretched. 'We don't need helping. We don't need you. We don't need your fucking cheese cubes, your crisps. And we certainly don't need you tinkering with our casserole. You're always standing around with that dumb look on your face. We're fine. We don't need helping.'

Silence from the rest of the room. My father peeled the recipe from the wet counter where a pool of brown Worcestershire sauce threatened to seep into his plastic covering. He wiped the recipe against his chest, cradled it, rocked it in his arms. He looked as if he might cry.

'I didn't know,' Eunice said. 'I didn't mean to upset you. I thought I was doing the right thing. Mike always said I was good at putting my own stamp on things.' Ig moved towards Eunice to touch her hand. She yanked herself away from him, running from the room. The stair door banged shut behind her. Feet thudded against wood. A bedroom door slammed.

'Looks like trouble,' Valerie said, rubbing both hands together.

'Leave it, Valerie,' my father said.

'It's only a casserole,' said Ig.

'That's not the point,' my father replied.

Anna led my father to a wooden chair at the table. He slumped, both hands covering his face.

'You'll never get rid of her,' Valerie said.

'Valerie, stop,' said Anna.

'Margaret wouldn't have wanted her staying,' Valerie continued.

'Margaret's not here,' hissed my father.

'I'll do the casserole,' said Anna. 'You just relax, Julian. I know how Margaret made it. David, fetch Julian another drink. We all know you didn't mean those things you said. Today's a very difficult day for you. Eunice will understand.' My father nodded, a little boy again, tearful, grateful.

Anna finished the casserole, wiped clean the kitchen counters, shucked the remaining oysters, then laid the table. She used a dab of wax to stick white candles into cut glass dishes, arranged them down the centre alongside bowls of white flowers freshly cut from the garden. On the kitchen counter, the oysters nestled into their bed of crushed ice. Everything twinkled. The table sparkling with polished silver cutlery, the crystal glasses reserved for best, the glisten of the oysters. The fading light outside gave way to the candles. Calm and order restored.

'Dinner's ready,' said Anna.

Valerie leaned forward to singe the end of a fag in the flame. Ig went to put some music on.

'You go,' my father told me. 'Fetch Eunice.'

'Me?' I said.

'I'll go,' said Valerie, standing up.

'Lizzy, you go. You're a woman.'

'I'll go,' said Valerie, grinning, heading towards the door. 'I'm a woman.'

'No,' my father said, rushing up from his chair to stand in her way.

'You can't fuss like this every time someone throws a tantrum,' said Valerie. 'I'd leave her sulking, if it was up to me.

You were perfectly within your rights to—'

'Just you go, Lizzy,' my father said.

I stood at the bottom of the stairs and called out. No reply. I called again. Nothing. I came back into the kitchen. 'I think she's gone out.'

'For goodness' sake, what are you all so afraid of?' said Valerie, getting up again.

'We'd have heard her go out,' replied my father. 'Just go.'

I started upstairs. 'Eunice, dinner,' I called out. I pushed her bedroom door open. Inside, Eunice sat on the bed, staring out of the window. The room gloomy, her face barely visible as she spun around, disturbed by the noise of me tiptoeing in. She sniffed, turned quickly back.

'I was just trying to help you all,' she said to the window.

'Come and eat.'

'I don't understand why I've annoyed everyone,' she said.

'You haven't annoyed everyone. Dad's very contrite. He's just upset today.'

Up close, I could smell her. The faint odour of onions and meat, that peculiar smell some people have when they cry. In her hands, a set of yellow plastic beads. She pulled them through and around her fingers, then slung them to the ground. She tugged at her fingers, pulling them angrily. She scowled, a screwed up, confused expression, like a cross child.

'Eunice,' I said, pulling her hand away. 'You're hurting yourself.'

'I want to hurt myself,' she replied. She dug her nail into the fleshy part around her thumb, then again, harder. I wanted to move away from her. She jabbed at herself again, banging her thumb and forefinger across her knuckles.

'You think I'm weird,' she said. 'You don't trust me.'

I kept looking at her hands, unsure what to tell her.

'You didn't stick up for me,' she said. 'No one cares about me. About how I feel. And now even Julian's being mean to me.'

'Just come downstairs,' I said.

'But you haven't helped me.'

'Eunice, I—'

'You keep pushing me away.'

'Let's just go downstairs,' I said. 'Come on.'

David shuffled along the table to make room for Eunice's chair. 'Here you go,' he said. 'This'll make you feel better.' He handed her a glass of wine. 'It's an emotional day for everyone. I understand.' As she took it from him, her eyes met his with animal quickness, holding his gaze for just a second.

'Thank you, David,' she said. 'You're very kind.' She looked dishevelled. Her hair not quite so neat as before. Her white top fell a little too low, revealing a tiny slice of scalloped lace from her bra.

Anna's slender arms encircled the plate as we all took our oysters. The long fringe of her pale brown hair tickling her eyes, making her flick her head to be rid of it. Anna had changed from the denim shirt into a round-necked navy-blue top with long sleeves. Small pearl earrings. A single silver bracelet. David took six oysters, Valerie just three. Anna bent so my father could reach, stacking one oyster after another on to his plate. David's eyes kept flickering towards Eunice. They ran down the line of skin between her breasts before he remembered himself, hauling his gaze back to his plate. 'Lemon,' said Anna, handing him a segment.

'Don't they have oysters in St Albans?' said Valerie, looking at Eunice's empty plate. 'They're full of iron and minerals,' she told Eunice, picking up an oyster and holding it out in Eunice's direction.

She leaned in towards Eunice with the oyster. As Eunice backed away, Valerie moved the shell closer in. Eunice looked down it, held inches from her mouth. A moment of stand-off, until Eunice relented, holding her plate for Valerie to deposit the oyster.

Eunice prodded the grey flesh with a fork. She looked around at us, watching her. She eyed my father as he swigged down oyster after oyster, then, as if mimicking him, she raised the shell to her mouth in the same cavalier way and swung her head back. The oyster remained stuck to its shell. Juice shot into her mouth, making her splutter. Without saying a word, Valerie sliced through the connecting muscle for her, handed the oyster back. 'Go on,' she said, winking at us all.

A trickle of disgust crossed Eunice as she poured the oyster into her mouth. As Eunice chewed, Valerie's tongue popped out of her mouth, lolling right and left along her lip, her peculiar little pleasure tic.

'It's funny to think they're still alive while you're chewing them,' said Valerie. Her tongue shot back in her mouth. Eunice reached for her napkin, about to spit. Laughter threatened to pop out of Valerie. She raised her hand to her mouth, to spoon it back inside. Eunice held her head high, swallowed down the oyster then swilled her mouth with water.

'Another?' Valerie said, holding the plate up.

'No, Valerie. No more, thank you,' said Eunice.

Anna sprang up from the table. 'Chicken,' she said. 'Let's have chicken.'

'You'll be better with chicken,' said Valerie. 'Won't you, Eunice?'

The strawberry tart seemed to come as a relief to Eunice.

She wolfed down two slices, then looked around hopefully as if waiting for a third. David took all three strawberries from his slice and put them on Eunice's plate. 'For the girl who hates oysters and loves strawberries,' he said. Eunice gobbled them down in an instant.

Valerie unfolded the Scrabble board. No one except Valerie really felt like playing. Anna wanted to drink her coffee. David and my father sat with a bottle of whisky between them. A thin line of smoke wandered upwards from the joint my father had wasted no time in lighting, but Valerie pressed on. She handed us each a stack of letter tiles.

My father passed the joint to me. Two puffs and the evening began to feel hazy. I liked the feeling. The day retreated, my sadness furred at the edges. I kept going, drawing the smoke deep into my lungs. I felt a swirling. A flood of energy. It rushed up through me, from my stomach to my throat, threatening to overwhelm me then sinking downwards, twisting through me like water draining down a plughole. I took four more puffs in quick succession, holding the smoke in my lungs for longer. Another rush, stronger this time. I closed my eyes and swam into it. Outwardly, my head felt heavy. I could feel myself slumped against the table, inert, the cold wood pressing against my head. But inside, I was a feather. Completely mobile, I swirled and swooped as if I was carried by the wind. I morphed and shrank, transmogrifying as I slipped into the tiniest space. Once within it, I could puff myself out or make myself invisible. Appearing and disappearing. Scary and delightful, funny and frightening. I felt myself looping and arching, I did somersaults, an effervescence within me.

I opened my eyes again. My Scrabble letters seemed to pulse. The 'G' looked like a tiny, pounding heart.

'No more for you,' said David, taking the joint from me.

Everyone looked like smudges. Eunice a smudge of white, Anna blue, David grey, Ig brown. Eunice wanted to try the joint. Her fingers crept towards David's hand to take it. He told her it wouldn't be a good idea because she wasn't used to it. Eunice pleaded. I closed my eyes again. An eruption of coughing. David saying, 'I told you.' I heard the sound of liquid being poured, then a bang, the sound of a bottle being slammed back on to the table.

The time of the night when we all would begin to fall apart. My father would drink too much, smoke too much then let his emotions cave him in. He'd shout up at the heavens, wrestle with them, tell them he was powerless, that he hated them. He'd tell us he missed our mother every day. He'd wonder why we had to be physical, why we were made of skin and bone that couldn't last for ever. 'I want to be pure energy,' he'd say, through heavy-lidded, stoned eyes. 'Energy that pings across the universe forever renewing itself.'

Ig poured me another glass of wine. Perhaps I shouldn't drink any more, but I didn't care. I wanted the oblivion. Ig drank beer, refused to join in the Scrabble. He wanted to think, to be quiet, to play records, and not have to speak to anyone.

I tried to pull myself up but couldn't. So I stopped trying and just let myself slump back. The conversation moved on. I don't know how much time had passed. I heard a slur of melted words from my father. 'I loved Margaret in a way people don't know how to love any more.' With my eyes closed, the voices weaved in and out of one another. I thought of a loom with sounds threading through it.

'Margaret and I were a dance. Never a tussle for power and control.'

The crisp sound of letter tiles placed on the Scrabble board, like horse's hooves hitting a road. Valerie's voice sounding pleased because she'd used her 'X' to make the word 'box'. Anna added her 'E' and 'S'. The scratch of Valerie's pencil against paper as she marked the score sounded giant and distorted as if the pencil was the size of a chimney. Three people to carry the pen, a blanket of paper as big as the sky. I heard it the way an insect resting on the paper might hear the sound of a pencil, as a deafening, terrifying screech.

'We didn't treat each other like commodities. We touched, we played, we were rapturous.' More whisky, a river of it, flowing around the table. My father slurred, talking without caring if anyone heard.

'David.' Anna's voice gave her husband a short, sharp smack as she removed the whisky bottle from him.

'We weren't just rapturous. We were rapture. We were ecstasy and bliss. Margaret and I still dance somewhere in the stars together.' The words swept and soared through the air. I heard Valerie snorting. Derision slicing into my father. Then I heard a whisper. The two women conspired against the men's fun. The whisky bottle flashed past my eyes. Valerie took it from Anna then planted it at the opposite end of the table, away from David and my father, both of whom sounded as if alcohol had sunk them.

'Margaret and I never tried to dominate one another.'

Valerie's turn to play. She spelled out: 'ZOO. That's my "Z" used.' Her grin travelled across the airwaves, a long, stretched-out sound like elastic being pulled.

'No, Eunice.' She snapped up Eunice's letter. 'Proper place names are not allowed. You can't have LONDON.'

'Bed for me, I think,' said Anna.

'You're always tired,' said David.

'I'm going to read.'

I jumped at a kiss, a brief dab on my forehead as Anna passed me on the way out.

'You all right?' It was Ig, prodding me with a finger. I felt an indent, long after Ig's finger must have gone.

The finger poked me again. I thought I'd said 'fine'. Perhaps I'd just gurgled. I curled my legs up into the chair, rested my head on the armrest. 'Fine,' I said again. I didn't want bringing round. In the dark space behind my eyes there existed a whole universe for me to gallop across.

'Water. If you need it.' I heard a glass being pushed on to the table near to me.

'Julian, play properly or sit out.' Valerie pinged her words at my father, the only person now who seemed to be able to talk properly.

'Oh fuck off, will you,' he said.

'Now, now, Julian.' David's voice, making laughter spill out of Eunice. I imagined her giggles like coloured tadpoles darting about.

'You know you can't have that word, David,' said Valerie.

'Fart's a word,' said Eunice.

'Fart's colloquial,' said Valerie. 'I'm taking it away.'

I heard sobs of heaving, wet laughter. David and Eunice, the pair of them delighted, stoned, conspiratorial.

'N-I-N-E. My last four letters. That's me out.' The scratch of Valerie's pencil on paper tore at my ears.

'S – A – T – U – R.' Eunice's voice. Triumphant, the tiles slapped on to the board. Eunice seemed proud, alive. I opened my eyes to see her sitting upright like a thick slab of stone.

'Saturnine,'said Valerie.

'Yes,' said Eunice.

'That's a very long word.' Valerie paused. 'Game over, then.' She clapped shut the Scrabble board. 'Eunice, look beneath your chair and make sure you haven't dropped one. I hate to lose my letters.'

Eunice pushed her chair back from the table, and her voice faded as she said she wanted to go inside to fetch a glass of water.

'Saturnine,' Valerie hissed. 'From a shop girl.'

'Leave her alone,' said David.

'What would you know?' said Valerie. 'You've been ogling her all night. I've half a mind to tell your wife.'

'What's she ever done to you?'

'She mocks my sister, just her presence, sticks two fingers up to the memory of my precious Margaret.' Valerie knocked back a shot of whisky. 'She should have fucked off for the day and left us in peace to mourn Margaret.'

'Just go to bed,' said Ig. 'Let the day be over.'

I left them all outside to be quiet for a moment. In the sitting room, I knocked back another drink. It burned my mouth, turned the space behind my eyes liquid. When I went to fetch still more whisky, I saw Eunice in the doorway watching me stumble about. I had no idea how long she'd been there. She held her hair from her face with one hand, gripped the door with the other, swinging it back and forth. 'You need helping,' said Eunice. 'Look at you.'

She took the glass from my hand, led me to the sofa, then sat beside me. 'Oh Elizabeth,' she said. She squinted her eyes with concern, cocked her head to one side. 'You've got to let people help you. You're too closed. You've got to let people in.'

I looked at her, through hazy, drunk eyes.

Eunice took me in her arms. I felt them tight around my back, her hands spread out, reaching to the sides of my body. My head nestled into the crook of her neck. I felt her warmth, scented skin, a soft, floral smell. I felt my whole body give. Her breath swished around my ear.

'Better?' she said.

She carried on holding me, her grip firm. I closed my eyes, my head still on her shoulder. I just breathed, losing track of how long we stayed like that.

When I pulled away from her, I looked around the room. My home. Even the smell of the air comforted me: the smell of being a child, it reminded me of being looked after, of once having two parents, seated at either end of a long table, one fixing, the other protecting. Four walls, a roof, just bricks, one laid on top of another, nothing more; but it can be the glue that holds a person together.

'What else can I lose?' I said to Eunice.

She took me back in her arms. 'I'm here now, Lizzy,' she said. 'And I'm going to be the friend you need. I'm going to help you. I'm going to get you unstuck. I'm here for you,' she said. 'I know about pain.'

She took the bottle from me, held out her hand, leading me back out into the garden to my chair.

'You're not as clever as you think you are,' she said. 'And you need me to help you.'

I had no idea how much time had passed when my father nudged me awake, giving me a blanket to lay across me. 'Stay up with me, Lizzy,' he said. I wrapped myself in the scratchy old blanket and followed him towards the fire pit: a pyramid of logs lit in a square of mud hollowed out of the lawn. Either side he'd stacked wooden wine crates with cushions as seats. The two of us fitted just neatly on to one crate. He took half my blanket to wrap himself in, one arm around my shoulder, holding us both within its warmth. Across from us, the only two left up were Eunice and David. David tended to her with his eyes. The brown blankets brought up over their heads, their arms wrapped tightly within so they made the shape of Russian dolls. The whisky bottle beside them.

'I wish I could go inside your caravan,' Eunice whispered.

'It's not my caravan,' said David.

'But it's lovely,' she replied.

'I hate it,' he said. He stared into the fire. 'I fucking hate that caravan.'

In front of them, a bag of marshmallows. David speared two with a fork, rested them at the edge of the fire on a stone. While the marshmallows blackened, David sandwiched Eunice's hand between both of his. 'Soft skin you have,' he said. He blew on the marshmallows, pressed one to Eunice's lips. She bit half of it away, leaving a pink goo dripping from the insides of the remaining piece. David held his head underneath to let it fall into his mouth. Eunice took the fork, touched his lip with the second marshmallow. Just as his mouth opened, she whipped it away so he bit at thin air. The next time she went to feed him, he grabbed her hand so she couldn't move, while he devoured the sweet in one go. 'I want to come to your caravan,' she said, her head lolling to one side, looking up at him with pleading eyes.

'Eunice, my wife's asleep in there.'

Underneath the blanket, I felt warmth. The line of my father's body pressed against mine, his arm firm around me, compressing me in towards him.

'It's like a Seventies porn film over there,' I said.

'Ignore them,' he replied. 'And just sit with me. I don't want to go to bed.'

My father and I stared into the fire while David and Eunice murmured together, lit in checkerboard pieces of light and shade. The tangle of a honeysuckle plant weaving up the wall behind them. David had his arm around Eunice's shoulders, his hand dangling, just casually around her chest.

'She's going to have to go,' I said.

'She'll get bored,' my father replied. 'She's one of those girls. All or nothing. One day, she'll just up and disappear as if we never mattered.'

I couldn't hear everything David and Eunice spoke about, only odd words, clips of sentences. He talked about being disappointed, his life lived as a system. His marriage had become its own narrative, a story he had to follow, a thing in itself, a shape he was forced to fit himself into. Eunice told him she'd thrown off her past. She wouldn't go back to her old life. Not for anything.

That night, sleep mocked me. The mattress felt hard and heavy as if it deliberately held itself taut to keep me off it. I turned in bed, walked my bare feet up the cool wall. Up there, I sat on the ceiling. I picked daisies from the grass, tutting to myself as I watched Elizabeth lying there wretched and sweating, refusing to see how flimsy the string had become that connected her to this world, the string that stopped her from floating off. She couldn't keep her mouth still as she tried to stop the thoughts that threatened her. Her limbs flailed around, whipping one side, then the other as she failed to get comfortable. Sleep tugged at her eyes until she abandoned it. Furious with sleep. She climbed down the ladder of the mezzanine, stomped out into the cool of the courtyard.

'Ig,' I whispered, pushing his door open.

The scent of sandalwood. Inside, New Age bell music played softly in the background, the sound he always slept to. His Japanese water garden tinkled in the corner, a tiny jet plinking droplets of water down the rocks. He still had teddy bears in here from when he'd been born. Ig threw nothing away. He hadn't been able to preserve our mother but he preserved every object of his past. Everything in his room could stay with him, pristine and indestructible.

On his mattress, on the floor, he was curled up on his side, enormous feet poking out from underneath the duvet. No face, but rather a ball of blond fluff for a head. I lifted the duvet and slipped in beside him. In the warmth and the comfort, the home-like atmosphere, with Ig next to me, I managed to drift off.

The next morning, fresh out of the shower, my father had wet hair, smelled of soap. If he was a colour, he'd have been bright yellow. Eunice held the fish slice, offering around eggs while Anna organised the table: a jar of marmalade in a saucer with a silver spoon, the silver toast rack full, a butter dish with its own matching knife, the silver coffee pot. Valerie wore a pink towelling dressing gown, scowling as she searched the floor for her fags. Finding them, she sucked one out of the packet with her teeth. She'd slept on the sofa, and you could tell. Puffy-faced, she hadn't slept well. She drew on her fag, then whispered to me: 'I'm knackered. Why should I sleep on the floor for my sister's anniversary while that car crash of a woman sleeps in a bed?'

Eunice poured coffee from the pot, taking a furtive glance at David. He had loaded his knife with butter ready for his toast, but Anna whipped it from him, scraping half of it back on to the dish. 'Cholesterol,' she said.

David sighed and put his toast back on to the plate, with nothing on it. He didn't touch it until Eunice, waiting until Anna couldn't see, took it, spread it thickly with butter, turned it over so it looked untouched and handed it back to David, with a wink. David grinned, biting into the toast.

Breakfast over, Anna and David said it was time to go. We waved them off in their caravan, told them we hoped to see them again soon.

'David's lovely,' said Eunice, as we turned back into the house. 'He and I really clicked.'

ACT FOUR

She'd made an indelible stain on the fabric of the building. She'd seeped inwards. If she stayed much longer, the bricks themselves would start smelling of her.

mother

'I HAVE A SECRET,' SAID EUNICE.

She scanned our faces with a look of pleasure, twinkling and happy as if she was enjoying the idea she had a little power over us for once. 'You all look so worried,' she said. 'Don't be worried.'

In her hand, she held a letter which she waved through the air, smiling.

'What do you think it is? Guess!'

My father, Ig and I remained quiet, sitting across from her at the kitchen table. I felt a mild fear, a knot at the back of my throat, wondering what this strange, unpredictable woman might present us with next.

'They found my mother and I wrote to her.'

'Gosh,' said Ig.

'This,' she said, waving the letter through the air again, 'is her reply. It was one of the toughest searches the agency has ever done. She moved a lot. Lived abroad. Married twice, changed her name both times. She sounds like she's had quite a life. She has four children with her second husband, the agency said.'

Still, we stayed silent.

'I've never seen you all so quiet,' she said.

We stared back at her.

'You've gone sheet white, Julian.'

I looked across at my father, who'd knotted his hands together so tightly his knuckles had begun to turn white. He looked stunned, terrified, as if someone had crept up behind him and whacked him over the head.

'She only lives in South London. I had half a mind just to jump on the tube and turn up at her house! I wanted to rush over and tell her I was alive! But the agency counselled me against it. They said I ought to approach the situation with delicacy.'

My father coughed into a handkerchief.

'And here is her reply!' she said, wagging the envelope at us once more. 'Who wants to open it?'

'Why don't you go and open it in private, Eunice?' my father said. 'I think that letter is something for you, on your own.'

I feared what these two women might do to our family. Would they gang up against us, with revenge on their minds?

Eunice ignored him. She tore open the letter. A white envelope inside a larger, brown manila envelope with the agency's stamp on it.

She gazed at her name written on the envelope, a scribble of blue biro, the agency's address written underneath it. 'To think it was her saliva that sealed it. Her hand that wrote the address on the front. She's physical. She exists. She's not just a fantasy any more.'

Eunice scanned us all to see our reaction. I tried to stay blank. She might have a mother, but I still hadn't. My father's hands remained knotted together, his gaze fixed on the table.

Eunice took a deep breath in. 'Here goes,' she said, pulling the letter out of its envelope.

As her eyes flickered across the page, her head moved backwards, just a touch. She held the letter a little further away from her as if a whiff of something nasty seeped off the page. Her expression melted. Tears filled her eyes. A crinkle appeared on her forehead. Eunice stopped reading. She folded the letter, pushing it away from her.

'My mother said "no",' she told us.

'Oh good Lord,' said my father with such expression I couldn't tell whether it was empathy or relief.

'It's fine,' said Eunice. 'I mustn't take it personally. I half-expected it. She blames you, Julian.'

My father had visibly relaxed. I don't think he cared who she blamed as long as she wasn't going to turn up at his house to remind him of his failings as a man.

Eunice picked up the letter and read out loud.

Dear Eunice,

I do hope you can understand that as a young woman I was very confused, very let down by the man who is your father. I did go to the house to see Julian when I was pregnant to ask for help. His wife let me in. We talked, but no help was forthcoming. They said what they needed to say to get rid of me. Nothing more. When I married my second husband – my first marriage was brief, a rebound, you might say – I didn't say anything because I was happy, relieved to have found my conclusion. And now I can't say anything to him because I've kept quiet for so very many years. He would wonder why I lied. It's been too long. He would doubt his trust in me. Then there're my children to think of. I worry about damaging my relationship with them. I have four with my husband. With children the relationship can be so flimsy and fraught. The slightest wrong move can end up being irreparable. I have to be so careful. Please be assured, I do think of you. I have thought of you all these years. I've hoped very much that you were cared for and safe. But I cannot meet you and I cannot introduce you to my family. I would like you to know that receiving this letter has been a great comfort to me. I hope you can find it in your heart to understand that I simply can't pursue this with you, although I am grateful you took the time to write. I can't even offer you the possibility that we might write to each other occasionally, as you suggested in your letter, for fear of the letters being found. I am profoundly sorry to be the one inflicting this wound on you and hope you can find comfort from the people around you. I'm quite sure you're very loved. Things might have been different, had I not been deeply let down by the man who is your father. It was hard for a girl in those days to be alone and discover she was pregnant and for the father of that baby to leave her in the lurch.

With love and warmest wishes,
Louise

'At least I know,' Eunice said with a thin-lipped glance at my father. She folded the letter back up and ran out of the room.

'I remember a woman coming here,' I said to my father. He stayed silent, staring ahead of himself. 'She wore a brown dress. You told me she was a friend of Tom's. Was it her?'

But my father didn't respond.

* * *

174

Eunice didn't want to go for a walk but my father insisted that it would do her good. 'Walking is the best thing if you're upset,' he said. 'Fresh air. Trees. Mud.'

Ig asked her if she needed sweet tea for the shock. She didn't but he fetched her some water anyway. We fussed her into the car. Ig insisted she travel in the front seat, told her he and I would go in the back. We slipped into the back seat, hoping to disappear, as if we'd been the ones responsible for her abandonment, the people who had stood in the way of a normal life for her. The least we could do was not stand in the way of her getting the front seat and ample leg room.

'The Heath,' my father said, starting the engine. 'I bet you've never been there before.'

Eunice sat in the car looking stunned, still holding the glass of water. None of us knew what to do with her. My father glanced at her shoes. He worried out loud that they weren't sturdy enough for the walk. Eunice said she didn't care. She could walk fine in flip-flops.

At the park, we tramped up the hill. My father never stopped talking, telling Eunice he liked this route, his favourite walk. 'It'll cheer you up,' he said.

At the height of the Heath, we picked out landmarks in the sweep of London beneath us, wind sending us sideways. My father pointed out buildings to Eunice as if London's wealth belonged to him. Beyond us, at the base of the hill, families sat on tartan travel rugs around a lake encircled by neat lawn, eating picnics. Two different climates. Up here, a fierce wind flattening our hair, the drone of it sounding like a war in the skies. Below, the genteel pulse of summer. Bumblebees buzzed through dusty, backlit air, the distant hum of an aircraft, the ping of a ball flying off a bat.

'I'm cold,' said Eunice. 'I think I'd like to go down.'

My father said he'd buy us all a drink in his favourite pub, a red-brick Victorian building with black woodwork and wisteria growing up the walls. 'We'll sit outside,' he said. 'There'll be no wind down there. A drink'll help.'

We picked our way back down the hill, along a path scarred into the meadow by hundreds of feet. We went slowly, avoiding the grassy knolls, searching for a smooth passage. Eunice had strayed off the path.

'She need a hand?' my father shouted from in front. The flimsy plastic soles of her shoes slapped against her feet as she slid around the clods of earth and small hillocks.

'She's fine,' I said. But just as I said it, I heard a squeal. I turned to see Eunice on the ground, yelping.

'What happened?' I asked her.

She gripped her ankle, making a low moan.

'What happened, Eunice?' my father said, rushing over.

'My ankle,' she wailed.

'Can you move it?' my father asked.

'No. I can't feel anything. My ankle just gave way.'

'We'll fix it. Whatever it is, you'll be OK,' my father said.

Eunice began to cry.

'Oh Eunice, you don't need to get upset.'

'I feel so far from home.'

Her cries grew in force. Slumped on the floor, she sobbed and sobbed.

'I'm completely alone. I have no one to protect me. You have everything. I have nothing. No one. No history. I am null and void.'

My father knelt by her side. He took her arm and clamped it around his neck to pull her upright. With the other arm around her waist, he held her up so that together, they could walk down the hill, supported by him so that her feet barely skimmed the grass.

I took the bus home so that Eunice could travel stretched out on the back seat of the car. She said her ankle was too painful to sit up. 'I fear making it worse,' she said.

When I arrived home, the car was already in the drive. My studio door stood open. Inside, my father was pulling my mattress from the mezzanine while Eunice steadied herself with the table, her bad leg hovering off the ground.

'I would never have been able to get up the stairs to bed,' said Eunice. 'Please don't look so cross, Lizzy.'

My father flitted about, fetching sheets.

I retreated to the sitting room.

'It won't be for long,' my father said, following me in. 'My hands are tied.'

'She's playing you.'

'That poor girl's had a terrible shock. Two terrible shocks.'

'At this rate you'll end up kicking me out rather than her.'

'Not everything is a drama, Elizabeth, with you at the centre of it.'

He hurried off back into the courtyard, carrying a tray of tea and toast to my studio for Eunice.

I hovered in the courtyard, not knowing how to proceed. I needed to fetch my things from my studio before I could sleep in the guest room: night clothes, toothbrush, face cream. A shaft of warm light from my studio succeeded the dim evening light. I paused in front of the enormous red door and ended up examining it. I'd never looked at it so closely from this side before. I'd never spotted the paint peeling away, revealing the green undercoat. I usually just flung it open without a second thought.

The studio was my space; private. No one went in there. It

was all mine. I left things lying around, knowing they would still be in precisely the same place weeks later. I never lost anything, no matter how messy the room became. But now my mattress was dragged down from the mezzanine, my stuff knocked around. The place turned upside down. The things surrounding my bed I wouldn't want anyone to see: my diary, old socks, knickers tangled in a dusty heap and forgotten . . . I shuffled my feet on the doorstep. Did I have to knock to gain access to my own place? I didn't need permission to enter it. She might complain if I didn't. I raised my hand, about to knock, but it refused to come down on the door. Instead, I threw it open and blundered inside. 'Eunice, I need my pyjamas,' I said.

Stretched out in my bed, rubbing in my hand cream, Eunice had completed her silent takeover of the only space I could truly call my own. My place. What is it about a place that attaches itself so deeply within us? What is it about the smell, the walls, the view from a particular window that makes a room become a part of our body? Ig argued human weakness attached us to things, based on some Buddhist aphorism or greetings card philosophy he'd read. He believed we should be able to simply set our emotions to one side, to move on, never look back. 'You can't love a place,' he said, 'because it's not a living thing.' But all the time he protested, his own room looked so lived in, it was as if his roots had grown in so deep and thick they'd begun to weave through the building's foundations. Still, he claimed he could leave whenever he wanted. 'But have you ever tried?' I said. 'It's easy to *say* you want to go, but you won't know if you can bear it until you've tried.'

Surely attachment to objects is a sign of human strength, a sign of risk, of belief in something more. The place that keeps you safe. It's what anchors us, gives shape to a shapeless world. Isn't it survival? To lose our sense of place means death: then we need to grieve. My parents might have shifted, changed from one day to the next, but these walls didn't. They held me safe, no matter what happened within them.

My room, now hers. The sofa had been moved. Just an empty space beneath the window now. Tangles of hair and dust lying in clumps. A shadow where the light had bleached the wooden floor and left behind a small, dark rectangle where the sofa had been. The wardrobe door open. A frosted glass door, with a metal frame. My clothes pressed to one side to make space for Eunice's clothes. On one hanger, Eunice's electric-blue cotton-knit sweater. On another her white linen trousers. A pair of coral pink polyester knickers hung over the rail at the top. I gathered up my toothbrush, a few bits of clothes, a T-shirt for pyjamas.

'Sleep well,' she called out, still twisting her hands around one another to get my beeswax hand cream properly soaked in.

I didn't reply.

'Lizzy,' Eunice said. 'Please don't be so cross with me. I want us to like each other. This isn't personal. I didn't hurt my ankle to spite you.'

'Sure,' I replied, slamming the door behind me.

'I've had a very difficult and hurtful day, Elizabeth,' she called out after me. 'And I think you are being very insensitive to my needs.'

The guest room smelled of Eunice, a smell of the body. A tangy, musty smell mixed with a hint of floral talcum powder. She'd grown into the walls. The scent of her had permeated the paintwork. We could never get rid of her now, no matter how hard we scrubbed. She'd made an indelible stain on the fabric of the building. She'd seeped inwards. If she stayed much longer, the bricks themselves would start smelling of her. A tiny pile of dust lay in the corner, where she couldn't have been able to get the sweeping brush. Her dust. Dead skin and hair. Fingernails. Bogeys.

I put my toothbrush on the table, shifting an aromatherapy oil burner and bottle of lavender out of the way. I laid my clothes over her chair, then fumbled for the T-shirt. Standing naked in her room felt strange, as if I was exposed in front of her. I clamped my arms in front of me, quickly pulling the long T-shirt over my head.

I picked at the sheet. It hadn't been changed. I went into the airing cupboard for clean ones. I held on to the corners of the sheet, flinging it outwards, letting a shot of air go underneath to take it flat across the bed. I did it with abandon so it might topple a few of her bottles. An earring slid to the floor. The sheet settled and as I stood by the bed to tuck it in, I noticed the shoes arranged in neat rows underneath, so I kicked them, making them skid towards the far wall.

The sheets felt cold. Everything felt wrong as I lay there, trying to get my feet to warm the bed, wrapped in starchy cotton and hatred. I itched within those sheets. I couldn't stand their rough surface pawing at my skin. In the early hours, I threw them off me. I kicked them to the floor in a lump then clambered out of bed.

I was six when I'd answered the door to that woman in a brown dress with a swollen belly. Her legs looked pale and spindly because the dress fell right to the knee. 'I think you know who I am,' she said to my mother.

'Who is she?' I whispered to my mum.

'No one important,' she replied. 'She's trying to find Tom.'

While my mother went to fetch my father, I stayed in the kitchen staring at the woman. I curled around the legs of the table like a cat. The woman didn't speak to me. I thought she looked dirty in her strange woolly dress. She wasn't one of us, rather something from outside. My mum wouldn't have worn brown or looked such a mess. She flowed around the house like scented water.

When my father came in, I was sent upstairs and told not to come down. I crept to the bottom of the stairs and listened at the door. I couldn't hear anything. Just voices, muffled, talking for ages. I wanted to push the door open to get a better chance at hearing, but each time I did, it creaked, until eventually my mother came storming to the stairs, picked me up and took me back to my room.

That woman felt like a threat to this thing that held me steady on a daily basis, the thing I called a family, yet my mother kept telling me she wasn't a threat. 'She's a friend of Tom's,' she said again. 'He's upset her, so she's come here to talk to your father.'

My mother sat with me in her room. She let me play with her make-up. By early evening, the woman left. My father sat at the kitchen table drinking a beer. But that night, my mother refused to cook. Hunger gnawed at me as Ig and I waited for the silence to be replaced with food. The ice in Mum's crystal tumbler jangled each time she picked it up. She didn't sip, rather she swallowed it down in deep gulps, filling the glass time and again. I sat in silence, willing her to be normal. The way she'd been the night before: opening cupboards, chopping vegetables, the sizzle of a sliced onion hitting oil in the pan. I wanted her and my father to look happy, the way they had done the previous evening when he'd made her laugh by doing an impression of Valerie, cupping his hand around his joint, scowling and coughing like an old witch as he sucked the smoke in.

Where had our mother gone? Fear knocked against my insides. Why had she changed so suddenly? I hated the way she smelled when she'd been drinking. My father told her to slow down, but each time he spoke, she looked up at him defiantly, sloshed more gin into the glass.

Ig and I did what we always did when things were bad. We stayed still, looking straight ahead of ourselves with our heads a little lowered. If no one noticed us, we couldn't make things worse. I longed for a button I could press to make myself disappear. If I wasn't there, they might have nothing to fight about.

Eventually, my father pushed two plates of toast across the table for Ig and me. Three slices each, a piece of cheddar, some cucumber. He held the gin bottle upside down with the lid off. 'That's a whole bottle, Margaret,' he said.

'Like you give a fuck,' she replied.

Later, with my father gone, I sat beside her. 'Mummy. Are you OK?' Her eyes didn't focus. She tried to reply but I didn't understand because the words melted into each other, making nothing more than a long, messy noise.

She took me up to bed but I couldn't sleep. Knotted into a ball that couldn't unfurl. Bashing against sleep until I couldn't stand it any more and crept downstairs to see if my mother would help. She might let me creep in next to her. Cuddle me to sleep. I poked my head around the door into the sitting room. Through the dim light coming from the window, I could just make her out, lying across the sofa. Head buried into a pillow, crying.

'Mummy,' I whispered. She lifted her head, turned it towards me. 'Go to bed, Elizabeth,' she snapped.

A few days later everything was fine again. Nothing more

was said. Late in the evening, I heard laughter. The whiff of pot smoke came up the stairs. My mum all dressed up because they'd been to a nightclub. A special place for grown-ups. Outside through the window I saw them in the early hours. Smoking, my mother in a black dress with gold jewellery: the two of them happy again. My father grabbed her round the waist, she tried to dash off, he threatened to chase her, then they both tumbled on to a sun longer, laughing together. Relief flooded me. She wouldn't leave. The danger had passed.

In Eunice's room, I opened the curtains to let in some light. I felt the edges of myself loosen and threaten to disappear. What would happen to me? I wished everything had stayed as it was. A streetlight beyond cast the room in a vague peach-coloured glow. My bare toes pushed against the cold floor. Dust underfoot. Shadows came in through the window, growing longer and shorter as the clouds teased the moonlight. Something soft brushed against me. Tickling, soft fabric, diaphanous against my cheek. I shuddered, tried to flick it away, but when I turned, quick enough to catch it, I found nothing there.

Through the window, I remembered seeing the shadow of my mother as she paced the garden one night. She was having one of her episodes, as my father called them. I watched her as she travelled in a wandering line towards the door at the end that led into the park. I was frightened for her because my parents had told me to fear that door. Strangers lay in wait behind it. Anything could happen, particularly at night. My parents feared that door so much they kept the key on the highest shelf so we couldn't reach it, but my mum was walking towards it with the key in her mouth like a dog with a bone.

'Mum,' I shouted, banging on the window.

I tore out of the room, barely touched the stairs as I shot

down them, jumping two, three at time, holding on to the railings. The door in the kitchen stood open. I pelted through it. 'Mummy, Mummy,' I shouted. 'Come back! Come back! Where are you going?' I shouted at the top of my lungs but the wind must have carried my voice away because she kept on walking. I ran as hard as I could to the bottom of the garden. Closer and closer to the door, the key cupped in her fingers so the shiny end of it caught the light. 'Come back,' I bellowed. She had to see me. I wanted to be seen. If she saw me, she'd stay. If she knew I was there, she'd stay. 'Mummy. Don't go. Look at me!' She turned but her eyes were distant, as if I wasn't there. Off her head, not focusing, leaving because she'd rowed with my father and this was really it. She was going to go, once and for all, a big, dramatic, frightening exit into the park with a bottle of pills in one hand and whisky in the other. As she turned to look at me, she seemed bewildered, as if I ought to know me but couldn't quite compute it. She shook me away from her, put the key in the lock while I shouted, trying to make her understand. Sentences not forming, nothing making sense. Swallowing away snot, tears blurring my vision. I cried. She told me not to be so silly. She wanted to go for a walk. She'd be back soon. I ran back inside to wake my father. He'd go through the gate and bring her back in. He'd lead her inwards, back to safety.

I stood over my father, shaking him awake. 'I can't sleep,' I said.

He pulled back the covers to allow me to slip inside. In his bed, I dabbed away the sweat from my forehead with the sheet. I pulled the duvet tight around myself and attempted sleep again.

roof

THE DIRECTOR WAITED FOR ME ON THE CORNER, CLOSE TO THE TUBE station. We walked along the street towards a members-only cinema.

'Popcorn?' said the director as we stepped inside.

'Absolutely not,' I said, with mock horror.

'How about a drink?'

In one corner of the cinema an area had been formed with cushions and beanbags. Along the wall, tall glass bottles full of old-fashioned sweets lined a shelf; a notice invited us to take as much as we wanted. We had our very own waitress who would bring us drinks and ice cream. The director kicked a beanbag against the wall. As he sat, he pulled me down with him, so I would sit in front of him between his splayed legs.

With my back leaning against his chest, head resting on his shoulder, he twisted a piece of my hair around as we watched the film. I felt his hot breath on my neck, the heat of his body, his arm across my chest pressing me against him, chin on my shoulder. He held me together for the evening.

He hated the film for not being subtle enough so I stayed quiet about having enjoyed it. We went to a sushi restaurant lined with pale wood, crisp with air-conditioning, where all the staff knew him. The waitress greeted him with a coy smile, put menus in front of us, brought him chilled saki without needing to ask him what he wanted to drink.

'It's near a place I worked in for a while,' he said. 'I came here twice a day sometimes. They know what I want.'

He beckoned the waitress, asked her to fetch me a glass of white wine.

Dinner was a functional event. The staff hovered around the edge of the room watching us, making it impossible to say anything private. We didn't linger, sharing secrets, delving into one another's past as I thought we might have done on our first evening out anywhere other than his flat. Instead, in the blank white light of the restaurant, we filled our stomachs, softened our edges with wine and saki, then went home.

Even at nearly midnight, the streets still felt hot as if the concrete had been sucking heat inwards all day. Back at his flat, he wanted to drink a nightcap on the roof. He grabbed a bottle, two glasses, the duvet and pillows from his bed and took me to the top of the building. Through a creaky fire door, up a few narrow steps, we emerged on to a flat roof. He threw the duvet out, let it settle on to the ground, then arranged the four pillows for us to sit on. He poured two glasses of liquor.

I laid my head in his lap. Beyond us, nothing but the blankness of a night sky, a huge, black lid keeping the heat in. The strange, sweet liquor he poured over ice tasted of cinnamon and oranges. My mouth felt cold and fleshy with each sip. I nestled my head deeper into his lap, while he told me about his plans for his next project. 'A short film exploring chance,' he said. 'I'm sure there'll be a part for you, Lizzy,' he said.

He spun the thick, clear liquid around his glass.

The heat of the evening pressed down on us, enclosed us in a tight little box, just the two of us up there, the duvet cushioning us from the hard roof. It felt like a wilderness, like we weren't in London but somewhere else – space or the Antarctic – somewhere blank and empty. I could see nothing but the sky, this wild expanse of nothing with the director and myself forming two tiny life forms within it. The two of us huddled together against the world. If I sat in close, stuck myself to him, we might stay like that.

'What are we doing?' I asked.

'We're sitting on a roof,' he replied.

I couldn't get him to lay things out. I liked the feeling of a soft palm clamping on to mine, knowing it was going to stay, but he wouldn't tell me that. I couldn't cope with ambiguity, with doubt or in-betweenness. But he said he had no desire to dissolve himself into me. He wanted to keep a line. Two separate people. Weekends wouldn't disappear with the two of us seeing no daylight and wearing nothing more than underpants. He didn't feel frantic to become one person then end up wondering why the sex had gone wrong.

'Don't get bogged down, Elizabeth,' he said. 'You'll ruin things.' He jumped to his feet. 'Let's play a game.'

He went towards the edge of the building. 'Why don't you lie very close to the edge, hang your head over, look down so you scare the shit out of yourself and I'll take you from behind.'

I stared back at him.

'Oh, go on,' he said, grinning.

'No way,' I replied.

He laughed, tucking an arm around my waist as he pulled himself in closer. 'I'm just joking,' he said.

'You're a sadist.'

'No, I'm not.' He grinned back at me. 'I just like watching pretty girls get scared.'

'That's sadism.'

'Don't take everything I say so seriously.'

He led me back to our duvet in the middle of the roof. When we fucked, he sweated a lot. Afterwards, we lay there for hours, his body tacky with sweat, wetly glued to mine.

'The actors are the ocean,' he said. 'And I'm the moon. I'm the magnetic field that draws actors back and forth. I make them move. I decide if it's going to be still, or crashing waves, or just a gentle lap.' I listened to him without moving a muscle because I liked the way we were lying. I didn't want to unstick us. 'I couldn't be an actor, I couldn't be the powerless ocean,' he said. 'I have to be the moon.'

'I love the sea,' I replied.

Limbs intertwined, his warm, limp cock resting against my thigh, a dab of wet at its end. He rescued a strand of hair fallen across my cheek, slipped it behind my ear. I wanted to disappear into him, no matter what he said about lines and difference.

He took one of my buttocks full in his hand. 'You're the ocean and I'm the moon. And that's the way I like it,' he said, turning over to go to sleep.

I drifted off, not waking at all until the first sun of the day burned my skin. I stuck my leg across the space, hoping to run my foot the length of the director, but he wasn't there. I sat up. An empty, wrinkled space where he'd been and gone. I jumped up, quickly pulled on my clothes and headed through the fire exit door. Down the stairs, I pushed open the door to his flat to find him lying on his sofa, naked, sipping a mug of coffee.

'Morning, Knight,' he said. 'Sleep well? I'm going to fry us an egg for brunch.'

He got up to go through to the kitchen. Still naked, he cracked three eggs into a pan and stood at the cooker, a fish slice in hand, poking at them. The eggs spat and spluttered, sending spots of boiling hot fat flying through the air, but he stood fast, dodging sideways when he needed to.

'I'm going to be bold and cook these eggs in hot olive oil without so much as putting my underpants on. I can't face clothes today. You and me are going to be like Adam and Eve in the Garden of Eden, except this time it's going to be me, Adam, willing you, Eve, to eat.' He squeezed me on the arse and grinned. 'But don't get any ideas and start putting on a load of weight. I'm only feeding you today.'

When the eggs were done the director slid them on to a single plate, grabbed two forks and a loaf of bread and asked me to follow him out on to the balcony.

Still naked, the eggs on the table, he fetched a blue parasol which he popped open then rested against the wall to give us shade.

'Right, Lizzy,' he said. 'The parasol's up. Get your clothes off. It's an order.'

As I undressed, the director flung my clothes around the balcony with fake abandon. 'Freedom!' he kept shouting. 'Isn't this wonderful? The sun on your naked skin. Look at you! Aren't you beautiful.' He cupped my face in his hands and kissed me. As I stood there, entirely naked, the backdrop of London spreading out behind me, he stood gazing at me. 'You have a marvellous body, Lizzy. Look at that! It's poetry to behold. I want you to lie on top of my glass coffee table so that I can get underneath it and examine your arse all squashed against the glass.'

He sat on a low sun lounger, legs splayed, cutting the fried egg with a fork, inviting me to dig in too. He tore a piece of bread from the loaf to dip into the yolk. He ate his eggs as if he hadn't eaten for weeks. I sat on the seat opposite him, feeling somehow boring, buttoned-up and fearful, wanting to hide myself. He kept looking up at me without saying anything, then returning to his eggs. I couldn't fathom what those looks meant, what it was he was thinking about saying, then not saying. I didn't touch the eggs. Not because I wasn't hungry but because of the way he commanded the plate. If I dug my fork in, I felt I might be trespassing. He cleaned the last of the yolk from the plate with another piece of bread.

When he finished eating, he lay back on the sun lounger, pulling me down to lie next to him. He lay on his back. On my side, I fitted in around him. 'I'm really very fond of you, Lizzy, you know that, don't you?' he said, squeezing me against him.

My nose flattened against his warm chest which smelled of rosemary and sandalwood. I felt completely relaxed, as if he might not let go of me all day.

love

A PAIR OF ENORMOUS WHITE TRAINERS STOOD ON THE FRONT STEP. MY eye flickered along them, then up the leg of a pair of blue jeans across to the textured fabric of a turquoise polo shirt, a spattering of stubble; two desperate eyes.

'Mike?' I said.

'I need to see Eunice.'

A hand dangled at his side, gripping a gold box of chocolates.

'She told me she'd been in trouble.'

'That was two weeks ago,' I said. 'She's better now.'

'Can she walk?'

I fetched Eunice and she took Mike outside to the bench at the bottom of the garden, nestled in among the silver birches, where they could talk. I watched as she let him hold her hand. I thought she'd been in love with us. He looked pleading and sorry. She looked stern.

I went to my room – reclaimed by now – to sleep. I lay on my bed with the top half of my door open, listening to the breeze rustle through the plants. The thick banana leaves made an occasional, idle slap each time the wind picked up enough strength to move them.

When I went back inside Mike stood in the sitting room, holding something up to the light. He hadn't seen me enter so he kept looking, asking Eunice to tell him what the stone was. A fossil of a shell. A smooth shape with gentle ridges along it, the perfect mould of a shell hewn out of the jagged rock surrounding it. My father found it when he was nine years old, nestled into long grass in a wood. Not even looking, he stumbled across it, a gift lying there for someone to find, and he found it. I hovered by the door, listening to them.

You can't stay here for ever, Eunice. I'm not going to stay here for ever, but I'm going to stay here for now. I'm not coming home with you yet, not after all I've been through, even if you are very sorry. But Eunice . . . Mike, I've changed. I'm not the girl you dumped. I've seen a different world. I'm not going back to the girl I used to be. I'm going to stay here in London. I'm going to make something of myself. Live a different life. I can't come to St Albans. I don't want the thing I thought I wanted any more. Eunice, they don't want you here. You don't know that. They just need to get used to me. They're afraid. But we're related, they're my family, we need each other. I'll make sure of it.

I retreated back out of the door before either of them saw me.

pigs

THE GARDEN HAD TURNED FROM GLOSSY GREEN TO GOLDEN. EVERYTHING was at its most richly hued: pink, russet, red, yellow. To me autumn – rather than spring – felt like nature at its fullest. Fat, red berries, intensely coloured leaves, well-fed birds. Everything swollen with colour. My father always timed his hog roast with the September equinox. He held the party every year as an antidote to the end of summer. He liked to say it was primal, an old pagan ritual, celebrating summer giving way to autumn with a whole pig turning slowly over a wood fire, its teeth clamped on an apple.

All morning the house had been busy. The bell rang constantly with deliveries which Eunice, Ig and I took in turns to bring into the house. First, rented plates and glasses arrived wrapped in thick, white paper, in need of polishing. Then caterers brought trays of vegetables, crates of oversized pans and knives, zesters and graters. They lugged these in and out of the kitchen in pairs, piling everything on to the kitchen table until it was no longer visible underneath all the carrots, tomatoes, onions and catering size tins of chick-peas. Then came boxes of flowers, white lilies, crystal vases, packets of candles. Jane, the caterer, laid out all of her platters to see if she'd brought enough to hold the salads. On the stove, a vegetable stock bubbled.

Jane did my father's hog roast every year. She always employed two schoolgirls to help. It didn't matter that they had no experience. Jane, in her sturdy shoes and floor-length white apron, double-tied and folded over, could command a battleship and still turn out dinner for a hundred and twenty-five. Everything she did seemed to work. She just told 'her girls' what to do. Something about the way she instructed them meant they succeeded every time.

My father panicked because the butcher was late. Jane tried to make him relax: even if the pigs didn't arrive, she knew a man who could deliver pork loin for all his guests by four o'clock. She'd have it cooked in time. 'There is no panic, Julian. Trust me.'

Finally, the butcher. My father ran into the courtyard, giddy with excitement. He peered inside the van, his hands jiggling at his sides. The butcher dragged out a pig to deposit into my father's cradled arms. Proud and pleased – delighted, in fact! – my father rushed through to the garden with his prize. Head held high, swelling with excitement, he kicked open the small gate. The butcher followed, carrying another pig with rather less dignity: his fists gripped two sets of legs; the poor animal hung upside down, head drooping earthwards, its mouth lolling open.

I wiped away condensation from the kitchen window so I could see my father lay the pig on a sheet of plastic spread on the grass. He bent so carefully, all the time cradling the animal, he might as well have been putting a sleeping child to bed. Next to him, the butcher slung his pig down. It thudded to the earth. Slumped, dead, its eyes surprised open: a corpse.

Eunice squealed. 'Are we sure we should be serving those at our party?' she said. 'Wouldn't it be more civilised to give our guests something a little less –' she paused '– animal?'

Two piglets, three months old, mouths agog, their solid little bodies about the length of my arm. Each with soft, fleshy snouts, a delicate shade of pink. A sparkle of mucus still clung to the white down that covered their noses. Their bellies made me think of puppies. They didn't look like meat. They still looked like two pigs, pink and flabby, lying side by side. Left there, they could have been returned to the wild: snouts, trotters and all. The fox wouldn't have known they'd cost my father a fortune.

Once the butcher had gone, my father rolled up his sleeves. A bucket of warm water by his side, he dragged a sharp knife along the pig's belly. He protected his hands with yellow plastic gloves as he pulled out the red, sloppy guts. Eunice squealed again. Next, my father cleaned the snouts with kitchen paper wrapped around pieces of skewer. He singed the coarse hair from their bodies using a cigarette lighter and a kitchen blowtorch, working carefully so as not to blister the skin. Neat and slow he went, my father the undertaker. The acrid smell of burnt hair drifted inside through the open kitchen window.

Nearby, Ig was setting up the dance floor. He carried boxes of records, the sound system, an old set of battered, aluminium disco lights that looked like hand grenades. He put coloured gels in front of them: red, green, yellow, orange. In the far corner of the garden, a hose dangled into the inflatable swimming pool to top it up, ready for the evening.

Jane's knife flew along a carrot, transforming it into a row of slim, orange coins in seconds. She nodded to a stack of spring onions, asking her assistants to chop away the green fronds to prepare the whites for slicing.

My mother used to love their parties. She'd spend hours getting ready, doing everything so carefully. Painting black around each eye with such precision, a sweep of pink, then a dab of gold glitter on her cheekbones. Sometimes she plaited the sides of her hair away from her face in a thick braid. She let me hold the strands, keeping them out of the way while she worked.

'Who do you want to be like?' I remember asking her.

'What a funny question,' she replied.

No, it's not, I thought. I knew that I imitated the people I saw on the television or the older girls at school, so who did she imitate? It seemed such an obvious, straightforward thing to ask but she looked affronted, so I kept quiet. I handed her the shade of blusher she wanted, asked her what dress she would wear, offered to fetch her another glass of wine.

Eunice jumped at the sound of the doorbell. 'I know what this is,' she said. 'This time it's for me!' She darted outside, returning a moment later with a large, flat box made of thin cardboard. Lifting the lid with both hands, she folded back the tissue paper and pulled out a silver dress.

'Wow,' said Jane.

Made of a silver fabric, a shimmery mix of linen and silk, it caught and reflected the light. She held the dress against her, showing off the slim bodice. It had a sweethheart neckline giving way to a full skirt. Eunice twirled.

'You're going to be quite the belle of the ball tonight,' said Jane.

Eunice swung right to left, cuddling the dress to her body; dreamy, happy.

'Did you buy that because David's coming?' I asked.

'No,' she shot back at me. 'Of course not.'

'He's married, Eunice. You haven't forgotten?'

* * *

By the time my father's closest friend Tom arrived, too late in the end to help light the fire pits, the scene in the garden might have been a still life from the Romantic period. Peasants at rest. My father, Tom and Ig were eating cheese sandwiches and sipping bottles of beer while Eunice sprawled next to them – the peasants' wench, perhaps – refusing to eat a thing. She lay on the grass examining her toes against the sky. The pigs were beside them, strung on to thick stainless-steel poles, flames jumping, excited by the thought of the two young pigs they'd soon be licking at. When they finished eating, Tom and my father heaved the pigs on to the cradle of the spit. The flames shot up and crackled with the first drip of fat. The pigs' skin puckered and blistered. The paper-thin membrane covering the ribs curled instantly away into nothing, disappearing the way hair or a spider's web vaporises in fire. Then the subcutaneous fat turned liquid, sending them a translucent pink. Two poor piglets turning over a slow fire. Their medieval punishment. Strung up in public to deter other little piglets from the same wickednesses.

'I'm so excited,' said Eunice, twizzling her ankles in the air. 'I love parties.'

As evening fell, Valerie was the first guest to arrive. She didn't go into the house but rather came to my studio. Hitching up her navy-blue pencil skirt, she raised her foot on to my sofa, opened the window and perched herself on the sill to smoke. With her head tilted, she sent each exhale outwards into the fresh air. In the courtyard and street beyond, car doors slammed. Gentle laughter tickled the air. Heels crunched on the gravel. My father stood at the door to welcome in each new arrival. He kissed, hugged, patted shoulders then sent his friends inwards to the laden drinks table in the sitting room.

Her fag finished, Valerie paced my studio while I finished

getting ready. She picked up books, inspected cosmetics, ran a hand over the contents of my wardrobe, then she stopped. 'What the hell is that?' she said.

Eunice's ornamental blue duck looked at us both with its huge eyes.

'What's it doing in here?'

'A gift,' I replied.

From its spot on the shelf it tried to seduce Valerie and me with its sad gaze and long, curled eyelashes painted in black. A lady duck. With a pretty beak made of bright yellow ceramic, a thin line of red paint tracing its curve. Valerie picked it up. Her wrinkled, dry hand, a smoker's skin, contrasted with the shiny ceramic surface of the duck. She jabbed it into my arm, pecking me with its beak. She coughed and wheezed with laughter, rattling like an old money box.

Valerie pushed her tongue out of her mouth, screwed up her nose and kept jabbing me with the duck until I laughed too. Then I turned quickly, grabbing the duck before she had a chance to hold on to it. I stabbed her with it in the arse. She jumped then erupted with phlegmy laughter as she plucked the fag out of her mouth to grind into the duck's beak. A perfect, fag-shaped circle of black tar remained behind. She grinned, then threw the duck to me. I caught, flinging it back to her. We went back and forth, the poor duck twisting and twirling between us both until Valerie's hand slipped and the duck fell to the floor, smashing into four pieces. The yellow beak broke off intact. Valerie smirked, her face creased up into a tight ball of crushed paper. She jumped, landing squarely on the beak, smashing it to dust.

I took one last look at myself in the mirror, fiddled with an earring, corrected some smudged mascara then smoothed my hair back into its ponytail. Ready.

'I suppose we should go inside,' said Valerie.

'I suppose we should.'

I entered the house and moved into the crowd with a wide smile. 'Mary,' I said, seeing my uncle's navy-blue clad wife hovering at the entrance. 'Elizabeth,' she replied, pulling me towards her in a freesia-scented embrace.

'How are you?' she asked.

In the sitting room, the cool smell of lilies mixed with the warmth of clashing perfumes and the tang of champagne. Everyone was speaking at the same time, arms waving in the air, peals of laughter. The voices all mixed together to make one solid noise that gathered in the ceiling. Jane's 'girls' had changed out of their jeans and sturdy kitchen shoes into smart black skirts and white shirts. They picked their way around the guests, filling glasses and offering canapés from large platters: small pieces of bread decorated with a bright red twist of grilled pepper and a single rocket leaf. As they offered them they explained, over and over again, '. . . then finished with a drizzle of balsamic reduction'.

Through a gap in the crowd, I spotted my father, sashaying about with a bottle of champagne, a grin so broad it threatened to slice his face in two. I imagined my mother beside him, the way she'd looked at the last of the hog roasts she was alive for. Gold earrings with a long matching necklace in thick, interlocking discs. A dress of loose silk folds. Relaxed, she slipped around after my father. We liked it when she was happy. Everything felt calm. We didn't need to panic. No risk she'd disappear if she seemed happy.

'So that's her,' Mary whispered, pulling me back. 'The half-sister.'

Mary's hand thrashed about inside her leather handbag,

searching for her distance glasses. 'I need to get a proper look,' she said. She squinted towards Eunice, screwing her face up as if she looked directly into the sun, then turned back to me, her forehead crinkled into a deep frown.

'Why's she dressed herself in tin foil?' asked Mary.

Eunice glittered in her silver dress. The low neckline revealed a scoop of perfect, creamy skin. A string of crystal beads twinkled in the light; teardops of the same stone sparkled at her ear. Each time she moved, she caught the light and glinted. High-heeled silver shoes. The whole of her shimmered. My father reached over to kiss Eunice daintily on both cheeks, exclaiming how wonderful she looked. Immediately afterwards, Tom gave her an avuncular little peck on the forehead. Eunice beamed. She picked up a champagne bottle and went to fill up glasses. Dazzling, she slipped among everyone, splashing champagne into the guests' flutes, touching their shoulders as she asked them whether they had everything they needed. 'I'm Eunice. Julian's daughter. I live here,' I heard her tell people. As more guests arrived, she carried on, introducing herself, offering drinks, fetching a napkin or offering a canapé.

'This is Eunice,' I said, introducing her to Mary.

'Hello, I'm Julian's daughter,' she told Mary.

'We thought he'd got himself a younger woman,' said Stephen, a client of my father's, sidling up to Eunice with a dirty grin.

'Oh no,' she said. 'I live here.'

Eventually the party became so full that people had to spill out into the garden, everyone chatting, kissing, greeting old friends. They talked about their holidays, their summer, about their plans for Christmas or New Year. All of them had plans; the kind of people who'd be ashamed not to. On the far wall, empty bottles of champagne began to line up.

Eunice quickened; David had arrived, followed by Anna. She rushed to the back of the room, replaced the bottle of champagne on the drinks table and rearranged her dress. David smoothed back his hair as he handed one of the waitresses his light trench coat. I turned to see Eunice again, her eyes fixed on to him as she moved through the crowd, heading directly towards him. Anna leaned in to say something to a waitress, who pointed to the drinks table. David began weaving through the crowd towards the champagne. Eunice twisted her necklace against her throat as she moved in to intercept David in his path.

'Here we go,' I said to Mary.

Mary's head swivelled just as Eunice turned, pulling herself up to stand straight in front of David. She held his gaze, a bright blue challenge. She said nothing, she just arrested him, stopped him in his tracks with her eyes. He jumped back, shocked, stumbling and awkward, then gathered himself to lay a kiss on her cheek. His kiss seemed an act of defence rather than affection, the only thing he could reasonably do to physically push her back. He tried to move round her but her eyes followed him. He stayed still. His stiff, starched collar protruding from a light turquoise sweater seemed suddenly uncomfortable. He ran two fingers along the inside of it, pulling at it, his cheeks burning, beginning to glisten waxy red. Eunice held him in her gaze, turned with him, followed him to the drinks table.

He appeared to be reluctant but Eunice didn't give up. She worked hard. She poured him champagne, kept talking to him, waited for him to take a few sips then topped his glass up. She held him captive, kept touching his hand until gradually, he seemed to soften, to succumb. He stopped glancing over at Anna and then he laughed as Eunice whispered something into his ear. He held his almost empty glass out for Eunice to fill again. He stayed by her side as he continued to drink it.

'She looks like trouble,' said Mary to me, watching them as I handed her a drink.

Outside, the breeze dropped. The smell was a mixture of citrus and damp earth. By the fire, Tom sat on a log to paint the pig's skin with hot fat from a tin cup. Next to him, a woman wearing a moss-green crocheted sweater talked about California. She spent every summer there, in a house built into a piece of cliff. 'Terrifying,' she said. 'I imagined all this rock above me as I slept. I thought, what if there's a landslide? I could almost feel it crushing me.'

The spit turned. The flames leapt as fat dripped on to them. Across the lawn, Ig made final checks to his music system. Four teenagers lay on blankets watching him. They sipped bottled beer and browsed Ig's music collection.

Floating candles in the shape of pink flowers twinkled in the pool. Eunice had sat for an hour or more, lighting them then launching them into the water from the wooden platform, scattering bright red rose petals, a luscious, deep red, in the spaces between them. From the garden, I heard my father shouting above the chatter that the food was ready. People gathered around the two pigs. Five hours over a slow fire had turned them a deep, rusty pink, stiff and crisp.

My father and Tom unhooked the first pig from the spit. They wrapped each end of the pole in a towel then hoicked it up, carrying it high on their shoulders towards the carving table. A gentle swell of clapping followed them and the pig.

'Let the evening begin,' my father said, sharpening a knife with brisk strokes over a stone.

Together, Tom, Jane and my father dismantled the pigs.

Tom cracked through the skin, lifting it away in large pieces while Jane scraped the ointment of fat covering the meat beneath. They sliced and pulled, breaking the meat into chunks. The waitresses peeled away cling film from plates of salads: green leaves, spiced chickpeas, coleslaw with deep purple cabbage and nuts, couscous speckled with crumbs of white cheese, sliced tomatoes scattered with parsley. Jane arranged the carved pig on to a large platter so that it, and the salads, formed a production line ending with a huge basket of soft, white rolls.

Valerie bristled with irritation as Eunice wafted past her, directing people towards the line for food, ensuring they had plates, offering them more drinks. 'Here,' Eunice said, grabbing the arm of a passing waitress, 'this young lady will fetch you a drink, won't you?' As the waitress went off inside, with her instructions, Eunice dashed after her to say something quietly to her – presumably another order – before returning to check the movement of the food line.

'I could smack her,' said Valerie.

'Yes . . . but don't,' I replied.

Valerie grinned. 'I might.'

By the time we sat down with our food, my father was already in full swing.

'None of it's true,' I said to the four teenagers surrounding my father.

'It's all bloody true,' my father insisted.

The teenagers huddled in close as he began to roll a joint. He hunched over it, his hand close into his chest, fingers rubbing together to desiccate the resin, looking like an ageing moneylender.

'You turn inwards with this stuff,' my father said to them.

'You unlock doors, travel down internal tunnels. You find your own inner world. There's no such thing as linear time when you're stoned. Time's circular. That's why smoking's so good for you. It's good for the brain and good for the soul to see time in a cycle, rather than a long, relentless march forward. You can never be busy if you go in circles.'

The teenagers kept glancing up, presumably watching out for their parents, while my father carried on singeing the block of hash, crumbling it on to the rolling paper.

'Pot smokers live a more vivid life,' my father went on. 'Because they feel everything.'

He put the smoke in his mouth, cupped his hand around it and lit. He didn't pass it on, rather he held it so the teenagers could duck their heads each in turn, to take a secret puff. My father, the High Priest, the pedagogue, handing down his wisdom to the next generation. Each of the teenagers concentrated hard as they pulled the smoke into themselves. They kept serious expressions as they held their breath, keeping the hash fumes inside them as if it was an education in itself, a rare elixir that would change the very workings of their DNA.

'You really shouldn't be doing that to them,' said Marilyne, an old university friend of my father's.

'I went over to New York with Tom,' said my father to the teenagers. 'We ended up in the middle of a bunch of Irish Trotskyites who told us to go to San Francisco where the chicks were hotter. We hitched our way across America – it took weeks – to get to this address they gave us.' He took another long draw on his joint. 'Inside the commune, people just wandered around naked. No hang-ups. Just loving each other. No one had their own bed. We slept wherever we ended up. It was a different time then, wasn't it, Marilyne?'

She nodded.

'Nowadays, everything's about money. We didn't want jobs back then. We weren't planning our lives out at twenty-two. The idea of a *career* was actually horrifying. We didn't want to own a house. We didn't panic about where we'd be at forty-five. That's why we lived in communes. *Wanting* is what toddlers do. We shared.'

'The communes of course were a marvellous solution,' said Marilyne, patting my father on the knee with a kind of amused tolerance.

I felt a tap on my shoulder and turned to see Jane. 'Can you please remove that girl from my kitchen,' she hissed. 'It's not her house, it's not her party, she's not paying my wages. I've got dishes to wash and cheese plates to organise and I need someone to get her the hell out of there.'

'I'll come,' I said, following her inside. I told Jane that I knew just the thing to say to make Eunice leave.

I found Eunice in the kitchen, in mid-flow, telling Jane's 'girls' that the pieces of cheese they'd cut were too big: no one would eat that much. The waitresses looked confused. Eunice had a knife in one hand, about to halve the pieces, when I sidled up to her to whisper quietly in her ear, 'Eunice. David was looking for you. Just a minute ago.'

Her eyes snapped wide open. 'Was he?' she said, dropping the knife and dashing out of the kitchen.

Around the garden, the guests had scattered with plates of food. They lounged on blankets, perched on my father's crates, glasses held between knees, plates unsteady in one hand. One pig had been entirely eaten, just a carcass now. The other animal had half of its body carved away, the other half still recognisably pig. A group of my father's university friends gabbled at each other. Marilyne teased pieces of lettuce into her mouth. Valerie, looking all hunched and pugilistic, seemed to bite at the air with her words, telling a story. My father was still telling tales of communes, of sex, of the rich hippy women who funded it all.

Everywhere around the garden, the colour palette of the guests was muted. If a scarf was a riot of colour, the rest of the outfit was restrained. A pale grey dress to offset a knot of fuchsia at the neck. Navy blue. Brown. Black. Then Eunice, a beacon of glimmering silver, circling the crowd searching for David.

'I can't find him,' she said. 'Where's he gone?'

From the kitchen window, Jane waved at me and mouthed 'thank you'.

'This girl said to me that before we had sex we had to take California Sunrise, a kind of LSD she said would turn everything blue while we fucked,' said my father, telling anyone who'd listen.

'There he is,' said Eunice. She nudged me, pointing to David and Anna, who formed a picture of intimacy sitting side by side next to one of the oil drum fires. 'He's with her.' Anna held both their glasses while David cut the meat into smaller pieces. They ate slowly, picking at their food, talking.

'She had these wonderful breasts, I remember,' my father said. 'I leaned up to run my hands along the sharp curve of her hip. I gripped her smooth, rounded belly. She had this serious way of looking at me, her hair falling right the way down her body while I pressed her warm flesh into my palms. I gazed at her belly button, fascinated by the shape of it.'

'What have they got to talk about so intensely?' said Eunice. 'She seems so dull.'

'Then the acid really hit and I just dived into her. I swam

206

into her, through her belly button, along her, up her, inside her. She tasted of lemons and smoke. And sugar. The sex went on for hours. The world turned blue and started dripping, everything melting like blue candle wax. The doors disappearing, the walls softening, turning liquid. All the time we fucked, I smelled this hot smoke smell, then sandalwood, then flowers, like spring had sneaked into the room. Like my body and this girl's body and the room had all melted together, scented and wonderful, into one new burst of life. We were the world, we were springtime, something new, new life from being joined up together and then joined up with all the rest of existence too. Then suddenly, the whole room just went from blue to pink. Everything pink. A bright, magical pink, as if something from another world had landed in the bedroom and told us everything had to be pink from now on.'

'Do you think I should go over there?' said Eunice.

Still staring at Anna and David, she took the joint from my father's hand without looking at him. She puffed angrily on it, her face screwed up into fury.

'It was very loving,' my father said. 'But of course the communes had their disasters. People went missing. People came in and robbed because everyone was off their heads. Other people couldn't cope. Things got volatile. It's why they didn't last long. Women were walking around pregnant and no one had the faintest idea who the fathers were.'

'It must have been fun,' Eunice said stonily.

Ig started the music. Beach bar music, a soft, rhythmic roll of sound. Music that washes through the air, slowing the pulse, sending everyone into reveries. I lay back on the grass watching the leaves twitching above me. In the pool, the candles had burned away to nothing. My father lay flat out across the grass looking at the stars. The leaves fluttered above me, like hundreds of tiny, silver reminders that my mother wasn't here any more.

'We were kind to the girls. Everyone was in it, everyone up for it. No one was exploited. If they didn't want to be there, they could leave. No one was held captive. I love women,' said my father. 'I really do. I loooooove women.'

'Here,' Eunice said to my father. 'Have your thing.' She handed him back the joint and stood up to go.

'Tin Foil's drinking a lot,' whispered Mary to me. 'You ought to stop her. Every time I see her she's got a full glass.'

'Well, she's not paying for it, is she?' said Valerie.

Dinner over, Ig's disco lights made patterns on the lawn: squares of blue, green, yellow. The music built until it roused people from their seats and on to the dance floor. Arms outstretched, Ig waved the crowd on. Full of energy, he jumped on the spot to the sheer force of the beat that came from the speakers. Shouting into the microphone, urging everyone on. In a corner, the four teenagers made a tight circle, carbon copies of each other as they danced: arms by their sides, heads flopping, their bodies artfully moulding into studiously maintained shapes that looked somewhere between fear, shame and an urgent need to look exactly like their friends.

Anna and David moved together. Anna stood very upright, her head held slightly away from her, making her long, elegant neck taut. Her arms sat at the perfect angle to her body, a complement to her lean, tall frame. Her narrow skirt ended at just the right point of her calf. The smooth line of a slim ankle disappeared into a flat snakeskin shoe. Her cerise silk scarf billowed out behind her in a comet's tail as David twisted her away from him. Everything about Anna seemed cool, smooth and considered while David played the role of the dashing, debonair husband swinging her across the floor. Dancing together, they made a thoughtful, restrained version of the thing people call fun.

David's hands disappeared into the mass of his wife's hair. Anna swished around the dance floor as if she was determined hers would be a victory dance. A yellow disco light burst into life and she moved into it, backlighting her. The outer wisps of her hair were encircled in light. David swung her. She leaned into his arm. He caught her before she fell. When the two of them came upright again, they gazed into each other's eyes.

Tom fetched me from the dance floor. He wanted company while he swam. By the pool, he stripped down to his underpants and Ig announced over the microphone that Tom had officially opened the pool. Anyone who wanted to cool off should join him, he told the crowd. Tom dived into the water and people cheered. Lit by security lamps fixed to the garden wall, the water was bright blue and crystal clear. Tom flipped on to his back, beckoned others to join him. Next in was Marilyne, wearing a white vest and her underwear. 'It's freezing,' she squealed.

'It was warm today,' said Tom.

Loosened by drink, more and more people stripped off to go in. I remained on the wooden decking, sitting cross-legged with no intention of going any further. Eunice wafted down the garden towards us. She came up the small ladder to sit beside me. She dipped her bare feet into the water with her silver shoes placed beside her. 'Come on in,' said Tom. 'Don't be a chicken, Eunice.'

'It's freezing. I'm not going in there.'

'I can make you,' he said, swimming towards her. He grabbed her toes, kept hold of them while Eunice continued to glance back at the party – checking to see if Anna and David still swept around the dance floor like love itself.

'I'm not swimming,' said Eunice, looking down towards Tom, who still gripped her toes.

David appeared at the water's edge, without Anna. 'Who's going in next?' he said. Eunice stood up to her full height on the decking and turned to David, running her hands down her dress. 'I think I might,' she said. 'But I don't have a swimsuit. What do you think I should do?' She was floodlit by the wall lamps, so she looked as if she could be on a stage. The dress reflected the light, and she appeared to be all light and happiness, a huge smile across her face.

'I don't know, Eunice,' said David.

'I knew he'd come,' I heard her whisper.

And suddenly as she stood there beaming with pride, she was all glory and victory, all light and hope, and I didn't want to watch it so I got up from the decking to leave.

The strobe light freeze-framed the dance floor. One time, the picture captured someone smiling, someone else holding their hands in the air, a foot kicking out at a jaunty angle, a skirt flaring. Then pop, the lights flashed on again, freezing a new picture until the next frame. In flashes of light and dark like that, I saw David heading into the house. Eunice dashed after him. Light, dark, light, dark, light, dark; her movements jumpy, stealthy, like a silent movie of a cop going after a fugitive.

Jane emerged from the house, carrying a large, square cake. Strawberries and raspberries scattered over the top covered in specks of white coconut. In the garden, on to a trestle table, she manoeuvred the cake into position and began slicing. She beckoned me over, to ask if I could help with the plates. I was trying to hand a slice of cake to Valerie, when Anna fled out of the kitchen door and nearly knocked my hand. David rushed after her. 'Anna, I wasn't trying to kiss her, I was trying to push her away.' Anna ran down the garden, followed by Valerie. David turned back into the house – I went in after him – to the sitting room where Eunice sat on the sofa, biting her nails.

'It's got to stop, Eunice,' he said.

'What?' Eunice replied.

'This.'

'What's *this*?' said Eunice.

'You know what I mean.'

'I didn't imagine it, David.'

He grabbed her by the arm, pulling her outside into the courtyard.

'Imagine what?' I heard him say, as I leaned in closer to the open window.

'I didn't imagine your laughter. I didn't imagine you telling me you hadn't laughed like that in years. I didn't imagine you telling me your life felt bereft of proper fun. You said you had more fun with me in a single evening than you'd had with your wife in a decade. I didn't imagine all that. You said those things.'

David sighed, trying to turn away from her.

'You said you felt more alive than you had in years, sitting round that campfire, drinking rum, talking and laughing.'

'Eunice—' David began.

'Don't do this to me,' she said.

'I'm a married man, Eunice.' David looked stiff and awkward, as if standing in front of him was an uncomfortable reminder of an incarnation of himself he'd rather forget. For an evening, the veneer had slipped away. He'd just been David, the person his twenty-year-old self might have recognised. 'I'm a happily married man,' he said, straightening himself, as if saying it out loud would remind him who he was, the thing by which he identified himself.

Eunice stayed silent.

'I'm not the person to give you the life you crave. If Julian has disappointed you, I'm sorry. But I'm not the person to replace that.'

'But you said you're not happy.'

David stiffened again. 'Anna and I are very happy,' he said firmly.

'You don't look happy.'

'I'm fucking delirious, Eunice,' he said, frantically.

'You're pretending,' she insisted.

I peered up out of the window to see them both, standing among the bamboo, David towering over Eunice, trying to gather himself. He smoothed his palm along his cashmere sweater, his voice went quiet as he spoke, he seemed suddenly fearful. 'I'd be nothing without my wife. No, our existence isn't always wildly fun, but let me be clear, I'd be nothing without my wife. Listen to that, Eunice. Don't listen to the things I said after half a bottle of rum and a load of marijuana which, incidentally, I don't usually smoke.'

He began to walk away, then stopped, turning back to Eunice. 'Perhaps I flirted, and I shouldn't have done that.'

'Flirted?' said Eunice. 'Is that what you call it?'

'It would be disingenuous for me to say I hadn't felt more rowdy than I might ordinarily have felt. I'd smoked that stuff. I'm sorry if I led you on. I may not have realised your vulnerability.' He said that final sentence with a certain sadistic pleasure. The perverse but beautiful enjoyment of the man – not full of regret, but pumped full of masculine pride. So dazzling, he needed to exercise caution around unstable women.

'But you said you weren't happy. And you said you felt happy with me that evening. That's real.'

'You don't understand,' said David.

'You used me.'

'Even if I were unhappy, which I need to make it quite clear that I am not, it would make no difference.'

'But there's nowhere else for me to go,' Eunice said.

'Stay here,' replied David, waving his hand in the air. 'They seem to want you.'

Anna and David left the party, slipping away with a brief wave. Anna tearful; David furious; neither of them speaking. Two casualties, but their departure couldn't leave a dent in the evening. The party had its own momentum now. Big, full of energy, it could swallow away anything.

Eunice kicked off her shoes, left them by the side of the dance floor and danced as if nothing had happened. She twirled between different groups of people. Tom came up behind her, surprised her, then spun her around, his arm held up high as he looped her around, away from him, then back again. She laughed, she wouldn't let anyone know she cared. Other people joined them until there was a whole group of them spinning and twirling together.

The whole garden was alive. The party had reached its apex. A crowd had gathered at the pool. Water splashed as people jumped in. Others gathered around the campfire, finishing off their cake, talking wistfully in front of red embers. My father wandered through the party and looked happy. He'd managed a hog roast without my mother. Two years previously, he cancelled it altogether. The year just gone, he tried to be normal but he couldn't do it. I found him in the kitchen with Jane, in tears, hiding from everyone, unable to join in. People left early, drifted home, because the party never really happened. But this year, he seemed to be himself again. He drifted through his garden with an air of pride and pleasure.

My father sliced his hand across his neck, to signal to Ig he'd like the music turning down.

'A few words,' my father said, stepping up on to a small table.

'Careful up there, Julian,' heckled Tom.

'He's only had two bottles, he's not swaying yet,' another voice shouted.

'You're not as young as you used to be, Julian,' a male voice joined in.

'Enough!' My father held up his hands.

He talked about the party, about how important his friends were, his gratitude for the pigs. 'I'm sure they'd never have imagined their short lives would give so much pleasure to so many,' he said.

'Last year's party happened under a shadow.' A murmur came from the crowd. 'But this year, I feel that we're back. Look at you all. Look at us all. We've survived. I've survived.' He glanced up at the sky. 'Margaret would be proud.'

The crowd murmured again. People held up their glasses, toasted 'Margaret'.

Eunice leaned against the kitchen door, holding a champagne glass, smiling as she watched my father talk. His speech gathered pace; he made jokes; he told stories; he had the crowd laughing beneath him. Tom heckled; others shouted that he was getting old, joked that his speech was boring. I heard my name being called out. My father was gesturing me towards him. As I moved forward, he outstretched his arms. People parted to make space for me. I walked through the crowd towards him. Someone put both hands to my cheeks to kiss me, another squeezed my wrist. My father shuffled over on his box to make way for me. He took my hand to help me up on to his podium. Ig followed.

'My two wonderful children: Ig and Elizabeth,' my father said, putting his arm around my waist. 'They both live with me and what would I do without them? I'd be a lonely old git, rattling around here on my own.' A ripple of laughter. 'They bring me joy and fun every day of my life. And I don't mind embarrassing them in return.' My father swallowed away a tear. 'My wonderful children. I can't tell you how much I love them. And how they've helped me survive these past three years.'

Beneath us, a crowd of smiling faces. I felt my father pull me in again until my head pressed into his chest and he kissed my hair. A final embrace before he was about to release me back into the crowd.

'But you don't just have two children, do you, Julian?' came the loud voice from the crowd.

I turned to see Eunice. Her face pale and furious.

With a look of determination, she moved through the crowd towards us. 'I just wanted to say,' she shouted over the gathering underswell of voices. 'That you forgot to mention me.' She wiped away a tear from her cheek.

'Julian. You actually have three children. Ig.' She pointed towards him. 'Elizabeth.' Her finger picked me out. 'And . . . there's me. That makes one, two, three.'

The crowd stared back at her as she climbed on to a chair. 'Or maybe there are more. Maybe he's got a couple in San Francisco. Anyone out there, who wants to claim to be the fourth? Hands up! One, two, three, four. Any takers for number four?'

Silence.

Faces in the crowd frozen in bemusement, hardly daring to look. Other guests stared at the floor, their lips thin with embarrassment. My father approached Eunice, tried to hold her arm, to coax her back down into the party. She shook herself away from him.

'Come on,' she shouted to the crowd. 'Keep looking at me. You lot have been staring at me all night. All of you. Don't think I haven't seen you whispering and gossiping behind my back. I'm not stupid.' She turned a circle, spinning her arms out. 'So look at me. Gawp. Here I am. Stare all you like.'

The kitchen door opened and shut as three guests escaped inside. 'Here I am!' she shouted again. 'The weirdo. That's what you all think. The girl who wears silver, while you lot all shrink away in beige.'

'Eunice, I really don't think—' tried my father.

At the back of the gathering, a small group sniggered. Eunice kicked a shoe into the crowd so it whistled through the air, barely missing one of the guests. Then the other one, landing with a soft thud in the grass. Every time my father tried to reach her, to coax her down from the chair, she shook him off.

Eunice wiped tears from her face. 'Maybe I should tell you my story, mine and Julian's story; in fact, mine, Julian AND the perfect, canonised bloody Margaret's story—' A hand landed on her. Valerie stood at the base of the chair with both arms around Eunice's legs, her face fixed into fury. As Eunice began toppling, she turned her head skyward. She carried on trying to speak but Valerie's hand clamped her mouth. The crowd gasped, recoiled in shock. Eunice fell like a statue towards the ground.

Ig thrust at the dials in a panic. The music started, full blast in an instant. Mary's spectacles magnified her eyes so that they seemed to bulge with pleasure. Valerie dragged Eunice up by the arm, marched her through the party. A patch of mud stuck to Eunice's silver dress where she'd landed. The fall had flung her hair in her face and Eunice hadn't been able to sweep it back because Valerie pulled her through the crowd. I ran behind, trying to catch them up. 'Valerie,' I shouted.

At the cellar, Valerie wrestled open the door with one hand. The other grabbed Eunice.

'You can stay in there until you've calmed down,' said Valerie, trying to push her towards the open door.

Eunice looked back at her, dishevelled, afraid, reeling with confusion, her eyes darting right and left. Valerie lunged forward, pushing Eunice towards the door.

'Valerie,' I said, moving towards her. 'You've got to—' I felt a sharp jab. I stumbled backwards with Valerie's push. When I gathered myself, I turned and saw my father standing there. I expected him to be doing something, to be putting himself between Valerie and Eunice, to try to gather things back into proportion, into their correct perspective. He just stood there, watching as Valerie continued to try to push Eunice down into the cellar, cramming her in like someone trying to squeeze a sweater into an already full drawer. Eunice continued to resist, pushing her knee against the door, yelping with fear.

'Dad,' I whispered. 'Do something.'

He stayed still. Just visible over Valerie's shoulder was Eunice's face, a dab of fear against the blackness of the cellar behind her.

'Dad,' I shouted. 'She'll kill her.'

I pushed in again but Valerie pushed me backwards. Eunice continued to struggle, holding on to the stair rail and flinging her legs in the air to kick Valerie away. Valerie threw herself at Eunice, attempted to unstick her hands, prise them off, finger by finger. Eunice kicked the air to hit Valerie but kept missing as Valerie dodged. Valerie went to karate-chop Eunice's elbows so the joint might pop, giving Valerie the chance to push her backwards. My father grabbed Valerie around the waist, clamping her tight, but still she held on as my father heaved her backwards. Eunice screamed. The music in the garden carried on playing; no one would have heard a sound from the cellar.

Valerie's hand flew through the dark, landing on her cheek. A sharp, stinging sound. Eunice yelped, stunned, holding her cheek so that only one hand remained on the handrail. Valerie kicked my father. He stumbled and went back to try again, but Valerie had already begun unpicking Eunice's fingers from the metal, one at a time, pulling at each finger with both hands, using all her body weight to pry Eunice's thin, pale hands free. Crying, panting, exhausted, almost overcome, Eunice seemed ready to be defeated.

Eunice's hand unstuck; her eyes rolling with fear, she quickly grabbed Valerie's hand. She held it fast in both of hers, even as Valerie grappled to release it. Eunice gripped and gripped, her legs holding her fast until the moment came. She flung her head forward. Valerie screeched and jumped.

'She bit me,' squealed Valerie. 'She fucking bit me.'

Eunice kicked Valerie in the shins, flung her out of the way. 'She's fucking mad,' hissed Valerie, running off whimpering like an injured dog.

Eunice turned to me, her face pulsating. Desperate, heaving, hysterical tears. Snot streaming down her face, mixing with salt tears, a drip of blood where she'd bitten her lip. Her cheek red from the slap. I went to touch her arm but she flung it away from me. 'Don't touch me,' she screeched.

She wiped a hand across her face and stared at us both full on. 'I'm a person, a human being,' she yelled. She held her skirt out, flung her hair about with her hands to prove the point, jabbing at her stomach with her fingers. 'You people think you can behave however you like.' She wiped her face, stared at us all, her hair wild, her face streaked with tears.

'Eunice, I'm sorry,' I said.

'I'm going,' she sobbed.

I went to take her arm. She pulled herself away from me and stalked off.

I watched the back of her as she headed down the drive, the gravel between us lengthening. The thing I'd wanted all along. The shape of her just visible against the night weaving towards the exit. A bang. The heavy, wooden gate opened, then shut. Eunice was gone.

I didn't feel like going back to the party. I went to my studio, lay on the bed and stared upwards until the sun began to poke at the trees. From the garden, I could hear the guests. The party still alive, my father's voice, Valerie's piercing laugh. Daylight began spreading across the sky. The small square of window above my head diffused light across my bed until I heard the guests begin to leave. Finally, as the birds started to sing, I felt myself relax. The mattress sank with the weight of me. It held me within its warmth and softness. The thing I needed. Sleep.

When I woke in the early afternoon, I tiptoed through the sitting room, pulling my T-shirt tight around me as I stepped over motionless body after body. Two soft feet poked out from beneath a red woollen blanket thrown across the sofa. On the armchair, a head lolled forward so that a thread of saliva pooled into the royal blue blanket pulled up tight to its chin. The lucky ones slept on furniture, the rest had made up beds on the floor using whatever they could find. Whoever had been last to sleep lay on hard wood, his head on a book, no cover.

I made coffee. The kitchen was deserted. The vinegar scent of spilled wine hung in the air. Stacks of plates with damp, screwed up napkins squashed against them hiding bits of pig fat waited to be washed.

Overnight it had rained. I walked through the garden with my coffee, through the cool, damp air. In the pale, grey light of a retreating September day the garden looked glossy and alive. So much rain, it had run out of places to go. Puddles formed on the lawn, most of the fire drums sat full of water but the one sheltered by the mulberry tree still smoked where the rain had only just managed to dampen the last of the smoulders. Water pooled in a pig carcass, a greasy pool in its ribcage making a small, impromptu lake. The leaves glistened. Tiny drops of water clung to them, making perfect spheres on the bright green blades of grass. I wandered through the remains of the night before, enjoying the quiet and the emptiness. Old bottles thrown across the lawn, a lost scarf tangled into the mud, grass rubbed away from too many feet making muddy lines where people had trodden the route from the meat to the drinks table to the dance floor and the house. The garden smelled not of pig, tobacco and stale wine but damp and clean from the rain.

At the cellar door, churned up gravel exposed patches of mud; stones scraped away in the scramble of feet formed a complete map etched into the ground of the night before. Whose foot landed where. A story trodden into the earth. Someone might have been able to piece it together, to find the truth of it in the pattern: who was the stronger, who started it, who was the aggressor and who the defender. All there in the pattern of footprints, a record we could pore over. If we could have read them perhaps we'd have known who to blame. We could untangle it all: we couldn't all be victims.

The intensity of the previous night seemed out of place in this mellow light, the quietness of the afternoon, the wonderful freshness of newly rained-on grass. How had things reached such a fever?

I kicked the cellar door closed, scraped gravel over the bare patches of mud, swept the stones from the lawn. When I checked again, everything was erased. No sign of any struggle. No story to tell. I wished I didn't have the memory of Valerie in my head.

Back inside, people began milling around in the kitchen, holding mugs of tea, complaining that their heads hurt. My father fried bacon. Tom buttered slices of white bread ready for the sandwiches that would cure their hangovers. The kitchen felt calm and certain. Warm tea, a mist of bacon fat settling on the tiles, a table of people groaning at the state of their heads.

She's gone, she's gone, she's gone.

As I sat back in the chair, no place ever felt so sweet and perfect, felt so much like home, the way it had when our mother was still alive. A house crammed full of our memories. A place, my place, the home that held me safe. It felt so simple, so inevitable. Why hadn't we just asked her to leave weeks ago?

ACT FIVE

Maybe, I'm not here to find my past, maybe I'm here to help you by erasing the bad things from yours.

empty

EUNICE'S ABSENCE WAS LIKE CLOSING YOUR EYES AFTER SEEING A bright light. She'd left an image burned into the space behind my eyes that wouldn't dissolve away. She was always there, everywhere in our home, among the things she'd unsettled. She remained among the spotlessly clean cupboards, the scrubbed clean kitchen surfaces, the sitting room rug that had been vacuumed so often the pile had begun to disappear. Our house still smelled of disinfectant – even a week after she'd left – and no matter how many of Ig's incense sticks I lit, I couldn't get rid of it.

The warmth of our home seemed to have vanished. She'd scraped it off to leave behind a kind of bright cleanliness, a sterility, the sleight of hand of a practically minded woman. Nothing more than a change of the light, but I could feel it. I kept trying to capture in my memory the way our home had felt before – the warm familiarity, the smell, the patina of time held in the dust, the sense of us – but it had gone. She'd cleaned it away.

My father hadn't even seemed to register that Eunice had left. One morning he'd said: 'It's nice this, isn't it?' I had no idea if he meant nice without Eunice or nice because it was a lovely, sunny autumnal morning with a spotless blue sky.

I sat on a chair in the kitchen, drinking my morning tea, as the leaves began to fall outside. Floating down, they scattered the lawn. On the table, a line of ants streamed into the honey jar on the table in front of me. Small black dots. If I squinted my eyes, they looked like tiny holes in the table, pinpricks of nothing, forming an exact, busy line.

'I'm here to get my things,' said the voice behind me.

I jumped and turned.

'Eunice!' I said, startled. 'What a surprise.'

We stood in front of each other, not knowing quite how to proceed. Should I kiss her? Or offer her tea?

'Mike's coming later with the car to load my things in,' she said flatly. 'I got the bus. So I could make a start.' I glanced down to the stack of flatpack cardboard boxes she carried.

'We wish things had ended better,' I said.

'Better?' Eunice replied. 'Or sooner.'

While she packed, I took her up a coffee.

'I don't want a coffee,' she said.

'So you're back together with Mike?' I asked.

'What else was I supposed to do?' she shot back angrily. 'I had nowhere to go.'

I left the coffee on the table and retreated back downstairs. I debated calling Valerie. I felt suddenly vulnerable, alone in the house with this angry woman. What might she do to me while there was only me and her?

When Mike arrived, parking his car right outside the front door, he pushed past me as he came inside. 'Where's Eunice?' he said.

I showed him upstairs then retreated to my father's office, to hide from them. All afternoon, they trooped downstairs with boxes. Box after box. Eventually Mike's face appeared at the office window.

'We're going,' he said, then turned to leave before I had time to stand up.

As I headed upstairs, turning the lights on as I went, it felt as if the house was beginning afresh. She really had gone. The guest room was free again. I opened the window. I paced the room. My feet echoed against the walls; the hollow sound of an empty room. We were free of her. It was over.

She would be fine, I thought. It wasn't her home anyway. She might be upset for a day or two, but so what. She'd get over it. It was just the way things were. She had to move out. It wasn't my fault. It wasn't her home and I didn't care what she thought of me because I didn't have to. If she thought I'd been harsh, or unfeeling, it didn't matter. She might rattle at our locked doors angrily but we wouldn't let her in. We'd zip ourselves up and keep her out.

As I leaned in to close the window, a breeze sent a note fluttering off the sill and on to the floor in front of my feet.

Don't think that you lot are going to get away with it because you're not . . .

That evening, I showed the note to Ig and my father.

'She's still got her key,' I said, laying it out on the table.

'Just ignore it. What's she going to do?' my father replied.

'We don't know what she's going to do. That's precisely the point,' I said.

'She's a harmless nutter,' my father said. 'She's not a psychopath.'

'If you had a disgruntled tenant, you'd change the locks,' I said.

227

'They might come back and steal the television to pay you back,' said Ig, smiling.

'Well, I *am* rather fond of the telly,' my father replied.

We found a number for a locksmith who came the following day. Toolbag beside him, he spent an hour drilling through the gate into the courtyard. He fitted a new lock, handed us a bunch of three shiny new keys and disappeared.

'There,' my father said, pulling a key from the ring to hand to me. 'Satisfied?'

'Yes,' I replied.

leading lady

'LIZZY!' THE DIRECTOR PULLED ME TOWARDS HIM. 'OH LIZZY,' HE SAID. 'So glad you came. How lovely to see you. You look wonderful. Did you read the part I sent you?'

'Yes,' I said, feeling a little breathless.

'Now.' He held his hands together in a praying gesture. 'Don't be disappointed but there's been a change. I'd like you to read a different part. It's still a very important role, the lines she has to say are absolutely pivotal to the narrative, but I can't lie to you. It *is* a smaller part.'

'Which part?' I said.

'Geraldine.'

I stayed silent.

'Lizzy, don't be disappointed. She has three or four lovely lines. You'll have the audience in stitches.'

Again, I said nothing.

'Come on, don't pout now. I've always got your best interests at heart, Lizzy. You know that.'

My finger still held the place in the script where Magenta had her best speech. 'Come on, Lizzy. Let's not let personal life get in the way of work. This is work. Start from page fifty-four. Just get into it. You'll love it.' The director moved back towards his chair.

My eye scanned down. Four lines for Geraldine, a character at breakfast in a seaside B&B who made a joke about the landlady's eggs.

'Just page fifty-four,' I said. 'That's the only scene she features in.'

'Her lines are a hoot, Lizzy. Honestly. You'll love them. Real character actress stuff.'

I felt exposed, too weak to begin reading.

'I haven't got all day, Lizzy,' the director said.

My voice shook. A lump in my throat stopped the words from coming out properly. I went slowly, barely managing to read through to the end.

'Super,' the director said. He clapped his hands together, his face bright. 'Brilliant. You've got the part! Well done, Lizzy. Your second role ever in London's fabulous West End. Actresses all over the country would kill to be you.'

He jumped out of his chair to come closer to me. 'Lizzy, it takes a lot of practice. Don't be despondent. I had trouble with the sponsors. You know how it is. They want a name for the leading lady. They can be terribly unimaginative. But even if the sponsors don't want you, I do. I'm here. I'm helping you.' He came in close to me and touched my hair. 'Come on,' he said. 'Have faith in me. Trust me.' His finger caught a loop of my hair. He coiled it round his hand, all the time looking at me in the eye, smiling, his fingers running up and down the bone along my cheek. His thumb moved to my lips. 'Don't be angry, Lizzy,' he said. 'You've got me.' I felt myself soften towards him. 'Those stories you hear about people making it overnight are very rare. Most often they're just the press department making it up. The public enjoy stories like that. It's good marketing.'

I wanted to believe him as he put both his arms around my

waist and joined them at my back. With me in his clasp he straddled his legs either side of mine to walk, pushing me in the direction he wanted to travel. He manoeuvred me offstage to the private area in the wings. The lights were dim and he pressed me into the wall. 'Fuck, I fancy you, Lizzy,' he said. He went to unbutton my shirt.

'Stop,' I said.

'Oh, don't be like that.'

'No. Stop,' I said. I pushed him away from me. 'You manipulated me.'

'I have not,' he said, jumping away from me, with indignation. 'I make it my policy to be honest with actresses. There are too many liars in this world. I try to be decent.' He leaned in towards me to kiss me again, but I turned my head. 'Oh, come on, Lizzy. Don't be like that. You know we all like to have fun in the theatre.' He cupped one side of my face with his hand and grinned. 'Remember what fun we had before. You and me locked in that broom cupboard together, fending off the cleaner.' He allowed himself a smile. 'Come on. Let's just be filthy together. Let's just have some fun and forget about all this stressful work stuff.'

He pulled me in towards him and began heading towards the pile of blankets in the corner. 'I'll just lie down here,' he said. 'And then you, Knight, can get on top of me.' He began grinning. 'And you can fuck me like you mean it.' His hand went down the back of my jeans. His face was close in to mine, kissing up and down my cheeks. 'I have given you a part in the play. I am doing my best for you. Anyway, it's a miserable life being a leading lady, Lizzy. You don't want that. Believe me. I see it all the time. It's not just the getting there.' I could feel his hand pressing into my buttock, his fat fingers massaging me. His mouth was going to bite my chin. 'You think you get there and that's it. You think you've made it and all will be fine from now on. But it isn't like that. I see it all the time. Once you get there, you're desperate to hold on to your position. You've got to posture and work to keep it. All these young, ambitious actresses coming up behind you, snapping at your heels, each as desperate as you were to make it. Each willing to do anything – and I mean *anything* – to take your place. You don't want that life.' His other hand was down my jeans. 'Go on. Just fuck me back here, Lizzy. Just get on top of me and fuck me and let it all out. Grab my cock and be beastly to me.' A smile crept across his face. The smile turned into a broad grin. 'Do it with abandoned fury. I can see you're cross. Unleash yourself against me. Go on. Do it. Just get on top of me and fuck all the fuck right out of me. Leave me limp and helpless. Make me gasp for mercy.'

'You've met someone else,' I said.

'I can see something in you. I wanted to help you out. But it's about figures these days. Accountants decide who get the big parts.' His hands were still holding on to me, firmly, as if he was going to refuse to let me go, no matter what I said.

'You gave her the part. Your new girlfriend.'

'Oh, come on, Lizzy. Be a grown-up about this.'

'You put me on the trapeze.'

'And you did really well up there. But, listen.' I had taken myself out of his grip. I was standing away from him. He'd stopped smiling. 'You're never going to be a leading lady,' he said. 'I'm a director and I'm telling you that. If you're causing yourself misery and putting your life on hold to try to make it in this world, you're wasting your time. I'm telling you that because I care about you.'

'You've met someone else,' I said again.

'Give it up. Get a job for money, take the odd character part and enjoy your life.'

'You think I'm going to stop at one rejection,' I said.

'Elizabeth, you're nearly thirty. You've had more than one rejection. Elizabeth, come back. Don't flounce off like that. We can talk about this.'

I flung open the door, raced down the corridor and back into the theatre's entrance hall. I still hoped the director would come chasing after me, tell me he'd made a terrible mistake. I slowed my pace just in case he couldn't find his way to the foyer. I hovered, then went back to the door that he might come through, peeked through the square of glass with my hands cupped to my face, but nothing. He couldn't just leave me like that. He couldn't just let me walk off without even caring. I tiptoed back down the corridor. Through a gap in the curtain, I saw him. Still on his chair, mobile phone to his ear chatting to someone, the chatter interspersed with laughter.

I sat on a cold bus, damp eating into my feet, tiny specks of drizzle clinging to my black woollen gloves like mist, and wondered what would become of me. Would I have to be a shop girl, like Eunice? Would I eke out my days scattering fluffy chicks over Easter scenes? Would I have to humiliate myself on a daily basis, have to phone Eunice and beg her to give me a job in Mike's mother's shop?

Maybe I should have been like her in the first place; found a man and worn him like a nice warm coat. Found someone to look after me because I couldn't look after myself. Not let go, even when I realised I didn't love him. He'd pay for things, worry about things, tell me what we could and couldn't afford (decide what I could and couldn't have) and I'd return the favour by organising his social life and keeping the linen cupboard tidy. If I grew bored, I'd get a hobby or a fashion habit and send him the bill; we'd have a nice old-fashioned marriage and I'd be grateful for the structure.

I walked home from the bus. Acting won't give up on me, I thought. I'll give up on it. I'll get so fat no one would put me on a stage anyway.

At home, I built up a fire in the grate. In the fridge were the last traces of Eunice. One of the sickly cakes she'd bought, a chocolate tart she made, her homemade rice pudding, a ceramic jar of Stilton cheese she'd found as a gift for my father, the horrible, cheap mayonnaise she liked. I stared at this stuff: I hadn't eaten in years.

I spooned mayonnaise on to white bread. It clagged against the roof of my mouth. My body demanded more. I crammed the remains of the chocolate tart into my mouth. I dug my spoon into the cake, taking chunks out of it, putting the spoon in again and again until all that remained was a gold disc covered in crumbs. I scooped Stilton cheese from the jar. I toasted bread, then a crumpet. I ate the rice pudding, using the wooden spoon that stood upright in the middle of the pan, to take enormous mouthfuls. I just kept eating. Wiping out years of hunger. My mouth crammed full, my cheeks bulging, crumbs all over me as I devoured the last of Eunice's food.

I went through the cupboards to find more food. An old packet of chocolate biscuits that Eunice had bought. I stuffed them down, one after the other, not stopping to pause. I'd get fat then I'd only go out at night, drape my enormous frame in black. I'd be a smudge of black against black, a pantomime horse of heavy linen lumbering through the night. No one would be able to tell where I ended and the night began. I chewed and chewed, the freedom of eating after all these years of being so tightly bound. I let myself go. I took more great dollops of rice pudding. I slapped spoonfuls of strawberry jam over it. Each mouthful would release me from the tyranny of slimness. Sticky jam and honey spread on thick slices of bread freed my hungry body.

If I carried on eating, the director would be disgusted he'd fucked me. This awful fat woman hiding in the dark, my terrified eyes popping out from behind a tree trunk. I'd have pasty feet swelling out of their shoes. My legs would be all white and fatty, like slabs of pork belly at the butcher's. My arse dimpled, my face puffy. I'd resemble a rare fungus. Weeping, crusted sores from where I'd rubbed together. If I ate like this every day, my two great doughy buttocks would meet the cool, hard slap of porcelain each morning and disgorge themselves of all the previous day's pleasures in one thrilling whoosh. I might powder the folds of my pure white flesh to stop them sticking then I'd wait outside the theatre for the director, grinning and waving at him. I think he hated fat women more than anything else.

I wanted more food. In the greenish light of the fridge, I examined the shelves but they sat empty. Every last trace of Eunice gone. A few muddy vegetables rattled around in the base. I held an onion, imagining the shining, green-white orb of flesh underneath the onion's skin, but I couldn't eat it. My father had grown that: a tiny, undernourished onion.

I slumped back into a chair. I could barely move. I felt like an enormous balloon that had been attached to the wrong nozzle. I'd been filled with jelly, rather than air. I couldn't bounce. I collapsed, dented by the shape of the chair I sat in. A weight in my legs kept me stuck to my chair. Was this the start of a steady spiral downwards? Would the day come when someone would have to cut through the roof of my studio to crane me out? I thought of the sea of faces looking upwards, wringing their hands, watching me swing in a canvas sling against a backdrop of clouds. I'd hear the whispers: such a shame. A mix of pity and disgust; and relief it was happening to someone else.

The fire had died. I raised myself up, threw another log on and blew until it caught. I took down a bottle of something strong from the sideboard to pour myself a large glass. I drank until I was wet old rags, wrung out. I closed my eyes and saw the arc my father's arm made, the colourful wizard's sleeve of a kaftan dangling from his wrist as he raised his hand to shield his eyes from the blinding sun.

I wanted to sit upstairs in my mother's room. I wanted to lie on the bed and feel comforted. A single shaft of silver moonlight lit the corridor as I opened her door. At the sight of her room, my hands began to shake. I felt my stomach contract. I turned on the spot to make sure I'd seen correctly.

In front of me stood an ordinary spare room: a bed with a wooden headboard, a lamp with a silk fringe that almost touched the table. I turned the light off, then back on again, to ensure that it told the correct story, that it wasn't just shadows.

What the hell had that woman done to us?

Everything had vanished: the clothes, the jewellery, the washbags still full of half-used creams preserved by us as if she'd gone away for the night and forgotten them. Not a speck of dust. Just an empty dressing table; an ordinary piece of furniture. A freshly polished mirror on top. Stool in front. Decanter of water with two sparkling glasses. Floorboards in polished wood. Clean and clear, polished wood. A wardrobe, a bed, a lamp, a side table. The bed was made up for guests.

I couldn't think or feel or make a sound so I just stood in the middle of this empty space and felt as if I was drowning. I felt as if I might fall and keep falling. I had nothing to hold me, to anchor me, no familiar thread running between me and the past, nothing to make me feel that I belonged. She'd obliterated our history. I stood in a void with blankness going on for ever and nothing to hold me in place.

In the blank, empty light I pulled the yellow note away from the wall. *It's for your own good, Lizzy.*

A clean, bright window looked out on to the garden. Large and transparent. The first time in nearly three years I'd seen the whole of that window.

I had nothing. I retreated into the corridor. With my hands behind my back, I pressed my palms into the wall. I closed my eyes, tried to catch my breath. I felt the wall's strength. I wanted to draw that strength into me, make the house a part of me. My mother still remained in this corridor, in these walls. This corridor, this slice of space, all I had left of her. I wanted the corridor to come alive, to curve around me, embrace me. This building was her permanent, indestructible, immortal part. I wanted to knit myself into those walls, to touch her, feel her presence. I imagined her telling me that she was there, that I was safe. I ran my bare foot along the battered old floorboards, clasped the iron handles of the windows with my palm. I gazed at a lithograph of bluebells and longed for everything to go back to how it used to be.

I needed that stuff. I didn't need white walls and a bed for a guest. I needed my mother back.

We knew she'd meant to take those tablets. Officially, during the inquest, there'd been doubt. But the way she wandered the house, for weeks, for months on end. We'd grown impatient with her. My father told her to snap out of it, told her to take a holiday. We all had.

During the inquest, we spoke only of her headaches. We kept quiet about all the other things: the pot and the drink and the parties and the laughter and the prescription drug addiction and the night sweats and the furious crying and the arguments and the throwing of a pan of boiling water against the wall. She knew how to get angry all right.

She'd had her good days too. The coroner had no proof that she absolutely did mean to take that many tablets and no proof that she absolutely didn't, so he came down undecided. He thought it could have been a cumulative effect over many days. Just not quite getting the effect any more; the headache was still there so she took another, then another, then another, each time realising her mind hadn't gone soggy, the pain hadn't stopped, so she might just need to take another.

'You're just a washed-up junkie,' I shouted at her one night.

I'll show you, she must have thought.

I opened the door to the stairs, put my head around to call upwards that I had a glass of wine for her when I saw the tips of those four fingers. I'd poured the wine to say sorry. I walked another step, trembling, to find the hand dangling, to see the perfect arc of a woman's nail and know without doubt it was hers. There she lay like a character in a piece of carefully worked-out theatre, a fallen ballet dancer, her nightdress ridden up her thighs. *Look at me! Look at what I've done!* Slats of moonlight fell along her body and she looked beautiful; calm and pale.

I'd been in the house all afternoon. She knew I was at home and she did it deliberately. She decided I should be the one to find her.

That'll teach you to call me a washed-up junkie.

I anchored myself to the sight of that pale hand. I phoned

my father, barely able to speak. He rushed home, pushed past me, told me to call help while he fought to revive her. The paramedic wheeled her out on a trolley with white foam drying on her blue lips.

I didn't go to the hospital. My father wanted me to but I couldn't. Ig went. Instead, I lay in bed and stared at cracks of light on the walls, waiting. When my father came from the hospital in the early hours, he crept up the ladder to my bed, his face the colour of the moon, painted with reflected light from the window. I tried not to move because I knew what he'd come for. If I stayed still then he couldn't see I was awake, then he wouldn't speak and the thing I knew he was going to say wouldn't be true.

Why hadn't something told me to go upstairs? She knew I was downstairs. I knew she was upstairs.

'Keep an eye on her,' my father had said, as he left the house.

Had she fallen on the stairs as she came to find me? Had she regretted taking the pills and come to ask for help? Or had she positioned herself, vindictively? Lain herself carefully down, rested her hand across the top stairs, found a strand of hair to pull across her eye, then downed the last tablet. *There! Like that. I'd like to be found like that. Beautiful but tragic. Something for them all to feel guilty about.*

I wanted to drink more. The house felt cold. The walls seemed so grey and dull. Depressing light, all shadows with no warmth. The house looked so different, so hostile, a horrible place rather than the home I used to love. All the things I thought I'd known to be true had shifted. The chair my father sat in wasn't a wonderful battered old leather armchair but a cracked, plastic thing that smelled of sweat. Black felt tip pen dotted the grimy armrests where he did crosswords. The kitchen seemed a mess: orange lights, great long industrial pipes through the ceiling that made no sense at all, an enormous old wooden table with too many dents. The kitchen cupboards seemed battered, an ancient brown cooker with a broken oven door. I hated this place.

I emptied a bottle of gin into my glass. I wanted to be drunker. I took my father's dirty old bag of hash out of the drawer. I pulled out the resin, leaving behind a collection of his nail clippings in the bottom. I rolled a fat joint, loaded with hash. Put ice cubes and tonic in the gin. I drank down the gin, feeling myself soften and melt.

I took the joint and the gin back upstairs to sit on that bed, in that empty room, and drink myself into a stupor. I arranged the pillows around me. My head spun, the room pulsed and twirled in front of me. I wanted to vomit. My insides wrung themselves out, made spirals, the whole room would topple on to me. I sucked down the last of the joint, pulling all that smoke deep inside me. I wanted to feel nothing.

In one hand, the end of the joint glowed red. In the other, the cool clink of the gin in a crystal glass. I felt drunk but I didn't feel oblivion. I wanted to be knocked out, completely wiped from the page. Not just cease to exist but to never have existed. I looked at the red end of the fat joint burning happily. It spoke to me: *Go on. Do it. You'll feel better. I want you to do it.*

'I want to do it,' I said out loud.

On the windowsill opposite, I was sure I saw my mother. Not a ghost but her, dressed in bright scarlet – a long silk dress that came right down to her feet with billowing sleeves. As if she'd come back for the evening.

'Is it you?' I said.

She didn't speak. She just gazed at me.

'Say something,' I said to her.

Nothing moved. She just carried on with her steely, steadfast look.

I jumped up from the bed to go to her side. I held on to her legs, rested my head in her lap and sobbed. My face wet with tears, I looked up at her.

'I dare you,' she said.

My arms still gripping her legs, I threw the joint on to the plump, flammable duvet. My mother smiled.

The fabric singed. The barest hissing noise as the material vaporised. Then a faint crackle as the joint fell deeper in towards the filling. My toes began to wriggle as they inched towards the line where they'd touch my mother's. What would the director think? He might carry the idea of me around with him, the way my father had my mother: *look at me with my tragedy*, without a thought to his own part in it. He could tell the story: a young actress who killed herself over him. *She was wonderful, but doomed. I'd done everything I could. She had a touch of magic about her but was so damaged.*

When Ig and my father came home, they'd end up with the same mystery: had Elizabeth meant to do it or was it a terrible accident?

The bed caught fire. A whoosh, then a deep noise like fabric being flung through air. Flames jumped high towards a watercolour on the wall. My mother laughed and danced. The flames tickled the picture frame, turning it a dark charcoal colour. My mother whipped up to see it. She held out her hand to touch mine. Her arm coiled in around my neck. She held me tight, pulling all of me into her, hugging me like a child. My head sank into her chest, her hair fell about my eyes. A thick, toxic black smoke hid the room from me. My throat burned as I tried to breathe.

My body fell backwards into the chair. I managed to take

an ice cube from the glass to roll around my tongue; cool and wet, it soothed my throat. Perhaps I'd made a mistake but I couldn't move. I pulled at the windowsill to try and raise myself but I couldn't. A lead weight pulled me back towards the ground. My mother danced in the smoke. *I was lonely tonight but now you're coming to sit beside me.* The overwhelming desire to sleep. My eyes felt heavy. They began closing. I felt myself sinking.

I didn't want this. I wanted to survive. I snapped myself awake. I struggled off the bed, pulled myself to. The room was full of thick black smoke. I pushed through it, feeling it choke my throat. I could barely breathe. I pushed out through the room. The corridor had filled with smoke. I could barely see, barely walk. My legs wouldn't move. I felt sleepy. My head so heavy I couldn't put one foot in front of the other. No air went in. I choked, coughed. My eyes stung. Tears wet my cheeks because of all the smoke. At the top of the stairs, I could just make out the door. It seemed like a temptation. An opening into something else. If I could just get down the stairs and push it open I'd step outwards. I spluttered, feeling myself give way. My knees melted away but I urged myself forward, the sheer force of my intention, the will of my mind forcing me down the stairs and out into the open.

Elizabeth

I SPLAYED MY HAND OUT AND PRESSED IT FLAT AGAINST THE WINDOW OF
the bus. It left its shape behind in the condensation misted over
the glass. My father told me that from now on I must try only
to remember the good things. He wanted me to stop dwelling
so much on the past.

But it was not the same for him as it was for me. His version
of the past seemed to shift and change according to his mood.
Mine felt like something enormous, solid and unchanging like
a giant stone statue with its finger pointing at me.

My father told me to try and remember the fun we had: the
parties, the house-guests, the nude swimming. He reminded
me that our mother had dreamed herself out of her old life. She
dreamed herself away from Valerie, away from her parents,
away from the old, hellish grandfather clock and the pies and
the gravy and she dreamed herself into something new. 'I think
you should do the same,' he said.

For a week, I'd sat on the floor of our mother's old room
watching my father repaint it. I cried as he cursed me for
drinking and smoking on top of a flammable duvet. He joked
that for my new career I could be a fire-safety executive, giving
talks to pyromaniac teenagers in schools. He hated painting,
he said. The soot kept mixing with the white, turning it to

grey, so he had to do three or four coats to get rid of it. He was bored rigid by the end.

The bus turned along the river road. From the top deck, the boats that slapped against the water's edge seemed miles beneath me.

It had been a year since Eunice had dreamed herself into our life. After she'd taken our stuff, my father phoned her up and demanded it all back but she said she couldn't hear who it was on the other end of the phone – hello? hello? hello? – and then she put the receiver down.

My father and I both searched the Internet to see if there were any adverts for 'Vintage Coat, Barely Worn' or 'Peppermint-coloured Cocktail Ring' but the stuff had disappeared. My father didn't talk about how he felt – all the stuff I knew he cherished as much as I did – but I did catch him at night sometimes (even after we agreed we'd given up all hope of finding anything) trawling through pages of second-hand jewellery websites.

In my hand, I held a photograph of my mother wearing the peppermint-coloured ring. I'd phoned the woman who was selling it, told her the ring had been stolen, said she ought to give it back. 'We want it,' I said, 'as a memory, but also to restore us. Things in our family don't feel the way they used to and we all miss it.'

The woman said she'd be open to a conversation if I brought the picture in and told her the story but she couldn't make any promises.

'Was it a woman called Eunice who sold it to you in the first place?' I asked.

She couldn't answer. She had so much stuff, things came from all over, she couldn't remember.

What was Eunice doing with all the money from this stuff

she'd sold? Had she treated herself to something new? More things? A new armchair in purple suedette to match Mike's sofa?

I got off the bus outside the shop. A small place, crammed full of costume jewellery with brass-coloured bars up at the windows and the front painted faded yellow. I cupped my hands against the glass to scan the display inside. I saw the peppermint ring, nestled in velvet, among the other rings. It did shine, my mother's ring. Far more eye-catching than the others.

I looked at it there for a moment. It had a tag tied to it with the price turned away and only the description visible: *Authentic 1960s Cocktail Ring*. I squeezed the door handle, trembling at the idea that the thing that was ours might be returned to us. The woman inside hadn't seen me yet.

By my side, I still held the photograph. I glanced down at it – saw my mother as she touched the side of her face, the ring clearly on show. I let the shop door close. I went back to the window to gaze at the ring for one last time then I turned away and began to walk.

Acknowledgements

Thank you to the whole team at Tinder Press, especially to Imogen Taylor; also many thanks to Amy Perkins, Georgina Moore and Abbie Salter. I'm so pleased to have found such a good home.

Thank you to my brilliant agent Lizzy Kremer, and to Harriet Moore.

Thank you to Michèle Roberts for her numerous readings of the manuscript in its nascent form and for her insightful comments.

Thank you to my sister Hannah Duguid for all the reading and re-reading of various drafts, and for being the voice of reason at the end of the phone. Many of the ideas in the novel came from our conversations.

Thanks to others who read the manuscript in its early stages and offered useful comments: especially to Jenny Little, Emma Temple, Megan Lloyd-Davies, Isa Campbell.

Thanks to Hannah Strickland for our adventure in Sicily, right at the start of it all. Thank you to Leah Sefor and Barry Kukkuk for giving me such a nice place to write for a month. Thank you to my mother, Anne Duguid, for all the babysitting and all the tidying – it helped no end. Thank you to Anne Barrett for her kindness and generosity allowing me many,

many more hours to write. Thank you to my father, Ronald Duguid, for digging me out of a hole once or twice – it was very much appreciated.

And of course, thank you to Nicolas Haméon, who had to live with me throughout the whole process. Nico, you kept the show on the road; I couldn't have done it without you.

LOOK AT ME

Bonus Material

My Family Secret

Q&A with Sarah Duguid

Reading Group Questions

My Family Secret

I was tearing down the motorway towards Portsmouth, late for a birthday dinner, when my sister phoned me: 'There's a family secret,' she said. 'Everybody knows about it except you and I.' For the rest of the evening, we texted each other with speculations: Bankruptcy? Terminal illness? Crime? My sister put each suspicion to our mother: No, no-one's been arrested, no-one's dying, no bankruptcy. It wasn't until my sister asked if there was a child we didn't know about, that my mum became strangely silent. 'That's not for me to say,' she replied. I was still on my main course when the call came through: we had a secret half-sibling, my sister was certain of it.

A few months after the discovery of our half-sister, I was talking to a woman of around my parents' age who rattled off a list of five of her friends who gave up children for adoption in the 1960s. 'It was very common,' she said. It immediately struck me that it might be a good place to start a novel. What if the secret child turned up at the family home? What might she want from them? What might she do to them? What might they do to her? But back then, that was all I had: a place to start and many questions.

For seven years, I slogged out this story, a sparely told tale of the abandoned daughter Eunice arriving into the Knight family, wanting to find her place in the world, while all the time gradually exposing her birth family's terrible fragility. Readers have told me that Eunice filled them with rage – and she was meant to. She's tactless and insensitive, unable to see that it's not just her who's been damaged by her parents' experiment with free love.

I made the Knights a pair of former hippies because I wanted to use the novel to explore idealism. For research, I sought out a few men who'd lived in communes in the 1960s. They talked of wild adventures: road trips, psychedelic drugs, wonderfully liberated group sex. They told me how dull my generation was, 'squares' with our mortgages and careers, our sushi habits and gym memberships. They described their lives as a romantic search for a better way of being, a yearning for a kind of prelapsarian bodily innocence – everyone naked and just loving one another – yet they left in their wake a trail of abandoned women and children. 'Well I just moved on. Her and the baby were all right, there were other people around,' one guy said. Another one told me: 'Half the time, no one knew who the father was anyway.'

I became curious about the role of women in all of this and the idea of performance. I was interested in the way women stage their own versions of femininity: muse, earth mother, sexual enchanter. At the time, I was also meeting up with the writer Michèle Roberts for her to read drafts of my novel. We discussed the idea of the 'hippy goddess', an appealing fantasy for some women back then. These conversations became the basis for the character Margaret Knight, who went along with her husband's longing for a truer, freer way of being. Through her eagerness to please, Margaret performed a role that not only proved devastating to her, but ultimately also devastating to her daughter, Elizabeth, who was left behind trying to figure out what a woman ought to be – a question that most generations of women seem to grapple with.

There is an assumption that most first novels are auto-biographical and of course, *Look At Me* is based on something that happened to me. But, unlike Eunice, my own half-sister didn't move in with us; she wasn't conceived while my parents were married to one another; she didn't push us all to the edge of sanity. Quite the contrary, we met up a few times for lunch, then carried on our separate ways. When I see physical copies of the book that took me so long to write, it's my sister I should be most grateful to. It was she who noticed the conversations behind closed doors, and who orchestrated the clever detective work that led me to the story that took a hold and didn't let go. And why, as we thought at the time, should everyone know a secret that we didn't?

This article originally appeared on www.thegloss.ie

Q&A with Sarah Duguid

What inspired you to become an author?

I can't really remember ever making a decision to be an author. I do remember feeling offended when my A-level English teacher told me I should go into business because he reckoned I'd be good at it, and I thought 'Well no, I'm going to be a writer.' I suppose the thing that keeps me going as a writer is having something to say – the desire to speak – as well as having things that I am grappling with, whether that's what form a novel should take; or questions of identity, the past, the sub-conscious, performance; whatever it is I'm thinking about at the time.

How do you personally feel about your two female leads, Eunice and Elizabeth?

Eunice is the grit in the oyster – she's supposed to be annoying – and yet I can sympathise with her desire to find her place in the world, to find her home, her 'tribe'. I suppose both Eunice and Elizabeth are trying to work out an identity for themselves, and while Eunice breaks into a family to do this, Elizabeth experiments with performance and sex. In Elizabeth and

Eunice, I tried to create two characters that would absolutely clash. There was Elizabeth's snobbery versus Eunice's neediness; yet they are subtly similar. Eunice is also snobbish, particularly about her adoptive mother, while Elizabeth is very needy. They had to have similarities, traits within themselves they were refusing, in order to truly come up against the other. I wanted their clash to unravel them, I wanted the reader to wonder what they might do to one another, but I didn't want them to kill each other – not literally anyway. And I didn't want them squabbling over boyfriends, or calling each other fat.

Family dynamics are a key part of *Look at Me* – is this a subject that particularly interests you?

I think I just like the domestic as a dramatic space. I find it a good place to explore much larger questions. I keep trying to force myself out of the home, to write about the outside world but I keep finding myself back indoors, exploring the clash between language and feeling, the said and the unsaid, who's right and who's wrong. But the domestic hasn't always been something I've been drawn by. As a child, I preferred sci-fi – Arthur C. Clarke, Ursula K. Le Guin – as well as adventure stories. I wanted to read about the world beyond; to escape. As a teenager, I was addicted to the books of Ryszard Kapuściński. I used to flick between reading the book and gazing at the author's tiny, black and white photo on the back cover. To me, he seemed maverick and wild, yet profoundly sensitive to both the written word and the world around him, poet as much as journalist. With a single word, he could bring alive his fear, the sweat on a soldier's brow, the uniqueness of an African sky, as he told these incredible, impossible stories of war with a suicidal attunement to truth. But I did also spend a lot of time wondering about his family dynamics. Married, a father to a daughter, he had reasons to stay at home yet he claimed to find Europe stifling and spent most of his time away, flirting with death and – rumour has it – other women. If I was going to write a novel about a war reporter, I imagine I'd be indoors with them, exploring that rich territory, rather than out on the road counting tanks.

What other authors were your biggest influences in writing this novel?

I think every reader has a book that is a turning point for them, a book that they read in early teenage years that awakens them to reading, that makes them realise what books can do – that novel for me was *Wuthering Heights*. Nellie Dean, both observer and occasional participator, maintains an intense and slightly creepy gaze on the characters as they are both cruel and protective by turn; loving and hating in equal measure. My love of that book most definitely influenced *Look At Me*.

I like the closed world of *Wuthering Heights*. The geography of the novel is one of isolation so the characters are removed from the moral forces of wider Victorian society – and even the mellowing forces of some lighthearted, diverting company. In their isolation, they become almost institutionalised; so involved in the politics of what's happening in their own home that the wider world fades, leaving them to find their own moral and psychological order. I tried to make a similar thing happen in *Look At Me*. I wanted to base my novel in London, and so in order to portray the isolation – *Wuthering Heights* transplanted from Yorkshire to the city – I used class. The characters within Julian's household are a step out of time, unlikely to be friends with their neighbours, not quite in tune with the normal world. It's a slight risk to write a book that tells the story of a posh, closed world because poshness and exclusion can antagonise more people than they attract, especially, I think, in Britain. Readers in this country seem to prefer their heroes to be working class or to be children (likability seems to be a big thing at the moment) but posh suited the story I wanted to tell.

Michèle Roberts read several drafts of *Look At Me*, and while I was writing I read all of her books, so she was definitely an influence. It strikes me that her work is – among many other things – a writing into literature of the female body. I've read a fair bit of French feminist theory and have always been struck by Hélène Cixous' notion of making the female body present in literature. She links the female body with the act of writing; through this pouring forth of words you can uncover repressed impulses and desires and can create something specifically female. To my mind, *Look At Me* is a novel about the body, as much as anything else – that's the reason I chose the quote from *Fleurs du Mal* at the beginning. I wanted to make the point that bodily freedom is associated with emotional freedom. Bodies in *Look At Me* are loved, abused, ignored, fetishised. They are treated as a path to freedom, to pre-lapsarian innocence and truth (by Julian for example) and yet the body is also a way through which the characters are ruined and ensnared. The mother was a drug addict; her son a healer. I made Ig a Reiki healer to show his vulnerability, to show how trapped he is, to show his magical thinking. He wants to believe he can enter the body in order to fix his mother's madness and change the past.

What is your next project?

My next project takes the characters of Anna and David from *Look At Me*, and transports them to a remote and wild corner of rural England where they have to look after two troubled teenage girls. All might be fine, until they are joined by an old friend of David's, an anthropologist who specialises in tribal ritual as well as a self-help charlatan – a dangerous man – who pushes everyone to the edge of life and sanity. I wanted to explore the fight between the conscious and unconscious, between order and disorder, between freedom and dependence while also – I hope – telling a gripping story.

Reading Group Questions:

1. Did you find Lizzy a reliable narrator? Were there any similarities you identified between her and Eunice?
2. Discuss the various manifestations of grief in *Look At Me*.
3. Margaret is a presence in the novel although we never experience her first hand. What did you conclude about her personality in life and the truth about her death?
4. What does the novel have to say about class and wealth?
5. Eunice is a rather marginalised figure; did you sympathise with her at all?
6. What do the sexual relationships in the novel have to say about gender politics?
7. Do you think the book created an accurate portrayal of sibling relationships?
8. There is a preoccupation with the past in *Look At Me*; what do you feel the novel has to say about nostalgia?

You are invited to join us behind the scenes at Tinder Press

TINDER
PRESS

To meet our authors, browse our books
and discover exclusive content on our
blog visit us at

www.tinderpress.co.uk

For the latest news and views from the team
Follow us on Twitter

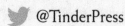 @TinderPress